Patti Malcolm is a book enthusiast, always reading and writing. She's been writing since she was fourteen years old and is ecstatic to finally see her dream of publication come true. She's currently working toward her English degree at MacEwan University and when she's not writing or studying, she's channeling her old lady side and crafting.

To Mr. Tim Chodan, for being my only high school teacher to have faith in me.

Patti Malcolm

HER SOUL

AUSTIN MACAULEY PUBLISHERS™

LONDON · CAMBRIDGE · NEW YORK · SHARJAH

Ordering Information:
Quantity sales: special discounts are available on quantity purchases by corporations, associations, and others. For details, contact the publisher at the address below.

Publisher's Cataloging-in-Publication data
Malcolm, Patti
Her Soul

ISBN 9781643782218 (Paperback)
ISBN 9781643782225 (Hardback)
ISBN 9781645368212 (ePub e-book)

Library of Congress Control Number: 2019920967

www.austinmacauley.com/us

First Published (2020)
Austin Macauley Publishers LLC
40 Wall Street, 28th Floor
New York, NY 10005
USA

mail-usa@austinmacauley.com
+1 (646) 5125767

I would like to start by thanking my wonderful beta readers, Cassie, and my mom. I also want to thank my whole family for their support and love during the process of getting this book ready for submission. There's also the amazing team at Austin Macauley, who deserve a huge thanks for all of their hard work.

Chapter 1

Carter

"Kaylee! Wait up!"

My best friend's voice floated forward from behind me. I was walking home from school and Lisa Perry was following me, giving up the ride we both usually got with her older brother.

Today had been hard. It was the last day of classes before exams technically started, but I had already taken mine. I had jumped from my desk and ran out of class as soon as the bell had rung for the end of the day. Not stopping for anyone who said my name. Not even stopping at my locker to gather the few belongings I had kept in there for four years. I didn't stop for anything. Because I had a secret. And it was a secret there was no way I would be able to keep if I stopped to talk with anybody.

"What is up with you today, babe?" she called, obviously worried. I hadn't touched my potatoes at lunch and she knew I loved me some potatoes. I also hadn't said much of anything all day. After more than seventeen years of friendship, Lisa knew me well enough to know something was up.

"I'm moving," I blurted as I abruptly stopped walking.

It was definitely not how I had wanted to tell my diaper friend I was leaving and would probably never see her again. I turned around just in time to see her shoulders relax and her face light up into a smile.

"I know," she chirped, shrugging as if my moving away and leaving her was no big deal.

My jaw dropped and my eyes felt as if they had tripled in size.

"You know?" I asked slowly, unsure if I had heard her correctly.

"Yeah," she shrugged. "Your dad told me right after he got the approval for expansion of his security firm up north. I'm kind of surprised he didn't tell you that I knew."

"Why're you so chipper about this? I'm leaving and we may never see each other again," I asked softly.

I was scared that my words would come true and I would never again see the girl I considered to be my sister.

"Geez, he really didn't tell you?" Lisa gaped.

I shook my head slowly, confused.

"I'm coming with you, babe."

I couldn't believe it. The person I dreaded telling the most about my moving away already knew and was actually coming along. That was the best news I'd heard all week.

Wait.

"What about your parents? And your brother? You have a family; I can't ask you to just up and leave!" I panicked.

At first it had sounded wonderful, having my best friend with me in a new and strange place, but the fact was that Lisa had a family and a life in Washington.

"Our parents have everything worked out. There's only one thing left to do," Lisa assured me.

"Pack?"

"No, babe. You have to tell Carter."

***

Carter. I had to tell Carter. How could I have forgotten that I have to tell my *boyfriend* that I was moving? I hadn't. I just didn't want to have to tell Carter that I was leaving him, and everything else, behind.

Lisa and I reached my house not long after she reminded me about Carter. With both of us propped up on my bed, the elephant in the room sat glaringly in my lap. My cellphone.

"Kaylee, come on. You have to call him. You're moving. You can't just not tell him. What if you move without telling him and he thinks you've gone missing? What if—"

Lisa babbled until I cut her off.

"I get it, Lis. I really do. I just need a sec, 'kay?"

"Kaylee. This is really important. How about you invite him over here and I'll wait in this wonderful room of yours while you guys talk. That way, if you need girl time after, then I'm already right where I need to be," she suggested softly, her hazel eyes full of understanding.

I nodded and called him, suggesting that he come over so we could talk.

About twenty minutes later, I heard his truck pulling into the empty space in the driveway. The door to his truck had barely slammed shut before I heard a knock at the door. I looked over at Lisa and she nodded her head in encouragement before getting cozy on my bed with one of my many books.

It was an act on her part. I knew the second I shut the door behind me, her ear would be pressed against it.

After making my way down the stairs, I opened the front door to see a very pale Carter Reed, green eyes shining with worry.

"Hi, Carter," I said quietly, looking down at my bare feet and bright blue toenails.

"Hi? You don't talk to me all day, and all I get is hi?" Carter asked, eyebrows narrowing and creating a bridge between his eyes.

I always did like how expressive his eyebrows were.

"I'm sorry. I have something I have to tell you and I knew if I opened my mouth at all today I would end up with a raging case of verbal diarrhea. We both know school is the worst place for that to happen," I blubbered nervously, pulling on a strand of my hair.

Apparently, I was getting verbal diarrhea anyway, but I had to tell him. Carter nodded in agreement and we moved toward the couch in my living room. I held a cushion to my chest.

We sat close together, knees touching, but Carter's body was stiff and tense. I felt terrible for not telling him sooner. This late in the game there was no time to prepare. We had grown up together, and now I was up and leaving with barely a word.

After taking a number of deep breaths, I went on.

"I'm moving, Carter. To some place in Canada. My dad knows where, but I honestly haven't cared enough. I mean, I don't think the 'where' really matters. And I've been trying to just live in the here and now, before the here and now becomes the there and then. You know?" I let out a sad laugh. "I don't even know exactly where I'm moving. How pathetic is that?" I added, my voice barely above a whisper.

Carter just sat there for a few minutes. Quiet. Unmoving.

"You're moving?" Carter whispered so quietly it was no more than a breath. He had gone ghostly pale.

"In a week," I nodded. "Lisa, too."

Carter's head snapped over to look at me so fast, I thought he might have given himself whiplash. Reaching over, I placed my hand on his shoulder in what I hoped was a comforting gesture.

"A week?" he whispered again. Having no words, I just nodded and we reached for each other at the same time. Just holding each other as we came to the same conclusion.

There was no other way this could go.
It was over.

Chapter 2
Moving Day

One week had come and gone, and moving day was upon us. The movers had already retrieved the bulk of our belongings and were on their way to a little place called Redheart, Alberta.

I had just slept the last night in the house I grew up in; in the bed I had been sleeping in since I was twelve. Dad had bought us all new furniture—though I hadn't seen any of it yet—and sold all of our old stuff with the house. He figured we might as well sell it as a 'furnished house' and make a bit of extra money, as well as make the move cheaper.

Lisa had spent the night before with her family. With her brother heading off to university somewhere in Europe and her coming to live in Canada with me and my dad, her family decided they needed one last big family night.

I was going to miss the Perrys. They had been like a second family to me my entire life. But I knew I would see them again. Eventually.

I looked over at the clock on my nightstand and saw that it was just past eight o'clock in the morning. Dad wanted to be on the road by noon.

Why we were driving was beyond me. Lisa had said she would be over at about ten to help us load the last of everyone's belongings into my dad's SUV. Which actually meant she would be forcing her brother, Carson, to drive her over with the rest of her things, and it would be him helping us load up the car.

I forced my butt out of bed and made my way to the bathroom that my dad and I had shared for seventeen years.

After what was possibly the longest shower of my life, I got dressed, brushed my teeth, and started down the stairs to have moving day breakfast which consisted of one of those personal boxes of cereal and a little carton of milk. Yum.

Any food we had left after breakfast this morning was either being brought back to the Perry's by Carson, or brought along as snack food for the what was sure to be an excruciatingly long drive.

Breakfast was a sad affair. Sitting with my dad at the old oak table that had been in this house since I was born, neither of us said a word. Until I got up to wash my bowl so I could pack it away.

"I'm sorry, Kale," my dad apologized quietly, head bowed. I knew if I could see the brown eyes that we shared, they'd be laced with regret. "I know your life is here. All of your friends. Carter. But you'll make a life up in Redheart, I promise. You'll be happy."

I walked back toward his still form, sitting at the table, and placed my hand on his shoulder.

"It's okay, Dad. I understand. The opportunity for expanding the security firm was too good to pass up. Just like you said. Seriously, I get it. I mean, it sucks, but I get it. Really," I told him this with as much enthusiasm as I could muster, which unfortunately wasn't much.

He just nodded and took care of his bowl before heading back upstairs to finish packing the rest of his things. I had finished high school already but was taking a gap year before university. Moving out on my own at seventeen would be too hard, so I was moving with my dad. More than 1300 kilometers away.

I was packing the remaining miscellaneous items from the kitchen and living room when the door burst open with a very excited Lisa standing there, and a not so excited male Lisa-look-alike coming up behind her.

Lisa was making Carson carry her boxes. Big surprise. As much as I loved her, Lisa was what one might call 'high maintenance.'

"You okay out there, Carson?" I called, with an amused grin on my lips. He grunted in response before placing the first box on the floor in the foyer and making his way back out to his car to grab more.

"So," Lisa asked, drawing out the word. "Are you excited?" She pulled me to the couch, her blonde ponytail swaying back and forth.

"A little. I mean, it's a new place and I know you want to start college in September. It won't be easy," I admitted with a sad little laugh, pulling on my black hair. I had always envied the Perry kids. Both blonder than blonde, deep hazel eyes, and more graceful than I could ever dream of being.

Lisa nodded her understanding and threw her arm over my shoulder, squishing me to her side. With her other arm, she gestured the way I have only seen on television during "I can see it now" moments.

"Just imagine, new boys, new stores—so new clothes—new house. And all those trees. It'll make Seattle seem like Times Square! And we can go camping every weekend! And we won't even have to go far! You probably have a forest in your new backyard anyway! Well, *our* new backyard."

"What makes you say that?" I asked, raising an eyebrow inquisitively. An ability I had always secretly reveled in, even though I could only do it on one side. I leaned back out of Lisa's hold waiting for a response.

"I may have *googled* Redheart this morning before I came over. Just about everyone's backyards face the forest and the city is only two hours away for shopping! Your dad may or may not have mentioned a shopping spree for the two of us when he gets everything set up," she winked making me laugh.

My dad was a security whiz. When he was twenty-eight, he started a security firm with Lisa's dad, Darrel Perry. It was the most successful private security firm in Washington.

A couple of trips later and Carson had brought in all six of Lisa's boxes. I gaped at her. She was lucky my dad owned an SUV. She was supposed to send off the majority of her things with the movers like my dad and I had, and only keep about two, maybe three, boxes worth of belongings.

Lisa simply shrugged and smiled at me before mouthing "Whoops." I laughed and shook my head at her. She really was high maintenance.

I stood from the couch to give Carson a hug. Growing up with his little sister since diapers kind of made him a big brother to me, too. He sure treated me like a little sister.

"Thanks for your help, Carson. We both know your sister won't say it, but she's thankful too."

"It's no problem, Leelee. I'm just glad to get the mothballs out of my hair," he grinned down at me, using the nickname he created for me when I was two and couldn't say my name properly.

Laughing, I looked over at his sister, who was still sitting on the couch, and saw a sad look cross her face. But it disappeared as quickly as it had appeared. All traces of the gloomy look in her eyes vanished when she stuck her tongue out at us. Carson pulled away when the strain on his neck from looking down at me became too much, which didn't take long at all. With his six feet and two inches compared to my five feet and five inches, it was a feat that he could look down at me for any length of time at all.

Grasping my shoulders Carson took a step back. "Your dad had mentioned that I could bring any of your guys' leftover food back home with me."

"Right!" I showed him where the bit of food we were leaving behind was and he took everything. The only food left was the bag on the kitchen island, which was full of snacks for our thirteen-hour drive. After going to the couch and kissing his sister on the cheek, he waved goodbye and walked out the door.

By this point it was almost noon, and Dad came clomping back down the stairs with his arms so full of both of our boxes I had no clue how he hadn't killed himself on the way down. Together, the three of us, mostly myself and my father, loaded up the SUV with the remaining luggage. Dad and Lisa were getting settled in the car when I remembered something.

"One second! I–I think I forgot my headband on the kitchen counter!" I yammered out. I knew I had actually thrown it in my backpack, but there was something much more important than my favorite headband waiting for me in the house. Waiting to be remembered in the secret compartment in my closet.

Running back inside, I shot straight for what was soon-to-be my old bedroom. Opening the closet door, I switched on the light and got down on my knees. I turned around and shuffled backwards, with my bottom touching the floor, so when I had finished scooching, I was leaning against the back wall of the closet.

To the left of the door was a little slit in the wall that you could only see if you knew what you were looking for, otherwise the shadow from the overhead light hid it. I slid my fingers along the slit in the wood until I found the tiny button that would allow the door to swing open. I pushed the button, feeling the slightest release of pressure under my fingertips, and pulled the door open.

It didn't creak; it never had. I eased it open and slowly reached inside for the only thing I had ever deemed worthy of such a secret hiding place.

My mother's locket.

The only person I had ever told about it was Lisa. I wasn't even sure if my dad knew it existed. Inside the locket was a picture. My favorite. It was of the three of us; my father, my mother and myself. I would have been about three or four in the photo; I couldn't remember. Both of my parents had sparkles in their eyes and we all looked so happy. I never understood how a family that was so happy could fall apart so completely. I never understood how she could leave us.

I reached into my back pocket for the spare piece of paper I always seemed to need for one reason or another, and so always kept there. I pulled the pencil from my hair that I had used to secure my bun right before we had started loading the SUV and wrote a quick little note about where the secret compartment was with instructions on how to open it.

I quickly clasped the locket behind my neck, tucking it safely beneath my shirt, and tore off the end of the paper with the note, leaving it on what used to be my bed.

I ran back downstairs and out the door, jumping into the passenger seat and giving a noncommittal shrug. "I must've packed it."

My dad rolled his eyes at me with a small, knowing smile on his face and Lisa was already snoring behind me. I silently patted the locket where it laid right above my breasts as my dad pulled out of the driveway and I said goodbye to the only home I had ever known.

Chapter 3

Home

The drive up north was painfully long. The three of us took turns sleeping in the back seat and driving. When we finally arrived at the new house in Redheart, Alberta, it was dark out and I couldn't really tell what anything looked like.

I reached back from the driver's seat to shake Lisa awake and got out of the car. I met my dad at the trunk and we both loaded our arms full. Walking toward the house, I heard Lisa jump out of the SUV. I looked back and saw her stretch like a cat, a yawn stretching her face wide open.

Shaking my head with a quiet laugh, I turned back toward the house and shuffled up the sidewalk. Dad had already gone inside and left the door open, letting light spill out into the yard. I walked inside and almost dropped the boxes I was holding. From where I was standing in the foyer, I could see straight through to the back of the house. The back wall was completely made up of windows and the light shining from the house danced off what I was hoping was a deck. Taking a couple more steps inside, I could see the corner of a dark wood kitchen island with a beautiful quartz countertop. Across from the island sat a deep grey sectional that looked like it could hold a football team. Lisa came through the door behind me as I kicked off my flip flops.

"Holy sh—"

"Yeah."

We both placed our boxes gently on the stone foyer floor and linked arms, continuing into the house together. When we reached the kitchen and living area, I gasped. On the wall across from the sectional was a massive television surrounded by dark brown, wall mounted shelves, already teaming with movie cases and CDs.

I heard shuffling behind me and turned around. Dad was coming into the kitchen carrying the box labelled 'last minute crap.' He softly placed it on the island and turned toward us.

"So? What do you girls think?"

"Dad, it's…it's…I don't even have words, I've never been in a house like this. How can we afford it?" I was in awe.

I knew we had money, but I didn't think it was *this* much. He smiled knowingly, looking at the space next to me that Lisa occupied.

"Sweetie, it's all handled," Dad told me calmly, an amused gleam in his eyes. I nodded slowly, still unsure. "Bedrooms are upstairs. There are four. All with walk-in closets and their own bathrooms, so choose whichever ones you want."

Lisa and I looked at each other and booked it. We ran to the stairs just off the foyer. Racing up to the second floor we laughed as we shoved each other, both of us wanting the best bedroom. At the top of the stairs was a second living room teaming with all of the upstairs luggage. Running through the mass of boxes, we made it to the first door at the same time. Twisting the handle Lisa pushed the door open.

Inside was a fairly simple set up. There was a queen bed in the center of the room with a white dresser on the opposite wall. Mounted on the light blue wall above the dresser was a large TV. Other than the few furnishings, the room was empty.

We moved on to the next room. Lisa opened the second door and squeaked. I looked inside and the room practically screamed 'Lisa.' Light oak furniture, white walls with a deep purple strip at the top going all the way around the room. The comforter on the bed was a pretty lilac, and there was a white desk under the window with an overstuffed 'spinny' chair the same purple as the comforter. In the corner sat a big fluffy chair that matched the paint on the walls.

Lisa ran over to the bed and jumped, already right at home. Laughing, I backed out of the room to let her get herself situated.

I opened the door across the hall from the bedroom that Lisa had claimed and gasped, my hand dropping from the handle as soon as I saw the interior.

Walking slowly inside, I took in the details of the room that seemed to have been designed for me. The dark bed frame and a black comforter with silver swirls. A window seat ran along the wall adjacent to the bed, long enough to hold my five-foot five-inch frame. The upholstery had the same pattern as the comforter on my new king-sized bed. The desk and dresser were made of the same woods as the bed frame, all dark and beautiful. The dresser sat directly across from the bed. There was a TV mounted above it—much like there was in Lisa's room—and dark wood bookshelves on either side. The desk was situated in the corner by the door, with another small window right above it and a basic black desk chair tucked underneath it. There wasn't a doubt in my mind that this house was professionally furnished.

18

Walking toward the bed, I knew I was home.

***

The next morning, I woke up with the sun shining in my face. I had forgotten to close the beautiful, navy blue curtains before I went to sleep the night before. I had also forgotten to change into pajamas. Wearing the clothes from the day before, I made my way downstairs for the boxes I had brought into the house last night.

Grabbing them, I carefully walked back up the stairs with my three boxes and, squatting, placed them on the ground at the foot of my bed. After getting a change of clothes out of the box labelled 'Kaylee's closet,' I opened the two doors across from the big window. One was a walk-in closet, just like Dad had promised—it was big enough to house a car. The other led to a bathroom that looked like it was probably bigger than my old bedroom.

The house was insane.

Opposite the door was a massive tub with jets, big enough I could almost definitely swim in it. To the right was a sink and a tower of shelves that were already stocked with towels, soaps, and other various toiletries. To the left was a shower with a bench, big enough to fit at least four people.

I quickly showered underneath all three shower heads, slightly intimidated by the size and beauty of it all, before dressing in clean clothes and making my way downstairs once again.

Only Lisa's boxes were left in the foyer. Laughing and shaking my head I went to the kitchen to unpack any boxes that were left only to find that there weren't any. Dad must have taken care of them at some point. I walked over to the two door, stainless steel fridge. Eyes closed and fingers crossed, I hoped beyond hope that there would be food inside.

Oh, thank goodness.

Eggs, bacon, cheese, cantaloupe, milk, and orange juice. Everything needed to make a huge breakfast for two people with bear-like appetites—and my dad. Especially after the disappointment of moving day breakfast. I pulled out the eggs, bacon, and cheese. While the bacon popped and crackled in a frying pan, which I had found in a drawer under the wall oven, I grated some cheese for the cheesy scrambled eggs.

By the time I was done, the cantaloupe was chopped, the bacon was crispy, and the eggs were covered in cheesy goodness. I plated everything and yelled for Dad.

Hopefully he would drag Lisa down with him. If he didn't, I would have to bring a strip of bacon upstairs and lure her out of bed with it. Or just jump on her until she woke up. I probably would have chosen the latter, had it been necessary.

A few minutes later I heard the unmistakable clunking of my father's steps and the groggy shuffling of Lisa's morning feet. After all the sleepovers over the years and the long weekends spent camping, we knew each other's morning personalities pretty well. Almost as well as we knew our own.

"Hey, Dad. Hey, Lis."

Dad smiled at me, his freshly showered-damp, dark brown hair, which was even darker when wet, brushed his brow. Lisa waved halfheartedly and went to climb up onto one of the tall barstools at the island. For just one second, it balanced precariously, and I thought she might fall, but she didn't. Unfortunately.

Dad, being Dad, came and helped me finish up with breakfast. We grabbed forks and cups for the drinks. Turning to hand Lisa her plate, I almost burst out laughing. She had her elbow on the counter and her chin propped up on her open palm. I'm fairly certain she was drooling.

Despite my best efforts, a snort slipped out. Dad heard and turned to look at me from where he stood at the fridge, brow raised in amusement. I gestured at Lisa and a grin spread over his face. With the door to the fridge open, I saw the exact moment when the mischievous glint appeared in his eyes.

SLAM!

"What the hell?" Lisa jerked on the stool and fell back.

Right on her booty; the bar stool toppling down beside her.

My dad and I both burst out laughing. Rounding the island, I offered my hand and sputtered, "A–A–Are you okay?"

Lisa glared at me and wrapped her fingers around mine, allowing me to help her up off the ground.

"You guys suck," Lisa muttered as she rubbed what I was sure was a very sore tush.

Still laughing, I went back to helping my dad move everything to the island. I knew she would forgive me quickly; I had made her food.

Breakfast was easy. Nice, even. The three of us talked about the unpacking left to do, which was the same for each of us—our personal boxes. The only difference being how *much*. Lisa had *a lot*.

The packers had unpacked everything else in the house according to a plan my dad had put together. Following breakfast, we all made our way back upstairs to finish putting our rooms together. Aside from the boxes I had brought in with me the night before, there were about ten more boxes in the upstairs living room labelled 'Kaylee's Room,' 'Kaylee's Closet,' and

'Kaylee's Stuff.' Bringing them all to my new and massive bedroom took a few trips. When that was done, I got to work.

By the time I was completely finished, it was just after four o'clock. All of my clothes were either in the huge closet, in the gorgeous dark dresser, or in a pile on the floor. The latter being dirty laundry I hadn't had time to wash before the move. All of my books, movies and CD's were unpacked and perfectly arranged on my bookshelves. I had also made a list of things I had to ask Dad about; either where they ended up or if we needed to buy replacements.

Taking my list of questions, I went in search of my father.

"Dad?" The shout resounded loudly throughout the house. The last door in the upstairs hallway swung open and my father stepped out dressed in dark pants and a dark t-shirt.

"What's up, Kale? Is everything okay?" A frown marred his features and the corners of his brown eyes were crinkled with worry.

"Yeah, Dad, everything is fine. But I kind of need a laundry hamper and I couldn't find mine."

"You know what? I think the movers put them all in the laundry room." He nodded to himself as if answering his own question.

He showed me to the laundry room, which was tucked in by the foyer, and we both retrieved our laundry baskets. I went over the rest of the list with him while we sat on the turquoise sofa in the upstairs living room.

At some point, Lisa had joined us. She sat in the big white chair and tucked her legs underneath herself, putting in her two cents whenever there was an opening. When we had finished, Dad stood and stretched. Little pops resounded all over his body.

"I almost forgot, I have something to show you."

I felt my face scrunch up in confusion. He motioned for me to follow him, and I looked over at Lisa. She just shrugged. I followed my dad and we ended up in the garage, where two shiny cars sat. One Mazda 3 and one VW Bug. They were both completely unfamiliar, and I knew neither one of them belonged to my dad.

I looked over at my dad's face, studying his profile and trying to figure out what was running through his head. "What's this? Whose are these?"

"Pick one." He motioned toward the two vehicles parked side by side.

My jaw dropped. Was he serious?

"Pick one," he repeated.

Oh my goodness.

I was getting a car.

"Uh, urm. The black one?" I sputtered, barely getting the words out. Dad reached into his pocket and pulled out the key for the *Mazda*. I squealed and grabbed it from his outstretched hand before hugging him hard. Running back into the house, I yelled for Lisa. I had just reached the stairs when I caught a hint of movement out of the corner of my eye.

There was a woman standing just inside the front door. A tall and slender woman, with dark brown eyes and honey blonde hair. A woman I recognized instantly. A woman whose photo rested lightly against my sternum.

I gasped.

"Mom?"

Chapter 4

Mom

Mom

I stood there, staring. Unsure of what to do. I don't know how long we stood in the foyer, neither of us saying a word, when Lisa's footsteps came pounding down the stairs.

"What's up, ba—?" Lisa cut herself off and I knew she had seen the woman standing in front of me. The woman that I so closely resembled. We had the same long, wavy hair, the only difference being the color. We had the same dark brown eyes and the same facial structure. However, where I am short and curvy, my mother is tall, slender, and somehow still curvy in all the right places.

"Helen?" Lisa gasped.

"Hi, Lisa," replied the woman who gave birth to me. She spoke softly with a small, sad smile on her face as her eyes gleamed with unshed tears. Looking back at me, she smiled again.

"Kaylee?" Her voice was everything I missed. Her face was everything I dreamed of for years. Everything I had wanted to see since she left us when I was twelve years old.

Shaking my head, I started to slowly back away. I couldn't handle it. Seeing her. I spun around and smacked right into my dad, who wrapped his arms around me, murmuring soothing words.

I hadn't even realized I was crying until he asked me not to, his voice strained. Sobs wracking my body, I buried my face in his chest.

"What are you doing here, Helen?" my dad's voice rumbled out and I could feel the soothing vibrations of his tenor in his chest.

"We need to talk, Johnathyn," came her response.

"When I called you to let you know we arrived, you weren't supposed to just randomly show up. You were supposed to give me time."

My crying stopped. I looked up at my father, sniffling.

I pulled away. "You *called* her?" I choked out past the lump growing in my throat.

I felt Lisa coming up behind me and then her hands were on my shoulders, pulling me from my dad's embrace.

"Come on, babe. Let them talk, they obviously have some things to discuss."

I continued staring at my father in disbelief. How could he? She left us and he called her. Then something clicked and when it did, I couldn't believe it had taken so long.

"You knew, didn't you, Dad? That she was here?" By the downcast look on his face and the regret reflected in his eyes I knew I was right. "How long? How? Long?" my voice rising with each word.

"Since she left."

It felt like a slap in the face, and I took a step back.

"Kale," he said, reaching out to me, but I cut him off before he could get another word out.

"No. No! How could you? You let me believe that my mother, your *wife*, abandoned us when I was *twelve years old!* I was a *child!* And you let me feel like she didn't want us anymore! I thought…I thought something was wrong with me. That she didn't want *me* anymore. That she didn't—that she didn't *love* me anymore."

My voice broke. I had started out strong, shouting my anger, but by the end I was broken. I couldn't even hold my body up on my own anymore. Collapsing against Lisa, I fell apart.

My father had betrayed me. He had known the whole time that my mother was here. For all I knew, he had stayed in touch with her the entire time and I was left completely in the dark. He let me grow up without a mother. They both had.

I was on the ground in the foyer, bent over with my legs tucked underneath me, my elbows on my knees and my face in my hands, sobbing brokenly. Then Lisa was beside me with her arms wrapped around my body, trying to sooth me, and I heard two sets of footsteps padding away before I let the grief utterly and completely consume me.

***

It was some time later when I found myself waking in an unfamiliar room. My head was resting in someone's lap and there was a fluffy red blanket tucked up under my chin. Glancing up I saw that the owner of my thigh pillow was

24

none other than Lisa. At that moment her face was the only one I wanted to see, or could stomach for that matter.

From where I was laying, I could tell that we were in a walkout basement that I could only assume was ours. There was a TV mounted to the wall in front of the couch we were on and adjacent to that wall was another that was completely made up of windows. In front of the windows stood a beautiful pool table. I had no doubt it was purchased with me in mind. Lisa and I would play pool every Thursday. Sometimes Carson and Carter would join us after we all finished our homework, but most weeks it was only Lisa and me.

"Hey, babe," came Lisa's voice quietly from above me, her hand gently stroking my dark hair.

"Hey, Lis. I–Is she still here?" I whispered, tears once again wetting my eyes. Lisa knew exactly who I was talking about.

"Yeah, babe. Yeah, she is," she replied solemnly. She knew how much this hurt me.

"Why?" I blinked back tears, voice cracking. "Why is she here? Why did he call her?" I was so confused.

"I don't know, Kaylee. But maybe this could be a good thing. Maybe she had a really goo—"

Always the optimist.

"*Don't* say she had a good reason for leaving. There is no reason I could possibly think of that would excuse leaving your twelve-year-old child without so much as a goodbye," I cut her off. No longer able to hold the tears back as they spilled down my cheeks.

"I know, babe, and I'm sorry. You're right. I know I wouldn't be able to forgive my mother if it was me, but it's not. It's you, and you've always had a bigger heart—a more forgiving heart—than me."

Before I could respond, the sound of light footsteps followed by heavier ones coming down the stairs interrupted us. As fast as I could, I sat up, straightened my hair, and wiped the tears off my face. *She* had already seen me break once, I wouldn't let her see me weak again.

I saw them coming over to us, my parents. They looked so natural together—so at ease—just like they always had.

"So what excuse have you two come up with?" I tried to be snarky, but it just came out sounding dejected.

I saw my mother stiffen and my dad, the man who raised me, flinch.

"No excuses, Kale. Only a long story that started the moment you were born," my dad responded, and I could tell he really didn't want to tell me the 'long story.'

His head was down, eyebrows creased, and hands clasped in front of him. Unfortunately, before anyone could say more, there was a pounding on the front door.

"He's here, Johnathyn. I told you he would come."

That was my mother's voice. She sounded worried, but I refused to look at her.

Dad swore softly under his breath, and his fists clenched at his sides.

"Who's here? Dad?" I looked at Lisa, who shrugged, seemingly just as confused as I was and then shifted my gaze to my father.

"No one, sweetie," he gritted out through clenched teeth. Next thing I knew he was running back up the stairs and I could have sworn I heard him growl.

Obviously, I wasn't getting answers from my dad, so I begrudgingly dragged my gaze to *her*.

"Who's here?" I asked, curious.

"His name is R—" she started with a small, knowing smile on her face, but was interrupted when my dad's angry shout rushed down the stairs.

"No! She's not ready!"

"You don't know that! She's mine and I want to see her!"

New. That deep, sensual voice was new. But, I realized as the last word was growled out, it was also somehow familiar.

"Please, just give us a couple more days. We haven't explained anything yet." My dad's tenor was quieter this time, but still loud enough to be heard. It almost sounded like he was begging.

There was a moment of silence before the stranger replied.

"Two days, that's it. You can't expect me to wait longer than that. You, of everyone, know what it's like to be separated. Even if she doesn't remember me, it doesn't matter, because I remember *her*."

That deep baritone came again, making my skin tingle. This man was yelling at my dad, but my body didn't seem to care. A few more words were exchanged quietly before I heard the door close and my dad coming back down the stairs.

When he reached us, I noticed he was paler than he was when he left. Actually, he was paler than I had ever seen him. He sat on the loveseat beside *her* and put his head in his hands, elbows on his knees.

"Dad? Who was that?" I asked quietly. Despite everything, I didn't want to disturb him, but something inside me demanded an answer. It took a few moments for him to respond. When he did, he sighed and shook himself.

"No one you need to worry about, Kaylee. At least not right now." He looked over at me with a morose look on his face.

The last part was so quiet I wasn't sure he had actually said it. It was then I noticed *her* hand on his back. The two of them were acting as if no time had passed. How could they be that close after five years of separation, of not seeing one another?

"Alright, guys. It's time for that 'long story.'" I sat up straighter on the couch, crossing my arms and legs.

They needed to know I was serious—that I wasn't taking any prisoners. With one eyebrow raised, I glared at my parents pointedly. They exchanged a long look and my dad sighed again before straightening himself.

"Okay, Kale. For starters, you were born here. In Redheart."

My heart stopped.

"What? Why didn't you tell me?" my words came out so softly I wasn't sure he heard me. But he did.

"Honestly, I didn't want you to be curious about the place you were born. When we left, we never thought we'd be able to come back, and it would have been dangerous if you had gone snooping around," he answered.

"Then why did we come back if it's too dangerous? And what about Lisa? I thought we had been best friends since birth?"

Dad gave me a stern look before responding. "Look, Kale, I know you're curious, but if you interrupt me every time you have a question, you're never going to hear the story. Not to mention most of your questions will probably be answered along the way and, if they aren't, you can ask when I'm done. Acceptable?"

He was calm, but obviously approaching the end of his rope. The stranger at the door must have upset him more than I'd realized.

I nodded, and he continued, "Alright. You were born in Redheart—in the mayor's home, actually. He was a good friend of ours at the time and his wife was a doctor, so it only made sense that she delivers you. Especially in a town as small as this one. You were supposed to be born in our home, but their four-year-old son had started running a high fever the day before you were born, and the mayor's wife, Lillian, didn't want to be too far from him. So when your mother went into labor, I drove her over to the Masons' house. Thirteen hours later, and you were born. Lillian and the mayor, George, gave us their best and went to take care of their son. You were beautiful, Kale. The most beautiful baby I've ever seen. You still are. My baby girl."

I blushed. I've never been able to take compliments well.

"Of course, in a town such as this, when a baby is born everyone feels the need to meet them; to pamper them and congratulate the parents. Especially when her parents are friends with the town's leader. We took that first day all to ourselves, basking in the joy of having a baby. Karen and Darrel visited first thing the next morning and brought Carson and Lisa along with them. At the time, Carson was a little over a year, and Lisa was four months old. Karen fell in love with you the moment you looked at her and she started jabbering on about how you and Lisa would be best friends for your entire lives."

Lisa and I squeezed each other, still sitting on the couch together, and smiled.

"Obviously, she was right. Not long after Karen handed you to Darrel, Lillian came in saying that as soon as your mother was up for it, there was going to be a party. Unfortunately, this never happened."

I watched as Dad's eyes misted over with ghosts of the past. I looked at my mother, and saw that hers were glazed over in much the same way. They were haunted.

"Four days after you were born, your mother was completely recovered from the delivery, and you were a perfectly healthy baby."

I found it odd that someone could completely recover from giving birth after only four days, but I'd never been around when a baby was born.

"The town was excited to welcome you into our little world and the celebration was scheduled for the next day. That morning, there was an attack. Word of your birth had travelled to a rival town, and they had sent men to come steal you. So, we ran. All the way to Washington. Lisa's family followed, knowing it would be safer for everyone close to us to disappear as well. Of course, the mayor couldn't just up and leave, for obvious reasons." Dad paused to take a deep breath. "Running worked perfectly for us. We lived our lives for twelve wonderful years—until the mayor fell ill and your mom had to return home."

He looked over at my mother with a sad smile on his face and motioned for her to take over. Even after all those years, I could still see the love in his gaze and the affectionate way they acted around one another. They gravitated toward one another, practically moving as one. They were two halves of a whole.

"You see, the mayor was a sort of brother to me. His father had saved my life when I was very young, and their family took me in, they took care of me.

"I grew up with George, so when I found out he was dying, I had to come back. A year later, he passed, and I still couldn't come back to you. Ryder and his brother, Lucas, just lost their father, and Lillian went into a depression."

Dad's face fell into a scowl at the mentioned names and I couldn't help but wonder why.

"I knew you would be fine without me, you were always so strong, and you had your dad. But Ryder and Lucas needed someone to watch out for them. They needed someone to care for them. Ryder was only sixteen, and Lucas was just eleven. How could I leave two children without anyone to watch over them? I couldn't. I just couldn't. So, I stayed. I begged your father to bring you home, but he said it wouldn't be fair to you to pull you away from your life, from Lisa. I knew he was right, but I still begged. And then he made the point that it still wasn't safe. Especially without a strong leader. It was selfish of me to want you to come home, I know that now. But now, with Ryder on top, it's finally safe enough for you to come home." She smiled at me, tears gleaming in her eyes.

After finally knowing her reasons for leaving, I understood. What I *didn't* understand was why she didn't tell me. Or why she completely cut me off. And there were parts of her story that didn't quite add up—like why the town didn't elect a new mayor after the old one died? Then there was the way she said 'leader.' There was also the fact that this Ryder person, he was obviously important, but there was something that didn't quite make sense.

"Wait. This Ryder guy must only be like, twenty something years old. How can he possibly be *mayor*?" Dumbfounded, I stared at my parents.

"Everything works a bit different here, Kale. You'll get used to it eventually," My dad answered, easily but vaguely. It though it was obvious he was holding something back, like he was being purposefully evasive.

Then something occurred to me.

I turned my head to Lisa who was still sitting next to me on the couch.

"Why didn't your parents move back here with us?"

I was suspicious. Why wouldn't a family as close as Lisa's was want to come home together? Especially when one of them already was. And if they followed us to move away, why wouldn't they follow us back?

Lisa blushed, biting her lip nervously. "They kinda, maybe, are moving here too. I think they're moving today. They're going to fix up our old house and move back into it," she paused, shrugging as if it were no big deal. "They want to come home," she told me sheepishly while picking at her cuticles and avoiding my gaze.

I rolled my eyes and kept going.

"Why didn't you tell me? Better yet, why did you move with *us* instead of just waiting for them?"

"Are you kidding?" she gaped. "And give up the chance to live with my diaper buddy?"

Laughing, she wrapped her arms around me and squeezed. I gaped at her. No one had even whispered the phrase 'diaper buddy' around me since my mother had left. She was the one who coined it for us. I flinched slightly, although it wasn't as painful to hear as I thought it would be.

I looked back at my parents and raised a brow. "Anything else?"

She looked like she wanted to say something, but Dad beat her to it.

"Not for now, Kale. But if you have any questions, *please* ask *me*," he practically begged for the second time that day. Why would my father feel the need to beg me?

My mother shot my dad a frustrated glare, which he ignored completely.

"Sure, Dad. Yeah." Then I looked at *her*. "I understand why you left. But what I don't get…what I don't understand…is—" I took a deep breath and leaned forward placing my elbows on my knees and clasping my hands together under my chin. I had to brace myself for what could be a very painful answer. "Why didn't you call? Why didn't you call me, Mom?" my voice broke when I called her 'Mom,' and I couldn't take it anymore. The tears streamed down my face like a waterfall and my shoulders shook uncontrollably. "Why?" I gasped out.

I put my face in my hands, unable to meet anyone's gaze.

Suddenly I was enveloped in what felt like the warmest hug of my entire life. It was *her. My mom.* After five years she was finally hugging me, finally holding me again. I was in her arms and she smelt the same, just as comforting as she always had. She smelt like vanilla and cinnamon. She smelt like home.

Chapter 5

Life Changes

I don't know how long my mom held me, but I do know that I was glad she did. I didn't yet know why she had cut me out of her life so completely, but with her rocking me and whispering soothing words as I cried, I didn't really care. She held me for what only felt like minutes, but really could have been hours. And it still wasn't long enough.

When I finally pulled my head back from her shoulder, I saw that she had been crying too and that we had been left alone.

Cupping my face in her hands, she sniffled and placed a gentle kiss to my forehead. "I'm so sorry, Kaylee." Her lips brushed my skin as she choked on the words. "If I could go back and do it differently, I would. I still would have left, but I would have told you *exactly* where I was going and *why*. I would have visited *all* the time and I would have called you every night to hear your voice and so that you could hear mine. So that you could go to bed knowing that your mommy loves you. That she has and will always love you."

"Why didn't you? Why did you cut me off, Mom?" I sniffed, facing her, wiping my face on my sleeve.

"We thought it would be easier for you," she sighed regretfully. "We thought it would be easier for you to move on with your life, and possibly even forget about me, if you thought I had left the both of you, instead of knowing that I had left you and your father for a family that you didn't know. We thought that thinking I had left you would be easier than going to bed knowing where I was but not being able to have me and knowing that I had chosen another family over you."

At some point, the tears had once again started falling freely down my face. I wasn't even aware of it until Mom wiped them away with the pads of her thumbs.

"I get it, Mom, I do. But you and Dad were wrong. I'm a tough girl, I always have been. You should have just told me." Staring down at my lap with my shoulders hunched and my hands sitting awkwardly on my legs, I shook my head.

"Can you ever forgive us, Kaylee? Can you forgive *me*?" She was so quiet, as if she was afraid I would say no.

For a second, I thought I might, but then I clasped my hands on her shoulders.

"*Of course,* I can forgive you, you're my parents. But, Mom, it's not something I'll ever be able to forget." I smiled sadly.

Things would never be the way they had been before she left and, if by some miracle they ever were, it would take a long, long time.

Mom returned my smile and pulled me back into her embrace. Her arms wrapped around my shoulders, and my arms tucked under hers.

"I know, baby, and I would never expect you to."

Having her call me *baby* somehow cemented her place back in my heart. It gave me the confirmation I needed that she wouldn't leave again. I finally had my mom back.

A few moments later, I caught her staring at that spot right above my breasts.

"You kept it." Her breath audibly caught in her throat as tears welled in her eyes. Reaching up, I fingered the locket that lay just in my cleavage.

"Of course I kept it," I replied, not knowing what else to say. There wasn't really anything *to* say. With no more words between us, we fell into a comfortable silence.

We stayed in the basement a while longer and caught up a bit. Mostly on the larger events throughout our lives, even though Mom said Dad had kept her pretty up to date on the ins and outs of what went on after she left.

She told me about how she helped Lillian through her depression and about the amazing young man Ryder is. How strong and how so much like his dad he had turned out to be. Although that last bit of information contributed nothing to my image of him, seeing as I couldn't possibly remember his dad. The entire time she talked about this Ryder guy, I couldn't help but feel like she was leaving out a very important detail.

She told me about Lucas and what it was like to watch a little boy growing up all the while knowing she had a little girl at home waiting for her. She talked about how badly she had wanted me and Dad in Redheart and to experience everything with us.

She let me know that she and Dad had stayed connected through phone calls, Skype calls so they could see each other, and even the occasional trip on my dad's part. Apparently, only about half of his business trips over the years were actually for business. The rest of them were to visit her; the woman he loves. How could I blame him for that? She didn't cut him out of her life the same way she did with me, and I found myself being grateful.

I couldn't imagine how hard it would have been for Dad if she had *actually* abandoned us. And looking back, he really did take her leaving far better than he should have.

In turn, I told her about school, about my aptitude for creative writing. I told her about my love of reading, which she remembered, and how I had collected many books throughout my life, mostly since she left. And I let her know about Carter. About how he had been my first real boyfriend. My first kiss.

We listened to each other and I don't think I had ever felt so appreciated for my words. When I brought up Carter, Mom's mouth did this funny puckering thing, like she had tasted something unappealing.

"Can I ask you something, sweetie?" she asked cautiously.

It was strange having someone other than my dad calling me 'sweetie' again. I nodded my consent, and she continued.

"You and Carter, did you guys ever...*do* anything?"

My jaw dropped. Shaking my head erratically, I actually burst out laughing.

"What? No, Mom. God no. I mean, he was really nice and attractive and everything, but you and Dad taught me to never do anything I wasn't one hundred percent sure about. And as much as I liked Carter, I was never one hundred percent sure about him."

She breathed out a sigh of relief and her shoulders slumped, visibly relaxed. I found it strange that she was so concerned; maybe she was simply being protective.

"That's good, honey. That's really good."

Beaming, my mother stood up from the couch and held her hand out to me. I couldn't help but wonder why she was so relieved. But then my stomach growled, distracting me.

Mom chuckled. "Why don't we go get some dinner?"

"Dinner? I haven't even had lunch yet," I told her. Then I looked at the wall clock that was mounted above the television set. "Six o'clock! How can it be six o'clock?" I jumped up off my bum, and foregoing my mom's offered hand, ran up the stairs.

Mom's footsteps echoed quickly from behind me as I raced into the kitchen only to see Lisa and my Dad busily moving around the kitchen and laughing. I was greeted by the smell of Lisa's lasagna—the only thing she knew how to make. The cheesy goodness that was the lasagna sat on the counter just waiting to be devoured.

I went and stood beside Lisa and said, "Thank you."

I didn't have to tell her what for, she knew it was for everything.

While I was making my way to stand by Lisa, my mom went over to my dad and put her arms around his shoulders. And she kissed him. I finally knew why they acted as if no time had passed when they were around each other. It was because, for them, it hadn't. They were only ever separated physically. Never emotionally. Their love survived all of the crap that being apart for five years had surely created.

My family was back together and again.

I couldn't stop staring—or smiling—until Lisa elbowed me in the ribs. I mouthed "What" at her with my eyes widened with feigned innocence, and she rolled hers, laughing silently and shaking her head.

Lisa gripped the handles on the lasagna and carried it to the casual dining table. I followed her, carrying plates and forks while my dad came up behind me with his hands full of glasses. Mom went to the fridge and pulled out the skim milk and orange juice.

By the time she made it to the table, it was set and Lisa, my dad, and myself were already sitting down. She placed the milk in front of me and the orange juice in the center of the table. I looked up at her, wondering how she knew I always drank milk with my dinner. It wasn't something I had started doing until I was fourteen. She winked at me with a small smile on her face, her chocolate eyes twinkling, and I realized Dad must have told her. I watched her as she walked to the chair across the round table from my dad and next to me.

Reaching over to take my hand, still smiling, she said, "You always drank milk with your dinner when you were younger. I guess I hoped you still did."

I had forgotten I used to drink it when I was really little. I grinned at her and poured myself a full glass and passed the milk along to my dad. Mom and Lisa both had orange juice and we all dished up the lasagna.

"One sec!" Lisa jumped out of her chair and went to the sink. Pulling a bowl full of lettuce out of the sink, she went over to the fridge and took out the dressing and an assortment of salad toppings. She came back and said, "'Kay, now we can eat." She grinned.

She was proud of herself for making dinner, as she should be. Her lasagna was to die for. I laughed at her enthusiasm and we all thanked her for her efforts.

Eating dinner was easy and wonderful. My best friend and my parents, all together. Everyone I loved most surrounded me. The conversation flowed around the table, smiles on all of our faces.

Mom and Lisa talked a lot about Lisa's family while Dad and I fell into an easy banter about one topic after another. All too soon, dinner was over, and my parents had to go hide away and talk, just like Mom had mentioned earlier that day. When they reached the bottom of the stairs and were lifting their feet to ascend, I stopped them.

I had to ask. "Wait. Mom, are you moving in with us?" I had my fingers crossed behind my back. No matter what she had done in the past, she was still my mom, and I wanted her around. No matter what, I wanted her back. She and Dad exchanged a brief glance. Dad nodded so minutely I almost missed it.

"If you're okay with it, I would like to, yes," Mom spoke cautiously again, as if she was worried she would spook me the way a person would spook a horse.

A smile lit up my face and I ran to her, wrapping my arms around her and burying my face in her shoulder—she was slightly taller than me, so this was easy.

"I would love it, Mom."

She squeezed me and let out a sigh of relief. She had done that a lot today. Sigh.

"I'm so glad you feel that way. My darling girl." My mom squeezed tighter and started turning from side to side.

I held on tight for a few moments before letting her go. Lisa came up behind me and slung her arm across my shoulders as I watched my parents, hand-in-hand, ascend the staircase of our new home. The home that was made so much better than I could have hoped for, with my family back together.

"You did good, babe. You did good," Lisa spoke quietly, and I was unsure of what she meant.

Scrunching my brow and crossing my arms I looked up at her, although she was only giving me the side of her face.

"What do you mean?"

"Letting your mom back in like that? Opening up to her the way you did in the basement this afternoon? And yes, I was eavesdropping. You guys bonded. Reconnected. I'm proud of you, Kaylee. So very proud of you. Not to mention bouncing off the walls happy. You have your *mom* back. The one thing you've wanted more than anything for more than five years."

She smiled, looking at me. I smiled back and we went downstairs to relax before bed.

We played a few games of pool and watched a movie. Lisa and I had always been able to talk about anything and everything or absolutely nothing at all while still being completely at ease.

I must have dozed off at some point during the movie because when I opened my eyes, I was lying on the basement couch. The room was dark and I was alone. Lisa must have gone to bed. I caught a slight movement from the corner of my eye.

"Lisa?"

Sitting up, I gasped. I was facing the windows, and through them I saw what had to have been the biggest coyote I had ever seen. With all of the lights off I could barely make out its shape, but it was large and fluffy like a husky. It had to have been almost the size of a bear.

Wolf, I realized with a start. It wasn't a coyote; it was a wolf.

"Holy crap," I mumbled under my breath.

I shot up off the couch and ran all the way up to my room. Feeling eyes on my back until I could no longer see the wall of windows.

That night, I tossed and turned in bed, unable to erase the image of the big brown eyes that seemed to glow in the dark of the night, until finally, I fell asleep.

I woke up the next morning in my wonderful king bed, once again having forgotten to put on sleep clothes. I checked the clock on my nightstand, and all I could think was that it was a darn good thing that it was summer. Because boy, had I slept in.

After a nice long shower, I dressed in shorts and a long sleeved, scoop-neck shirt and made my way downstairs. Lisa was already sitting in the living room. Seeing her sitting there nearly gave me a heart attack, but then I saw the reason behind her being awake already.

Karen and Darrel Perry were sitting on the couch, talking with my parents. Lisa had herself situated in the big chair in the corner with a mug in her hands, noticeably basking in her family's presence.

Darrel heard me first and turned to look at me. A smile broke out across his face and he turned to get Karen's attention. They stood together and walked to meet me half way as I made my way over to the couch. Both of them hugged me, and they each planted a kiss on my cheek after saying hello.

Karen and Darrel returned to their places on the couch while I went and perched on the armrest of the chair Lisa was lounging in. The armrest was wide enough to make plopping down quite comfortable.

"What have you guys been chatting about?" I asked nonchalantly, but secretly jumping up and down inside. Everyone I loved was with me. Except Carson, and…Carter. I had had other friends in Washington, but none of them were family the way the Perrys were.

"Oh, you know. Just how glad we are that you finally know what happened five years ago," Karen responded with a breathtaking smile.

Their children definitely took after her. She was as fair as they come. Pale, blonde, light eyes. Whereas Darrel the stereotypical tall, dark, and handsome—

for an older guy. Olive skin, black hair, and eyes so dark they seemed to reach into your soul. But in reality, he was just a big teddy bear.

Despite the genuine tone of her voice, I couldn't help but feel like Karen wasn't telling me the whole truth. But I brushed it off, too happy to worry about a hunch.

"I'm glad you guys are here, actually. It means that you can take Lisa back," I started laughing and stuck my tongue out at my diaper buddy.

Laughing, she shoved me off the arm of her chair and I landed as ungracefully as humanly possible. Right on my backside with my hair hanging in front of my face. I brushed the hair away from my eyes and went to sit on the opposite half of the sectional as the Perry's, beside my parents. Everyone else laughed as Lisa stuck her tongue out back at me. I just rolled my eyes and mouthed, 'copy-cat.' She glared at me. A glare that, if I were anyone else, would have had me shrinking into myself and quite probably wishing I was six feet under.

I laughed at her and snuggled into the deep cushions of the grey couch.

Conversation flowed freely around me, mostly between Lisa's parents and my mom. After five years of very little contact, they had a lot to catch up on. I don't know how long we sat there talking, laughing, and just generally enjoying each other's company, but eventually the good time was interrupted by the doorbell ringing.

My dad glanced nervously toward the door and Mom smiled.

"I'll get it," I said, standing.

I don't think I've ever seen my dad move as quickly as he did in that moment.

Putting his hand on my shoulder, he said, "It's fine, Kale, I got it."

I was slightly confused, but I moved out of his way and sat back down. All of the adults were tense. They knew something.

I looked at Lisa and, just like the last time someone was at the door, she shrugged. We all waited in silence until my dad's voice, along with one that was unfamiliar, drifted toward us through the foyer and into the living room.

Mom must have recognized the strange one, as she stood as well and went to greet the stranger.

"Lillian!" Mom exclaimed cheerfully. The late mayor's wife? "Why don't you come in? Come meet my daughter!"

Footsteps followed the voices, and I was greeted with the sight of a beautiful woman. She had alabaster skin, high cheekbones, long black hair and blazing green eyes. She wasn't much older than my mom, but she was one of those women whose age you would never be able to guess. She just had that ageless beauty and grace about her that a girl could only hope to achieve later in life. She was perfect.

In her arms was a clear container full of what looked like cinnamon rolls. Thank goodness, too. I was starving! Her eyes scanned the room, and it didn't take long for them to fall on me.

"Oh! You must be Kaylee! Last time I saw you, you were about the size of a loaf of bread," the woman that must be Lillian reminisced, giggling. "You're so beautiful, just like your mother."

She must have noticed me eyeing the cinnamon rolls because she handed me the container with a wink.

I stood from the couch and plated one before quickly heating it up and returning to my spot.

Looking at my mom, Lillian said, "When you didn't come back yesterday, I figured things had gone well. I'm glad that I was right." Lillian enveloped my mom in a hug, which she returned with just as much enthusiasm.

"They did!" Mom laughed, but I could hear the waver in it, and I knew that she had been legitimately worried. She sounded so relieved. "I'll be over in the next couple of days to move my things."

Mom tucked herself into Dad's side with her hand on his chest. His arm immediately wrapped around her slim frame, and a content smile lit up his features.

"Oh, don't be silly, Helen. I'll just have the boys bring your stuff—" She was cut off.

"No!" My dad shouted while Mom said a polite, "No, thank you."

"That's really okay. Johnathyn and I are perfectly capable. Thank you, though, Lillian."

My mom quickly recovered after my dad's outburst, continuing on with what was obviously some sort of excuse and nodding her head. She spoke as if her words had some untold meaning to them, and she looked at Lillian pointedly.

Lillian's face paled as she understood whatever point Mom was trying to relay, and I thought I heard her swear under her breath. Mom's eyes bugged and I knew she had heard it too, although I think her reaction had more to do with the reason for the curse than the actual word.

"Um, whoops?" Lillian said quietly in response to Mom's expression.

That's when the front door opened, and several things happened at once.

Everyone in the room stiffened. Everyone except for me.

Lisa buried her face in her hands and groaned, having placed her mug down at some point.

The adults swore.

And my entire world changed.

Chapter 6
Wolfy

He. Was. A. God. A freaking Adonis if I'd ever seen one.

He had dark hair the same color as his mother's and eyes the color of chocolate. His face was perfectly sculpted, almost as if created by Michelangelo himself. With high cheekbones and a strong jaw, he was a perfect man. There was no other way to describe him. He was tall, at least six-foot-three, and had wide shoulders that led down to a tapered waist. The t-shirt he was wearing stretched perfectly across his torso, forming around his pecs—his astonishingly real pecs—and hugging his abs and biceps. I was fairly certain I was drooling.

My stare-fest was interrupted by Lillian's voice. "Ryder, I'm sorry, but it seems as if Helen doesn't need your help after all. Would you mind taking Lucas back to the house, and we'll talk later?"

Only when she finished talking did Adonis' eyes leave me, and I realized he had been staring at me much like I had been at him. Why would he stare at me? *Me?* I am what one would call a 'plain Jane.'

"Sure, Mom." He smiled at her. He lit up the entire room with that smile and my breath caught in my throat at the sound of his voice.

He was the one at the door the day before.

His eyes sparkled at my reaction, and turning his gaze to my Dad, he spoke again: "One more day."

Nodding toward my parents and then Lisa's, he turned to leave. How did he know them all? We had been living in the U.S. for the past seventeen years! That was when I spotted the younger version of him standing in the doorway. Except this one had green eyes that matched their mother's, and his skin was a little lighter. I came to the conclusion that he must have been the 'Lucas' that Lillian had mentioned.

When the door closed, I turned back to everyone. "Alright, spill it. Who is he? Like who is he *really*? You guys wouldn't have all tensed up like Satan was here if that guy wasn't someone seriously important."

"Kale, we already told you who he is. He's the mayo—"

Cutting my dad off, I glared into the eyes of everyone in the room. I knew that each and every one of them was privy to information that was purposefully being kept from me.

"Don't give me that crap about him being mayor! He's only like, twenty years old! Now, you are all lying to me about something really big and I want to know what!" When no one made a move to explain, I went on. "Strange people are showing up at our door left and right, Lisa's parents decided to move to town at the *exact* same time we did, Mom is back in our lives, and to top it all off, there was a wolf in our backyard yesterday! So, excuse me for thinking there's something you guys aren't telling me! Especially when you've already lied to me about the last five years of my life!"

I huffed. I hadn't mean to say all that, but when I got started I couldn't stop and it all sort of just came rushing out, the same way it had when I told Carter I was leaving. Everyone in the room was silent, too shocked to speak.

"Oh! And I know he's the one who was at the door yesterday," I added for good measure, raising a brow.

I stood up and cocked my hip with my arms crossed, staring at those I considered family. Although, with all the lies, I wasn't sure I should anymore.

"Lis?" No response. "Dad?" Same thing. I took a breath, "Mom?" my voice came out quieter this time. Why weren't they saying anything? Mom sighed and looked up at my dad who shook his head.

"We can't tell you, sweetie. Not yet. It's not even that important anyway."

Lillian's head swung to the side, staring at my mom in disbelief, mouth agape.

"Well, this has been lovely and it was wonderful meeting you, Kaylee, but I think I should be going," Lillian's gaze stayed trained on my parents the entire time she spoke. The muscles in her neck were noticeably strained, and the hostility in her voice was painfully palpable.

"I'll walk you to the door." Uncrossing my arms, I did just that. I was raised to be a good host, and so I was.

With a quick goodbye and a thank you for the cinnamon rolls, I closed the door behind her and walked back to the living room where whispered words were being exchanged. Upon arrival, I looked to the Perry's.

"Darrel, Karen, it was great to see you and I don't mean to be rude, but could you please leave? Lisa, my parents, and I have some things to discuss."

They nodded, kissed their daughter on the cheek, said their goodbyes, and saw themselves out. I stood by the TV with my feet spread and my arms crossed in front of my chest.

"Well? Do you plan on telling me *anything*?" I looked at Lisa, who had her eyes downcast, and she shrugged. When Lisa avoided looking at me, it was either because she was guilty or because she wouldn't be able to keep herself from spilling the secrets. I'm pretty sure it was both.

My parents shook their heads slowly.

"Why not?"

No answer.

"Soon, at least?"

My mom stood then. She approached me and laid her hands on my shoulders.

"Absolutely. Soon. It's just—it's something we think Ryder should be able to tell you himself."

I didn't understand why that was important and I was upset that they were keeping something so obviously important from me, but after taking a few deep breaths, I came to the conclusion that I could respect their choice to let Ryder tell me his secret himself. Even if it seemed as if it wasn't only *his* secret.

"Why does Lisa know? She grew up in Washington just like me," I asked, confused and angry. And, despite my resolve to respect my parents' wishes, I was still peeved and was looking for buttons to push.

"Babe, my parents told me the truth from the beginning. I've always known where I was from. I've always known who the Masons are. All those family vacations we took? We came here."

She looked guilty. Good. She should feel bad. I could kind of understand my parents keeping things from me, but Lisa? She was my best friend. We share *everything*. And why would her parents tell her, but my parents wouldn't tell me?

As if reading my thoughts, Lisa continued. "It was never safe for you to know."

But *why*?

I knew she could see the question in my eyes, but she glanced away, silently refusing to answer.

Letting my arms fall to my sides and my head drop forward, I walked to the stairs.

"Kaylee." I heard Lisa call my name as she stood, but it didn't really register.

"Let her go, Lisa. She feels betrayed."

That was my mom speaking, and she was right. I did feel betrayed. And lied to. And stupid, for not realizing any of this sooner. I was pathetic. It only made me angrier that my mother was the one to point it out.

In a way, she was the worst. She left me feeling unloved and abandoned. But Lisa had been my best friend since the moment I was born. Her lies hurt more than my father's and even more than my mother's abandonment. Suddenly, more than seventeen years of friendship felt like it meant nothing.

When I got to my room, I went and curled up in the window seat, pulling up the overly large and fluffy blanket I had placed there while unpacking. As I looked out the window, I realized it faced the back of the house. I had unknowingly chosen the room with the best view. But I had a feeling that my room had been designed specifically for me, and the fact that the view from my window seat was amazing, was no mere coincidence.

I sat there for a while with the window open, just watching the trees and birds flying in and out of the canopy. The wind floated across the yard and into my room, its sweet smell calming my anger.

After a time, I noticed a familiar canine shape poking it's nose out from the shrubbery. As if sensing me watching, it glanced up to where I sat, and I gasped. I found myself looking into intelligent eyes. Eyes that were somehow more familiar than they should have been.

They were gentle, yet there was clear strength shining in them. The only way I could possibly describe them accurately would simply be to say that they were human.

Those eyes drew me in and I had to get closer. I stood and quietly snuck down to the basement without being seen. I ignored the whispers coming from the living area, and quickly descended the stairs, silently thanking my light footedness. I opened the sliding door in the center of the wall and stepped out onto the grey stone patio.

The wolf was gone. I felt an odd pang of disappointment, but brushed it off when I decided it was ridiculous.

Barefoot, I walked to the grass and sat down, crossing my legs, and calling, "Wolfy?" the whole way.

The grass was green and cool. It was just long enough for my fingers to play with while sitting. Laying down on my back, I stared up at the cloudless blue sky and played with the green wisps at my sides.

Sometime later, I felt a cold, wet sponginess against my cheek. When I opened my eyes, I found myself staring into that same pair of big, chocolate brown eyes that I had seen from my window.

Sucking in a breath of air, I shot into a sitting position. While raising myself up, I knocked my head against its muzzle, cutting my forehead on his tooth. Feeling the slight sting of pain, I reached up as I tried to scramble away. My fingers came back dotted with blood, and I winced.

The wolf watched me the entire time and my wince must have triggered something in it—him—because it slowly walked toward me and whimpered.

Such a small sound.

I stopped moving completely when it reached my side. Sitting back on its hind legs, it tilted its large head to the side like a confused pup. I gently began dabbing at my forehead again. Each time, I hoped my hand would come away looking the way it had the time before, signaling that I had stopped bleeding. Unfortunately, my head seemed to be a bit of a fountain.

The giant wolf just watched as I continued to prod at my cut. After watching me for what it must have considered long enough, it huffed loudly and stood on all fours again. It gently knocked my hand away from my face with its muzzle and I grimaced at how close his teeth came to my skin. My first encounter with his teeth obviously wasn't great.

He stood close enough that I could tell that he was definitely a he. His spongy nose sniffed at my skin until I felt his tongue flick out against the cut on my forehead. I hissed between my teeth at the sting of pain, but as the wolf licked the pain ebbed to nothing.

Wolfy sat resting on his hind legs again, towering over my frame and staring at me expectantly. I reached up again to touch my forehead and this time I got what I wanted. My hand came back the same as it had been before. *He had stopped the bleeding.* There must have been some sort of coagulant in his saliva.

"Thank you, Wolfy," I said quietly.

I knew I didn't have to worry about him not hearing me. His ears perked at the sound of my voice and a strange sound rumbled from his chest, sounding suspiciously like a laugh. He nodded wolfishly—which involved very exaggerated head bobs—and his ears twitched again. He suddenly looked over at the house, gave me one last glance and trotted away.

"Kaylee, honey? Are you out here?" Mom's voice came from the door as she scanned the yard. When her eyes found me sitting in the center of the space, she gasped. "Baby, is that…is that *blood?*" Standing, I walked over to her. When I reached her, her nostrils flared and her eyes lightened. "Did you have company out here, Kaylee?" Mom smiled.

"Yeah, actually. It was the strangest thing."

I dove into my experience with Wolfy—she laughed when I told her what I named him—starting with seeing him the night before while I was in the basement. There was no doubt that he was the same wolf as before. She listened to every word, and not once did she question what was coming out of my mouth. I was questioning it, and I was the one it had happened to.

"Am I crazy, Mom? I mean, a wolf. In our backyard. And it *licked* me! Like, really licked me!" Shaking my head and laughing, I looked up at her in disbelief.

"No, baby, you're not crazy. It's all part of what we need to let Ryder tell you. What your *father* needs to let Ryder tell you."

Now I was even more confused.

"What do you mean?"

"If I had my way, we would all sit you down and tell you everything, but your dad insists on giving you more time," Mom huffed, and I could tell that this situation really frustrated her. Maybe even more than it frustrated me. "Now, let's go get all this blood off of you. We don't need your dad panicking because his baby girl *was* bleeding," she laughed.

We both knew how overprotective Dad was. Especially right now, with the move and the fact that I didn't really know anyone. And apparently with whatever he was keeping from me.

I spent the next couple of days in the backyard, hoping to see Wolfy again, but he never returned. Strangely enough, neither did anyone else. The only people in the house were my parents, Lisa, and myself. I was beginning to think that I had imagined the whole thing with Wolfy and that maybe I really was crazy, despite what Mom and the scab on my forehead said.

Until he showed up again.

I had been laying on my belly and reading in the grass, completely engrossed in my book, when I felt that same, cool, sponginess as I had before, except this time it was on the bare toes I had been wiggling in the grass.

Turning my head around to look, I grinned. "I'm not crazy!"

The wolf made that same rumbling sound as the last time and sat cocking his head.

Laughing, I sat up with my book in my hand, my thumb marking the page. "I've been coming out here every day since I hurt my head. When you didn't show up again, I thought I was nuts! That maybe I had imagined the whole thing!"

I chuckled at myself and shook my head—which was almost completely healed by then—looking down into my lap. "And now I'm talking to an overgrown dog. Maybe I really am crazy."

Wolfy growled lowly in his chest at the 'overgrown dog' comment and glowered at me. I just stuck my tongue out and he barked out what I'm pretty sure was a laugh. I just kind of stared at him for a few moments before he laid down in front of me, resting his head on his paws. His dark brown fur shimmered in the sun. Even laying down, he was massive. At least six-feet long from neck to bottom, not including his tail and almost two-feet tall.

Entranced by Wolfy's beauty, I reached out a hand, meaning to pet him. He glanced up at my hand and I snapped it back. He gracefully bobbed his head up and down, giving me permission.

I slowly reached out again, pausing when my fingertips were no more than a couple of inches away from his head. This time, I didn't jerk away.

Wolfy's fur was possibly the softest, silkiest thing I had ever felt. I stroked gently before scratching him softly behind the ears. Wolfy leaned into my hand and grumbled strangely, it almost sounded like an odd purr. I smiled and readjusted to laying on my belly again, feeling weirdly comfortable in the presence of this beast. I held my book in both hands. Getting back into the story was easy, even with a massive wolf for company.

We were out there together for hours. I had almost finished my book and Wolfy just laid there next to me the entire time. Every once in a while, he would nudge my hand, asking for attention, and, after scratching his head for a few moments, Wolfy would allow me to return to my novel.

I had started petting Wolfy again when I heard Mom's voice calling my name. "Kaylee? Kaylee, sweetie! Your dad made dinner!" I jumped up and bookmarked my novel.

"Bye, Wolfy." I smiled and gave him one last scratch behind his floppy ears before heading inside for dinner.

For the next week, I spent all of my time outside. Sometimes with Lisa, or one or both of my parents, sometimes all three of them. Karen and Darrel visited a couple times and we went over to their house just as often. They were our neighbors—big surprise—but all of the houses in this town were all about a normal city block apart. So, for once in my life, we had this big chunk of land. And privacy. I enjoyed being able to go outside and not worrying about who was watching and possibly judging.

At some point during the week Mom went to Mayor Mansion—which is what I had started calling the mayor's ginormous, estate-like home since walking by it one day with Lisa to go get ice cream—to collect all her belongings and she moved them into our house. Mostly into her and Dad's room, but some things found places elsewhere. I couldn't keep the smile off my face when she announced that she had 'officially' moved in.

As much as I enjoyed spending time with my family and their old friends, I enjoyed my alone time in the backyard even more. Especially when it became alone time that wasn't *really* alone time.

Wolfy would come and visit at the same time every day. Even when people were in the backyard with me, I could somehow feel him watching from the trees. It made me happy to know he enjoyed my company as much as I enjoyed his. Somehow, I knew this without a doubt. He became as much of a friend as a wolf could be. When it was just the two of us, he would lay on the grass with me while I read whatever book I was on that day, or sometimes he would watch me write. Every once in a while, he would disappear for an hour or so and return looking no worse for wear.

One day in the yard, I was reading a raunchy paranormal romance. When Wolfy saw the cover, he actually rolled his eyes. I stopped at the strangely human gesture, but brushed it off. Surely, I had been seeing things. Or maybe animals could roll their eyes, too?

One day, after spending the afternoon outside with Wolfy, I headed back to the house before when I usually went in for dinner, leaving Wolfy in the grass. As I reached the top of the stairs, I heard my parents and Lisa all engaged in heated discussion.

"Why hasn't he shown up yet? He said two days, it's been two *weeks*!" That was Dad's voice. He was freaking out over something. Something big.

"I know, honey. Maybe he just decided to give us more time." Mom. She was trying to sooth him, but it was obvious it wasn't working. He was far too upset.

"Helen, have you noticed the way she smells when she comes in from reading in the back all day?"

What were they talking about? And what did Lisa mean the way I smell? Casually putting my nose to my armpit, I took a whiff. As far as I could tell, I smelt fine. I didn't even need deodorant that day. In fact, I rarely did.

Mom sighed before responding and I desperately wanted to know what she was going to say.

"I have to tell you both something. She has been coming in smelling like a male wol—"

I took another step up the stairs and the step creaked. I swore silently, cursing myself for not stepping more lightly.

My mom cut herself off mid-word. "Kaylee?"

I ran up the last remaining steps, trying my hardest not to look like the eavesdropper I was as I strode into the living room.

"Hi, guys! Watcha all talkin' 'bout?" I swung my arms on either side of me and went to sit on one of the barstools off of the island.

I watched as the three of them exchanged a look, trying to decide how much to tell me.

"Oh, you know, Kale. Just talking about heading to Lillian's for brunch tomorrow," Dad was lying threw his teeth and no one denied his words.

Why were they lying to me? Again? I knew *exactly* who they were talking about, but I didn't understand why it was so important. I decided I had had enough.

Shooting my father a piercing glare, I called them out on it. "Hey, Lis? What did you mean by me smelling odd when I come in from the yard?" I glanced around the room, looking each of them in the eye and watching with satisfaction as they all paled at the same time.

"What do you mean, sweetie? She didn't say—"

"Really, Mom? You're going to lie to me? After everything? I heard you guys. You were talking about 'him.'" I made quotes with my hands. "Why do you keep lying to me? I don't get it!" I demanded.

I watched as the three of them looked back and forth between one another. That's when Lillian walked in, dropping a bomb shell that pissed me off more than anything else that had happened yet.

"It's to protect you, Kaylee."

Chapter 7

Ryder

"*Protect* me? All of this, this *crap*, is to *protect* me? Why is that the stupidest thing I have ever heard?" I threw my hands in the air and started pacing, waiting for answers. "And where did you even come from?" I glared at Lillian.

"The bathroom," she said while gesturing in the direction of the half bath tucked into the wall by the stairs.

I huffed once before moving my gaze back to my parents. They got up and went to stand in the kitchen with their backs toward me. I ignored Lisa's grin and Lillian's look of disapproval as I snuck closer to hear what my parents were saying.

Whatever was going on, Lisa wanted me to know about it.

"Johnathyn, she deserves to know."

"I know that!" My dad whisper shouted. "I know she does, but she doesn't *need* to. Not yet."

"Honey," Mom breathed. "You know how Lisa asked about how Kaylee's been smelling off and I started to say something but then Kaylee came up the stairs?" Dad nodded. "I was about to tell you guys that it was *him*. Ryder. She's been spending her time with him in the backyard. Only, she doesn't actually know it's him." Then Mom giggled—she actually *giggled*. "She calls him 'Wolfy.'"

My dad stared at her in disbelief and I'm sure my face mirrored his exactly, until the horror overtook the disbelief.

Mom thought Wolfy was the mayor.

Dad ran his hand over his face and through his hair. Gripping the back of his neck with his hand, he groaned.

"Damn it. I guess we really do have to tell her."

Mom nodded in agreement and at once they both turned around. Both of my parents paled even more after noticing how close I was standing while the front door swung open without warning for the umpteenth time.

And in walked the devil himself.

Ryder

Once again, I found myself taking him in. His beautiful build, his strong face, and those soft, brown eyes that became more and more familiar each time I saw him. He was fascinating. He looked me up and down, taking in my appearance, and if the darkening of his eyes was any indication, he enjoyed what he saw.

He swung his dark gaze to my parents, eyes narrowing as he approached. He paused at Lillian on his way to my Mom and Dad and dutifully kissed his mother on the cheek, but his eyes never strayed from my parents.

Ryder reached Mom and Dad, and I gasped. I knew he was big but seeing him next to my parents only reinforced it. My dad was about six-foot-two and my mom almost hit five-foot-nine. Ryder dwarfed them both. He had to have been six-foot fiveish. Taller than I had originally guessed, and his shoulders were deliciously broad.

I glanced back up at his face only to see him glowering at my parents. Neither of whom shrank away from him.

"Why haven't you told her yet?" Ryder growled out through clenched teeth, though I could tell he was trying to be calm.

"How could you possibly know we haven't?" Dad snapped with his arm around Mom's waist.

"I've spent every day with her for a week. Trust me, I know. Not to mention that Mom told me she was coming over today to convince you to tell her." Ryder rolled his eyes and crossed his arms with his legs spread, like he couldn't believe they were having this conversation.

I had to butt in.

"Woah, woah, woah." I stepped toward the three of them with my hands raised. "I have *not* spent every day with this guy. I haven't even seen him since that first morning the Perrys came to visit." Moving my head to look Ryder straight in the eyes, "Right?"

His lips twitched up and for a moment I forgot where I was and who I was with. All I saw in that moment were his lips, all I wanted was to see them smile. Then he spoke, breaking the trance and my skin tingled.

"You're wrong, Kaylee. You *have* seen me since then." A shiver ran down my spine at the sound of my name rolling off his tongue, and I couldn't help the smile from spreading across my face when I saw the twinkle in his chocolate eyes.

"Ryder," Lillian snapped. "I know you want her to know, and she deserves to, but she definitely should *not* be standing. And her parents should be the ones to tell her."

A growl rumbled out of Ryder's chest. An honest to god growl.

"Don't growl at your mother young man. You may be the Al— eh, leader, but I still gave birth to you. Now, as I was saying, her parents should be able to tell her. Considering they're the reason she never knew in the first place."

Lillian walked forward and laid her hand on Ryder's shoulder. She stared at him until he gave in, nodding begrudgingly. I was missing something.

"Fine, but I'm staying. I have to make sure they tell her everything, Mom." Ryder's voice was strong, determined, and then softer. His angry resolve faltered, and, for some reason, my heart twinged.

Lillian nodded and smiled softly in understanding. She then looked at my parents expectantly, eyebrows raised and lips pursed.

"Couch, Helen? Johnathyn?"

Looking at each other, my parents came to a silent agreement and nodded, before taking their place on the sectional.

My parents sat on one end of the charcoal couch while Lillian and Ryder sat at the other end. I think they all expected me to sit in the middle, but instead I went and sat in the big chair and Lisa took a seat on the floor in front of me with her back pressed against the monstrous piece of furniture.

We all sat in tense silence for a few moments. I was waiting for someone to tell me what the hell was going on and I think everyone else was trying to decide what to say.

Surprisingly, Lisa spoke first.

"This is ridiculous!" She exclaimed, standing and throwing her hands up in the air in exasperation. Looking me straight in the eye, Lisa propped her hands on her hips. "Kaylee, babe, we're werewolves."

The room erupted.

"Lisa!"

"How could you?"

"Are you insane?"

These statements chorused around the room and I just sat there staring into nothing. Then I started laughing. I don't know why, but at that moment it was the only thing I could do. Everyone in the room stopped talking and stared at me with mixed looks of confusion and concern as I bent forwards, clutching my stomach.

I couldn't decide if Lisa was insane or joking, but by everyone's reactions to Lisa's outburst, I should have known it was neither.

"Kaylee, honey? Are you okay?"

"Kale?"

"Babe, what the hell? This isn't exactly what I would call comedy."

None of what was coming out of their mouths registered and I kept on laughing. Until those eyes were staring into mine from right in front of me. All of a sudden, the laughter coursing through me turned into body-lurching sobs. If I had been standing, there would have been nothing anyone could have done to keep me from falling over.

As I stared into Ryder's eyes, things began to click into place, and it dawned on me why those eyes became more familiar every time I saw him. It was because I had always been with Wolfy before seeing him. And their eyes were the same. Ryder and Wolfy weren't different at all. They were one and the same. Mom was right.

I hid my face in my hands, not wanting to look at anyone, especially Ryder. I didn't want to see the eyes. I didn't want to look into the chocolate pools of warmth that had kept me company for the past week. But it only lasted a minute before I felt strong, warm hands wrapping around my wrists, gently pulling my hands away.

"You're Wolfy, aren't you?" I sniffled quietly, choking on a sob. Ryder nodded calmly, still holding my wrists. "How?"

He swung his head back around and faced the couch where Lillian and my parents still sat.

"Well, we're werewolves, honey. Lisa, Lillian, Ryder, and myself," Mom explained slowly. Or, I'm sure she thought she was explaining.

My gaze shifted to Dad and, as if he could read my mind, he shook his head. Mom noticed the silent exchange and spoke again. "No, not your dad. He's very much human. Well, kind of." She scrunched her forehead.

"What about me?" I asked quietly.

Ryder still knelt in front of me, a pained expression crossing his features. I looked to my mom, she seemed to have been silently elected spokesperson.

"Well, Kaylee, you're unique. You're sort of half human, but you're also half werewolf. It's kind of complicated." Again, she thought she was explaining, but I was still just as confused as ever, if not more so.

"Then make it uncomplicated," I said. My voice gained strength with every word, but it was still shaky and I knew, much to my chagrin, that everyone could hear the waver.

Before Mom could respond, Dad spoke up, placing a reassuring hand on her knee.

"Helen, let me. You see, Kale, in a half human the werewolf gene sort of…" he paused, hopefully searching for a good way to explain. "It sort of lies dormant until it gets…triggered."

Ryder's head, which had turned to watch me, whipped back around to look at my father. His whole body noticeably stiffening. My dad simply ignored his reaction and continued.

"My gene never manifested, making me a first generation Dormant. I will never shift. *You* are what we call a second generation Dormant; but I'll get back to that later. I'm assuming you'd like to know how this all happened? How it all started?"

I nodded once, confirming his assumption.

"Well, okay then."

"I've always lived in Redheart, except for when we moved with you, so I grew up knowing about werewolves. Both of my parents were werewolves, but for some reason I have never been able to shift. Regardless, I was always treated as part of the pack. When I was about seventeen, a new wolf came to town. For a reason that was unknown to most at the time, she was in something we call Sanctuary at the order of Darius Mason, Ryder's grandfather and a deceased mayor."

Ryder cut Dad off with a growl.

After shooting Ryder a scathing look, Dad continued. "Obviously, for a new wolf to come to town *and* for the said wolf to be under the protection of our leader, well, I knew something serious had to have happened. A few weeks passed and people stopped caring so much about this new girl who was being protected and, to an extent, hidden. Except for me. I still wanted to see her, to meet her. And when I finally did, my entire world changed. My vision shifted and I knew I had found my home. You see, your mother and I are what we call mates. You're an avid reader, Kale, so I'm pretty sure you already know what that means." Dad looked at me expectantly and I nodded my head, even though I knew fantasy and reality never went hand in hand.

Ryder growled again, but Dad kept going without so much as a glance in his direction. "Good. So, we dated for a while, though we knew, even then, that we are meant for each other. Until eventually we married and had you. And you know what happened after that."

"So, wait, is this whole town like a…a werewolf town? Like, a pack or something?" I asked, finally pulling my wrists from Ryder's grasp. I hadn't even realized he was still touching me.

"Yes, Kaylee, it is. It's my pack, actually," Ryder answered, looking at me intensely.

My skin still tingling at the low rumble of his voice. If Redheart was actually a pack—Ryder's pack—that would make him…Alpha.

"I knew you weren't the mayor! There's no way a twenty-year-old could *possibly* be mayor!"

I stood from the chair, pushing past Ryder and Lisa who had been standing right in front of me. I began to pace back and forth in front of the television. I was fairly certain I was overreacting to this little bit of information, but after everything I had found out I felt entitled to a little tantrum.

"Actually, sweetheart, I'm twenty-two, and I am essentially Mayor. We just call it Alpha. But you already figured that part out, didn't you?" Ryder smirked. He actually had the gall to smirk.

"*Sweetheart*? You listen here, 'Alpha.'" I made quotes with my fingers as I spat out the title. "You do not get to call me 'sweetheart.' In fact, you don't get to call me anything! None of you do!" I whipped my gaze around the room and stormed out of the house, not wanting to talk to any of them. *Especially* not my parents or Lisa. Those three had lied to me my entire life.

Slamming the door behind me, I ran. I didn't know where I was going, but I knew it had to be away from there. Away from them.

Faces zipped by as I ran, shooting confused and strange looks my way as I passed them by.

I don't know how long I ran, or where for that matter, but when I finally stopped, it was in front of Mayor Mansion. It was really amazing to look at. It was at least three stories tall with massive windows. In front was one of those u-shaped driveways only seen in movies, and the grounds were covered in beautiful sprawling landscaping.

Lucas was outside the mansion throwing punches back and forth with some other guy. This guy looked taller and broader than Ryder, and darker in features than him. He had dark skin and long, dark hair pulled back in a low ponytail at the nape of his neck. I couldn't see his eyes from where I stood, but I knew without seeing them that they would pierce my soul.

Lucas noticed me first and stopped moving, earning him a fist to the face.

"Hey! What the hell!" I yelled running over to wedge myself between them. "You're twice his size! What in the hell do you think you're doing?" I put my hand up in front of big guy's chest with my back to Lucas.

There was no way I'd be able to hold Big Guy off if he really wanted to do some harm, but I had to try. Lucas was so small compared to him. Then again, I was even smaller than Lucas.

I was in a stare down with Big Guy. I had been right about his eyes; they were dark and piercing. Combined with his size and obvious strength, he was extremely intimidating. Our glaring contest was interrupted by a sudden burst of laughter coming from the sixteen-year-old boy behind me.

Turning around, I cocked my hip and raised a brow, crossing my arms. "What's so funny?"

Lucas was bent over with his hands on his knees, his body shaking with laughter.

"We were j–just sp–sparring, Kaylee," he laughed, trying to catch his breath.

"What do you mean, 'sparring?' He punched you in the face!" I screeched, appalled.

"Exactly that. Ryder makes sure the pack can protect itself. We're training, Spencer." I didn't even question how he knew my last name as he put his arm around my shoulder and patted it with an uncomfortable familiarity.

"Right," I drew out the word. "Sparring. Why are you doing it with someone so much bigger than you?"

"Because I can beat everyone my size," he boasted with a smug grin, looking down at me.

"Ugh! Fine." I elbowed him in the ribs and he sucked in a breath and hunched over slightly, taking his arm from around my shoulders. "You're kind of an ass, Lucas Mason," I glared with my arms crossed.

"Oh, believe me, I know," Lucas smirked at me.

The man behind me cleared his throat, making me jump. I had forgotten he was there.

I turned around at the same time Lucas said, "Whoops! I totally forgot to introduce you guys! Spencer, this is Blake, he's the Beta and Head Guard. Blake, this is Kaylee. Spencer."

Lucas threw his arm back over my shoulder, grinning. There was no way he could have known that I knew the big secret, so telling me that Blake was the Beta was risky.

"Does she know?" Blake's voice was scary deep, only contributing more to his crazy level of intimidation. His dark eyes ran over me in a gesture that wasn't at all intimate but was just as unsteadying. He was sizing me up.

"About werewolves? Yeah, I do. About the fact that my mother and best friend are both werewolves? Oh! And that I'm supposedly half werewolf? Yes, to all of the above. And I just found out, so I'd really rather not talk about it, if that's okay with you?" I asked with all the sarcasm I could muster.

Blake nodded, turned, and walked into Mayor Mansion. I took a step away from Lucas, uncomfortable with the proximity and how he towered over me, making me feel ridiculously small. Even though he was only sixteen, he was still a good six feet tall.

"Hey, Lucas, exactly how tall *are* you?" I asked, taking in his strong, but still slightly boyish, features.

"Six feet," he announced, puffing out his chest. I laughed quietly and muttered 'boys' under my breath. He must have heard me though because all of a sudden I was over his shoulder and he was running.

"Hey!" I pounded on his back and kicked my legs. "Put me down!" I screeched.

"Boys, huh? Let me take you to my brother and see what you think about boys, then!" Lucas laughed, wrapping one long arm around the backs of my legs to keep them still and let the other swing at his side.

"No! I. Don't. Want. To. See him!" I renewed my struggles, but it was no use. Lucas just laughed and bounced a couple times, jostling me. "Gah."

I huffed and leaned on my hand with my elbow resting on his back. I felt like Princess Fiona in *Shrek* after she's rescued from the tower.

It didn't take long to get wherever we were going. When Lucas finally stopped running I heard a deep chuckle.

"What the hell, Lucas?" Ryder laughed. I could hear his feet approaching and renewed my struggles against Lucas's annoyingly firm grip.

"I was telling her how tall I was and she questioned my manhood so I decided to take her on a bit of a trip. Watcha think?" Lucas asked, hopping where he stood, causing me to grunt when my belly landed back on his shoulder.

"Well, I definitely appreciate the view," Ryder laughed again, his brother joining him.

"Put me down," I shrieked again, flailing my arms and legs. I felt Lucas shrug beneath me and then I was plopped down right on my butt. Leaning back on my elbows with my legs sprawled out in front of me, I glowered at the *boys*. "You guys suck," I muttered.

Both of them offered me a hand, but I ignored them.

Standing up—all on my own—I started to stomp away from them only to realize I had no idea where I was.

"Ugh!"

Spinning around, I stomped right back up to the two boys, who were wearing obnoxious grins that split their faces wide open. Crossing my arms, I stood in front of the huge boys. "Where the hell am I?"

"You're at the training grounds, Spencer. Ryder spends a lot of his time here, and I did say we were going to see him. So here we are!" Lucas swung his arms wide and began spinning in circles with the biggest, most mischievous grin on his face.

We were in a field surrounded by trees. There was a large building that looked almost like a dormitory, and smaller shed-like buildings on either end.

"Wait, what happened to your face, Luke?" Ryder asked with a hint of concern in his voice, but mostly amusement.

"Eh, well, Blake and I were sparring when this girl ran up looking all upset and I got distracted. He landed one right here," Lucas explained, pointing to the purple bruise blossoming on his jaw.

"Wow, Luke. Good job." Ryder rolled his eyes and shook his head. His gaze shifted to me. "You were upset because of what you found out today weren't you?"

"Of course I was! I just found out that my family has been lying to me my entire life! About what I am! And! I found out that the only friend I've made since moving is you! As a wolf!"

"I'm sorry, I know this must be hard for you," he apologized with a guilty look on his face.

"Well, duh," I snorted.

I was being childish, but I, quite frankly, didn't care.

"I have an idea!" Lucas announced proudly.

"What, Luke?" Ryder groaned.

That sound said a lot about Lucas's ideas.

"What if you spar in front of Spencer?" he suggested, while looking over his brother's shoulder.

"Do I get to see you get hit?" I asked, seeing merit in the idea.

Ryder laughed at my all-too-obvious excitement, shaking his head.

God, I liked his laugh. Damn it.

"There are a couple people who can get a few swings in on me." He tilted his head, motioning toward the big open field with marked off arena's. "Come on, you can watch someone try to beat the snot out of me." He offered his hand again, but I glared at it and he pulled it back.

"Well? Are we going or what?"

Ryder looked down at his shoes and chuckled softly, but it sounded almost sad.

Ryder nodded and turned to walk away. And I got to see him get slugged.

Chapter 8
Lost

The match was a blur. Both Ryder and his opponent—who happened to look a lot like Blake, but I couldn't be sure—moved so fast that I could barely keep up. Punches were thrown, and legs were kicked and swept out.

By the time the fight was over, the sun had noticeably moved further west. A slightly out of breath Ryder came jogging up to me and Lucas, with a sweaty Blake on his heels. I was grinning when they reached us.

"Did you enjoy the show?" Ryder asked and I couldn't tell whether he was angry or amused, but there was a bruise blooming above his left eye and I found that I was strangely concerned.

I knew I shouldn't be and it made me furious.

Trying not to let my worry show, I nodded vigorously. "I sure did!" Lucas nudged me in the side with his elbow and I plastered the most innocent look on my face that I could manage. "What? I did!"

Lucas laughed at me and Blake's lip twitched. Ryder just stood there with his arms crossed loosely and a light sheen of sweat gleaming on his brow.

"I'm glad you enjoyed yourself," Ryder smiled for a moment before suddenly becoming very serious. "But you and I really need to talk, Kaylee." The smile completely slipped off my face.

"About what? I know about werewolves and I know everyone in my life lied to me for almost eighteen years. What else is there to know?" I crossed my arms defiantly.

I actually had a lot of questions, but he didn't need to know that, nor was he the one I wanted to talk to about any of it. I wanted to talk to Lisa about everything, not Ryder. Seeing as she was the one to spill the beans, I figured she'd be the least likely to lie to me. She was family and I actually trusted her—despite all the crap of the last few hours.

"Your parents didn't tell you a damn thing. Your werewolf gene is Dormant, Kaylee. Sure, they told you *that*, but they didn't tell you how it's triggered. Which is kind of important, don't you think? And all that crap about not explaining what mates are because you're well read? Guess what, this isn't a book. Your father should have told you about what you are and what it means. He should have explained *everything* and he should have done it a long time ago!" Ryder roared. His face was shadowed, eyes dark and lips lifted in a snarl as he paced with his arms flailing around in large dramatic gestures.

"My father told me what I *need* to know! I don't *need* to know the specifics about mates," I choked on the last word, "in the real world! Nor do I *need* to know how the hell my Dormant werewolf-ness is triggered. You want to know why? Because I don't care! I don't want a mate and I definitely don't want to be a werewolf!" I raged.

The only difference between my outburst and Ryder's was that I had no growl behind my words.

Ryder looked at me as if I had physically struck him with my little tantrum. He stepped back with a shocked expression overtaking his breathtaking features. Lucas stood stiff beside me, and Blake was a statue behind Ryder. With all three intimidating males looking at me with different versions of shock and disbelief written across their faces, I did the only thing I could think of. Something I do only too well.

I ran.

I ran into the trees surrounding the training grounds, leaving the stunned quiet men behind. I figured by escaping to the trees, at least my chances of running into anyone were slim to none. I didn't however, take into consideration that I had absolutely no idea where I was going. I was lucky that I had left my shoes on after leaving the backyard earlier that day. Normally, I left them just inside the basement door.

I ran for what felt like hours but what was most likely only a few minutes before I stopped, taking in the scenery. The gorgeous, diverse greens of the forest and the woodsy smell that surrounded me were soothing. With my heartbeat calming and my breath slowing I could think again, past the anger and frustration that seemed to have consumed me, if only for a moment.

Ryder wanted to talk about everything I wasn't told. Good for him. I didn't want to talk to him. About anything. I didn't even want to see his aggravatingly gorgeous face. As a human with flawless bone structure, or as a friendly, snuggly wolf. The only person I wanted to talk to just then was Lisa. My diaper friend. A small smile tugged at my lips as I thought about our adventures over the years. Like the time when we were seven and got lost at the mall after getting separated from our parents.

That's when I realized that I had a very big problem.

I was lost. Except this time, I didn't have Lisa with me, nor a security guard I could run to.

When I was thirteen, Lisa and I got lost in the city after leaving the mall after dark. Fortunately, Lisa always had a good sense of direction—which, in hindsight, I'm fairly certain is thanks to her being a werewolf—and she led us both home. Another time, when I was much younger, I ran off in a large shopping center when Dad wouldn't take me home. I got lost and found a security guard who helped me find my dad.

But this time, I was alone and I didn't even know remotely where I was. I could only hope I was still in Redheart as I couldn't begin to guess where the boundaries were. I know people tell you to just stay where you are when you're lost, but I never was good at listening. Besides, without my phone—which I had left in my room that morning—I had no way of contacting anyone to tell them that I was lost. No one knew I had run off except for a few guys, and I highly doubted that those *boys* would care enough to come find me. Or even to tell anyone that I was missing.

I started walking in what I hoped was the same direction I had come from, but I wasn't that lucky.

As I walked, I thought about everything that had happened over the two weeks that had passed since moving *back* to Redheart. The werewolf town. That I was apparently born in.

My mom was back in our lives.

I was from a place I had never even heard of before being told I was moving there. Or, *back* there.

Werewolves existed. My best friend and my mother both belonged to that fictional species that it turns out is not so fictional. And I sort of did, too.

Oh, and I became friends with a werewolf in wolf form, who is actually a bit of a demanding dick. Can't forget the craziness of *that*.

What did this all mean for me? Did I want to know how to trigger my werewolf gene? Did I even want to *be* a werewolf? And then there was the whole 'mate' thing! How much of what I've read over the years was true? What were mates, really? I know I told Ryder I didn't want any of it, but was that true? I didn't know. What I *did* know was that I had all of these questions, but I couldn't ask anyone. All because I got myself lost and I wasn't sure it was only physically.

I had been lied to my entire life. About who—what—I am, and about what my family is. My life had taken a path that I never in a million years could have truly believed it would take. Until it did.

I have no idea how long I walked, but when I finally stopped, the sun was setting. It had to have been almost ten o'clock in the evening, if not later. Of course, I didn't have a watch either—I hated wearing them—so I had no way of knowing. I walked a little longer until I found a thick tree and sat at its base, leaning back.

Bringing my knees to my chest, I wrapped my arms around my legs and rested my chin on my knees. I was well and truly lost. Both physically and mentally.

I sat there, curled against the base of a tree with my eyes closed. Crying. I found myself fingering the locket that had found a permanent home between my breasts. By the time I heard my name being called, it was dark out, and had been raining for at least an hour.

There were both familiar and unfamiliar voices coming from all around me. I could hear Mom and Dad, Lisa and her parents, Ryder with his mom and brother, even Blake's voice rang out from somewhere in the woods with others I didn't recognize.

My eyes were closed and my body had curled in on itself to keep warm. When warm arms lovingly wrapped around me, my eyes snapped open to see my father kneeling before me with unshed tears brimming in his eyes.

"I found her!" Dad shouted out behind him. "Oh, God, Kaylee. I'm so glad you're okay."

His arms squeezing me tight to his chest—ignoring the water seeping from my clothes to his—as his hands ran up and down my goose bump covered arms, trying to warm me. His voice rumbled under my ear and all of a sudden, I knew everything was okay, or at least it would be.

I heard more feet hurriedly approaching and I buried my face in my father's chest, trying to absorb his heat and the comfort that came with it.

"Oh, thank goodness, Kaylee." Mom's voice echoed breathlessly when she reached us.

Next was Lisa, accompanied by her parents, and then Lucas, Lillian, and…Ryder. Concern radiated from all of them. Last was Blake with a bored mask on his face, but his eyes told a different story, and I knew he was worried about me too.

Someone draped a heavy jacket over my shoulders and Dad helped me into it. After getting the jacket zipped around me, Dad helped me to my feet and pulled me into one of his big, crushing bear hugs. He reached down and put an arm behind my knees, lifting me and cradling my shivering body to his chest.

Blake took the lead and everyone else kept close to Dad and me.

As we walked, I heard different people offering to take me from him—Lisa, Mom, even Ryder and Lillian offered—but Dad either grunted or straight out said no, pulling me tighter after every offer. I managed a small smile when he barked at Ryder.

Dad's body heat and his familiar scent of mint and male soap was soothing and, for that moment in time, I forgot. I forgot that he had lied to me so much throughout my life and that he *still* wasn't telling me everything. I forgot about how angry I was and I just took comfort in being held by my daddy, the man who had taken care of me for almost eighteen years.

I must have dozed off on our way to the house because next thing I knew we were home. Mom rushed forward and opened the glass door at the back of the house for Dad, and he, along with our entourage, moved inside. Dad placed me laying down on the couch and ran up the stairs with Mom hot on his heels, while Lisa took the blanket from the back of the monstrous piece of furniture and draped it over me, jacket, and all.

Lisa pulled my shoes off and sat with my feet in her lap, running a hand up and down my shin. Her body heat felt amazing on my chilled toes and I sighed, snuggling deeper into my coverings. Everyone else was scattered around the room, exchanging hushed words.

Only a few moments had passed when my parents descended the stairs. My dad was holding two steaming mugs and my mom was carrying a tray full of them. Dad came up to me, placed the mugs on the coffee table and helped me sit up before reaching over and handing me one of the mugs. Mom handed out the mugs on the tray while I drank from mine. My hands shook as I held it, but it was hot chocolate with marshmallows—my all-time favorite.

Shaky hands would not keep the chocolatey goodness away from me.

The room filled with the smells of hot chocolate and coffee as everyone fell into a mostly comfortable, though still slightly tense, silence.

When I was finished, a big yawn burst from between my lips. Dad took my mug from me and placed it on the tray Mom had brought down. He began to lift me from the couch—blanket and all—despite my protests. He grimaced and grunted softly before gently placing back onto the sofa.

"Daddy, are you okay?" I asked quiet, slightly worried.

"I'm fine, sweetie. It's just been a long day," he replied softly, not wanting me to worry. But his forehead was scrunched and there was pain in his eyes.

Mom came up behind Dad and whispered something in his ear, making his jaw clench as he whispered no.

"It's okay, Helen. I can carry her up," Lisa assured them gently.

Then, lifting me up the same way my father had, she walked me up to bed. It briefly crossed my mind how strange it was to have my best friend carry me like a child, but I didn't have the energy to dwell on it. Lisa helped me change into warms sleep clothes—flannel pants and a long-sleeved cotton shirt—before running to her room and changing. She came back not two minutes later and climbed into bed with me.

"You know, you don't have to sleep in here with me," I murmured, rolling onto my back.

"Babe, we'll all feel better if you let me stay with you. It gets cold at night and your weird human-werewolf-ness still hasn't warmed up. So please don't fight me on this," Lisa propped herself up on her elbow in my bed and stared down at me.

I don't think I had ever seen her so serious in my life. I knew not to argue.

"Okay, Lis. Goodnight."

"Goodnight, Babe."

I was just slipping away when Lisa's voice came softly from the dark. "Hey, Kale?"

"Mhm?"

"I'm sorry," she said it so quietly I almost didn't hear her.

"I know, Lis. I know."

Then I drifted off into oblivion.

Chapter 9
Getting Ready

I woke the next morning covered in a sheen of sweat and had to fight my way out from under the mountain of blankets that had amassed overnight. My squirming jostled Lisa—who had also been on me—enough that she shot up, hands on either side of my ribs, looking confused.

"Wha—? Is it morning?" she mumbled right in my face. Her blonde hair fell in front of her like a curtain and a few blankets draped on top of her body.

"Yeah, Lis, it's morning. Now get your breath out of my face." I shoved at her shoulders and she fell on her back beside me, taking part of the mountain with her.

"Morning breath, huh?" Lisa smirked as I sat up.

Uh oh.

Lisa tackled me back down to my back and breathed grossly in my face. Again, I shoved her off me, only this time in the other direction and she landed in a heap of blankets on the floor. Laughing, she untangled herself from the mass of cotton and fleece. Her hair was a mess and the makeup she had worn the day before was smudged across her face.

"Why so many blankets, Lis?" I asked, laughing at her mussed hair.

"You wouldn't stop shaking all night, so every time I woke up to check on you, I got up and threw another blanket on the mound. Eventually I gave up on the blankets and just wiggled in to snuggle you instead," Lisa exclaimed proudly, although I could still hear worry in her voice.

"Well, I'm fine now, Lis. In fact, I'm sweating like a damn pig!" I laughed again and Lisa joined in when I ended up falling out of bed right on top of her while trying to stand.

Of course, the entourage chose that *exact* moment to open my door. Dad raised an eyebrow quizzically and Mom tried and failed to stifle a snort behind her hand when they saw Lisa and I sprawled on the floor by my bed, tangled in a hill of cloth.

Karen and Darrel both barked out a laugh when they peaked at us from behind my parents. Next was Lillian, who sort of giggled and squealed at the same time. I had a feeling it was a sound she made a lot.

"What's so funny?" My skin tingled and I rushed to stand, but only managed to trip over Lisa instead, much to everyone's amusement and soon to be concern.

I would have landed on my face if not for my quick, albeit clumsy, reflexes. My hands shot out in front of me, but my left wrist twisted awkwardly sending shootings spikes up my arm and causing me to land on my elbow instead. When I landed, a little squeak of pain escaped from between my lips and Ryder was suddenly in front of me, cradling my face in his hands.

"Kaylee, are you alright?" his deep voice rumbled.

Staring into his chocolate brown eyes. I was suddenly very aware of the fact that I was in pajamas, and I couldn't for the life of me remember why I was supposed to be mad at him.

Someone cleared their throat, snapping me out of my reverie. I pulled away from his hands and watched as his lips dipped into a frown.

"Yeah, um, I'm fine," I cleared my throat and tucked a strand of hair behind my ear with my uninjured hand. "Thanks."

Lisa and I stood together and I raised a brow as I held my wrist to my chest. "Is there a reason everybody I know in this town is standing in the hallway outside my bedroom door?"

Dad laughed and said, "We just wanted to make sure you were alright after spending *six* hours in the woods. By yourself *and* without dinner, might I add."

"I'm fine, Dad, I promise. Or, at least I was. Until…" I looked down at my wrist right as Lillian pushed her way past my parents and Ryder and stood directly in front of me.

Lillian tenderly prodded my wrist, moving it this way and that, before deeming it 'just sprained' and telling me it needed to be wrapped. Dad ran into my bathroom and came back out a couple minutes later with a tensor bandage, that I didn't even know was in there, in his hand. My wrist was wrapped and we all headed downstairs, apart from Lisa who stayed behind to clean her smudgy face.

Lucas was standing at the stove, scrambling eggs when we walked in. There was an apron knotted at his lower back and when he turned around, I had to lift my hand to my face to cover a snort that escaped. The apron he was wearing had painted-on muscles that were overly bulgy and pink.

"Are you *laughing* at me, Spencer?" Lucas asked me, splaying his palm against his chest in an offended gesture.

"You bet your ass I am, Mason." I stuck my tongue out at him, kind of proud of my wit, which really couldn't be considered wit at all.

Lisa came up behind me just in time to hear my comeback and she burst out laughing, leaning on my shoulder for support.

"He's wearing a man apron!" She shrieked. "Where the hell did you get that thing?" She was holding on to her knees with her legs bent, face turning red from laughter. I was just a little bit disappointed that she hadn't been laughing at my comeback.

Lucas rolled his eyes and shrugged out of the apron before grabbing plates—although I don't know how he knew where they were—and dishing up eggs for everyone except Lisa. He glared at her and said she could get her own. It was obvious he wanted to give me the same treatment, but one look at my wrist made him think better of it.

We had to eat in the formal dining room to fit everyone. Dad sat in the center of the table on one side with Mom on his left and myself on his right. Lisa sat on my other side and Lucas across from me. Beside him and in front of my father was Lillian, with Ryder on her other side in front of my mother.

We were all just about to dig in to our surprisingly delicious looking—and smelling—food, when the front door opened and Blake walked in. Letting out a breath, I stood to greet him.

He was halfway to the dining room when I reached him. I could practically feel Ryder's gaze on me as I walked, there were tingles on the back of my neck the entire way to Blake.

"Blake," I greeted, nodding my head.

"Miss Spencer," he replied in kind. His voice low and professional.

I raised a brow at him, having only ever been called 'Miss Spencer' by my teachers back in Washington.

I felt more than heard Ryder come up behind me, his heat radiating through his clothes against my back. He was so close, and he smelled amazing. Like pine.

"Blake, good of you to join us."

His low voice vibrating out of his chest caused my skin to tingle. Why did that always have to happen?

"Ryder, sorry I'm late. I was just finishing up at the house." Blake inclined his head in respect and I could tell there was more to his words than what was being spoken aloud.

"Thank you for doing that. I know Mom will be very happy." Ryder came out from behind me to stand next to Blake and I let out a breath I hadn't realized I had been holding.

Patting Blake on the shoulder, Ryder lead him to the dining room, and I followed closely behind.

I returned to my seat and noticed that Blake had taken the previously empty seat beside my best friend. Seeing all the food laid out on the table reminded me that I hadn't eaten in about twenty-four hours. Suddenly ravenous, I dug in.

The food was marvelous and conversation ran easy. I made another jab at Lucas about being shocked he could cook, and he jabbed back calling me 'Spencer,' much to Ryder's chagrin. And despite the secrets that had been kept and the rift it had torn in my family, I had never felt more at home.

When we were cleaning up, Lillian announced that she had planned a party at Mayor Mansion—which she called the 'Pack House'—to celebrate the Perry's and our family's return to Redheart. I was kind of wary of attending; I couldn't stand parties and with, my wrist being sprained and the fact that I didn't really know anybody, I *really* didn't want to go. When I said as much, everyone insisted I attend; especially Lisa, who decided it would be so much fun and that we *had* to dress up for it.

By the time everyone had left to go home, it was nearly one o'clock and Lisa was panicking about us not having enough time to get ready for the party. Which didn't start until seven. Rolling my eyes, I dragged her upstairs and shoved her in the shower before going to my room for some downtime.

I tidied up the mess of blankets from that morning and when that was finished, I curled up on the window seat with a book that I had almost completed. It was the same book I had been reading yesterday with Wolfy before I found out that he was actually Ryder—before I had found out about werewolves at all.

An hour later, Lisa came barging in and swore at me for sitting on my butt instead of getting ready. I rolled my eyes and told her we had plenty of time, but she refused to listen to me. Pulling me up, she threw my book on my bed before forcing me into the bathroom.

"I'm not letting you out until you're showered!" Lisa shouted through the door.

Chuckling quietly, I shook my head and stripped before jumping under the scalding water.

When I was finished with Lisa's orders, I got out, slipped into a small robe, and pounded on the door with both hands.

"I'm done!" I shouted at the top of my lungs, purposefully being obnoxious.

The door swung open and there was Lisa, standing in a sky blue, strapless dress that puffed out at the waist before ending right under her butt. Her makeup and hair were already done.

"Okay, one, you totally left, you liar. Two, how the hell long was I in there for you to be ready?" I asked, standing in the small robe with my hip propped against the door frame and my arms crossed in front of my chest. My mom's locket visible through the 'v' at the top of the robe.

"Well, one, yes, I totally did leave. Two, you were only in there for like, forty-five minutes. I knew I had to hurry so I could get ready, too," Lisa smirked, mirroring my stance.

Her eyes dropped down to the locket on my chest and surprise flicked across her features, but she recovered easily, and the shock vanished just as quickly as it had appeared.

I had opened my mouth to rip into her about not needing help and that I was perfectly capable of getting ready myself when my bedroom door swung open and Ryder stepped in.

My jaw fell a little bit more. Over Lisa's shoulder, I could see his navy button up shirt hugging his shapely arms and torso, stretching across his chest—the top button was left undone. He was wearing black pants that seemed cut to his muscular thighs and backside.

"Ryder!" Lisa screeched. "What the hell are you doing here?" She turned to face him and tried to shield my body with her own.

Ryder blinked at the sound of his name and shook his head, as if snapping out of a daze, while clearing his throat.

"Uh, Mom sent me over to bring you guys to the party. John and Helen are both already at the House and Mom wants you both there as soon as you're ready." Ryder cleared his throat again and pulled at his collar a bit, forcing a second button to pop open.

His eyes were moving non-stop, trying to find a way past Lisa's body shield. I blushed, knowing he was trying to get a peek of me.

"Well, we're obviously *not* ready yet! So shoo!" She said, making shooing motions with her hands without giving his eyes access to my body.

Ryder nodded stiffly, took one last try at getting a peek and left, closing the door behind him. Lisa turned to look at me and I hoped she didn't notice my hot face.

"He was totes trying to get a look at your goods," Lisa said, smirking, and I knew she had noticed my strawberry-colored cheeks. I could feel my blush deepening and Lisa chuckled. "Let's get you ready, babe."

Lisa got to work on my hair first, making me sit on the little purple ottoman in my bathroom while she dried and then curled my waist-long, black hair.

When she was done pinning my hair up in a simple updo, she moved to my face, giving me a smoky eye with a pink highlight and a light pink lip.

While she worked, I asked her what she thought about me learning to fight. I pointed out that I was a human among supernatural beings, and she agreed that it would be a good idea to be able to defend myself. She didn't, however, appreciate being called supernatural.

When Lisa was done, I picked up my cell phone which I had placed on the counter and checked the time. I gasped. It was four-thirty.

"Oh my god, Lisa! You took forever!" I exclaimed, shoving my phone in her face.

"Sure," she shrugged, not even glancing at the screen. "But you look hot."

Lisa walked out of my bathroom and walked into my closet. She came back holding a navy-blue dress with different colored flowers on it. I knew, without a doubt, that it hadn't been in my closet that morning.

"What do you think?" Lisa asked with a nervous smile, holding the dress up in front of her.

"Lisa, it's super cute," I said, standing.

Of course it was cute; Lisa had impeccable taste, and somehow always knew what would look good on me. I took the dress from her and changed into it, not worrying about my nudity. We grew up together and had seen each other naked enough times to not care anymore.

While I slipped the dress over my head, she grabbed some undies for me and I slid them on, not needing a bra as the dress had one built-in.

When I was completely ready, Lisa dragged me to look in the full-length mirror on the back of my closet door. We looked amazing. The dress flowed loosely above my knees. It formed to my breasts and waist, showing my curves and my mom's necklace lay in perfect view. Lisa's light blue dress made her hazel eyes shine beautifully. It hugged her womanly figure perfectly, and no doubt the vision she created would turn heads.

"We look fabulous!" Lisa sang.

I laughed and nodded, a huge smile on my face. I refused to let my wrapped wrist make me feel less than amazing.

"It's definitely a few steps up from diapers."

We both laughed and left my room.

We went down the stairs, and Lucas and Ryder were waiting for us. Lucas had a big, goofy grin on his face and Ryder was wearing a small smile that softened his features. He went from intimidating jerk to stunning teddy bear in less than two seconds. I should have known it wouldn't last.

I was busy taking in Ryder's beauty again, completely enraptured, when a blinding light flashed causing me to stumble down the last couple of steps.

Ryder caught me with an arm around my waist and I giggled and ducked my head, trying to cover my embarrassment and pink cheeks.

"Good thing I'm not wearing heels yet." My hands were on his shoulders and I was staring at his chest.

A strand of hair had escaped the twist that Lisa had so brilliantly sculpted, and Ryder caught it between his fingers before tucking it back behind my ear, leaving a trail of tingles in his wake. I blushed and stepped away, moving my eyes to Lucas.

"What the hell was that?" I chuckled nervously, not letting my gaze return to the fine specimen who still stood oh-so close.

"Pictures?" Lucas lifted the camera I hadn't noticed he was holding. I hit my palm against my forehead and groaned.

"Okay, Lucas. If you say so," I conceded, only slightly exasperated.

He continued taking photos like a trigger-happy monkey and when he finally decided he was done, his green eyes shone happily. Sort of like a child on Christmas.

"Alright, Luke. Let's go," Ryder laughed.

Lisa's laughter joined Ryder's as Lucas strangely chirped "Okay."

Ryder leaned toward me and whispered in my ear, his breath fanning my neck. "You look beautiful, Kaylee."

I shivered and blushed lightly. I was very frustrated by my reaction to him. I was more frustrated by the fact that I couldn't help it.

I sort of liked that Ryder called me by name. Everyone else in my life had a nickname for me. Not that I would mind a—*No!* He would call me 'Kaylee' and that's *it*.

Lisa and I both slipped on shoes. She put on a pair of strappy, silver heels and I went for black heels with an ankle strap.

When my shoes were on, Ryder offered his arm, but I ignored it just as I had done with his hand the day before. He sighed and walked ahead to open the door instead. I stepped out into the warm evening air with Lisa and Lucas chatting behind me and Ryder ahead of me.

The sun was still up but I knew from experience that, as soon as it went down, the temperature would too.

Ryder slowed to walk beside me and led us to a black sports car. It was low and sleek. And seriously cool. Lucas and Lisa took the back, forcing me to ride passenger with Ryder driving.

As soon as we were all buckled in, Ryder hit the gas and we shot forward. With his brother singing, "party!" from the back seat, we were off.

Chapter 10
The Party

We got to Mayor Mansion without me strangling Ryder, which was a feat on its own, but only made more impressive when I took into account his reaction to my suggestion that I learn how to fight. When I brought it up, Lucas laughed from the back seat and Ryder said there was no way in hell. And for the rest of the drive he had a muscle ticking in his jaw and his hands were tight on the steering wheel.

This was all made even more frustrating when all I could smell in the enclosed space was him.

When we pulled up in the driveway at just after six o'clock, I hopped out as soon as Ryder shifted into park. Stepping out of the car I breathed in the fresh air—air that didn't smell deliciously like Ryder. It also gave me the chance to get away from his maddening opinion that there was no point in me learning to fight because even an untrained wolf would be able to take me down as long as I remained human.

I walked up to the door and raised my fist to knock, but Ryder was already standing next to me and reached out to turn the knob. He opened the door and placed his hand at the small of my back, attempting to lead me inside, but I walked faster and escaped his touch. Lisa and Lucas both followed behind us.

As soon as we were through the doorway, I stepped further away from Ryder. But he followed, refusing to remove his hand from my back. Little shocks radiated out from where the heat of him seeped through my dress to run along my skin.

Ryder led us through the foyer, past a seating area full of white furniture and through a massive kitchen with large French doors at the back. We walked out onto a deck that lead down to the largest yard I had ever seen. There were small versions of old-fashioned street lamps scattered around the perimeter of the yard, which was actually more of a small field. Fairy lights were strung up in the trees surrounding the field and a large unlit fire pit sat in the center. I knew that as soon as the sun went down, this yard would be one of the most beautiful things I had ever had the pleasure of seeing.

Ryder's hand never left my back as we descended the stairs of the deck. Mom and Dad both looked up from by the fire pit and Lillian came from the trees with a big smile on her face, doing what I could only describe as frolicking. We reached the bottom step and Ryder finally pulled his hand away to approach his mother, while I took the opportunity to escape and went to see my parents.

Dad enveloped me in a strong hug that immediately calmed my nerves, if only slightly. "You look beautiful, Kale," he said lowly, before shifting me into my mother's embrace.

She smelled like vanilla and cinnamon, just like always. Smiling at me she said, "you look amazing, sweetie."

I whispered a quick thanks and, feeling slightly overwhelmed, excused myself to go find the bathroom.

I ran back up the stairs to the deck and wasn't paying attention to where I was going. I smacked right into Blake, who reached out a hand to steady me.

"Sorry, Blake!" I squeaked, flushing from embarrassment.

"No worries, Miss Spencer. May I ask where you are going in such a rush?" he asked calmly, removing his steadying grip from my arm.

"Oh, yeah. Um, I was just about to go looking for a bathroom," I stammered. I could only hope he didn't guess that I was trying to hide. I was running. Again.

"Come on, I'll show you." He led me inside and up a grand staircase, down a hall, and into a bedroom that smelled strongly like pine.

Turning on Blake, I opened my mouth. "This is Ryder's room, isn't it?"

Blake nodded, and I asked, "Why? Why would you bring me here?" My voice wavered slightly.

"You said you needed to use the bathroom and I know Ryder would be the most comfortable if you just used his," Blake responded calmly.

"Why does Ryder's comfort matter? He's not the one who has to pee! Did you ever think that maybe I would be uncomfortable using Ryder's bathroom? Huh? I don't think you did!" I knew I was being dramatic, but I was frustrated. Why did everything seem to lead back to that man!

"I'm sorry, but he is the Alpha, Miss Spen—"

"*Don't* call me 'Miss Spencer.' My name is 'Kaylee.' Use it," I cut him off. I refused to be called 'Miss Spencer' by someone who was practically the same age as me and clearly no smarter.

Blake's lip twitched slightly at my little outburst and he shrugged. "Okay, Kaylee. All you had to do was say so."

My jaw dropped as his entire demeanor changed. And suddenly he wasn't so intimidating anymore. His dark eyes became softer and I could see the person behind the Beta.

"Ugh!" I groaned loudly and stomped away from Blake and toward the door that I hoped opened to the bathroom.

"That's the closet!" Blake called, as I approached one of the doors.

I could hear the mocking laughter in his voice. I changed course to the other door as soon as the words were out of his mouth. Once inside, I slammed the door behind me but I could still hear his chuckle on the other side.

I listened to the sound of his footsteps retreating and went to the window across from the door. Opening it, I sat on the ledge and watched as people began to spill into the backyard. I found myself wondering how many of them were werewolves.

At least one hundred people arrived as I sat there watching and lazily counting. The sun had fallen lower in the sky and I knew it must have been about eight o'clock.

I was about to leave my hiding place, knowing I couldn't stay there forever, when I heard the bedroom door open. I sucked in a quick gulp of air and jumped off the windowsill to lock the door, but I wasn't fast enough.

Just as I reached my hand toward the door knob, it turned and the door swung open so quickly I had to jump back in order to avoid being hit.

When I looked up, Ryder was staring at me. His navy-blue shirt stretched with every tantalizing breath he took, and at that moment I realized we matched. Did Lisa…?

Damn it.

Ryder took a step toward me and I took one back. "What are you doing up here? In my bathroom?" His deep voice rumbling from his chest sending tingles all across my skin.

"I, uh, I needed to use the washroom and I ran into Blake while searching for one, and he brought me here," I explained quickly, noticeably rambling.

"So, you're hiding." Ryder smirked and crossed his arms across his broad chest, making the material stretch deliciously over his biceps.

"I am not," I snapped, crossing my arms.

But it was no use; I was caught. And, of course, it had to be Ryder who found me red-handed.

"Yes, you are. I can see it all over your face," Ryder said. I didn't think my face was that readable, until that very second. "Why don't you come downstairs with me and join the party? There are people who are dying to meet you." Ryder held out his hand again and just like always, I ignored it. I wondered if he would ever give up.

I walked out of the bathroom, brushing past him. Unfortunately for me that wasn't the smartest thing to do. I got a whiff of his pine-scented skin and my arm brushed against his defined stomach. I groaned silently at the feeling of his sculpted belly and forced myself to keep walking.

While walking through the house, I wondered what Ryder meant about people wanting to meet me. Why would they? I was no one special.

Ryder followed me the whole way to the backyard, not once making a move to touch me. I found I was disappointed at the lack of contact and mentally smacked myself.

When I reached the bottom of the deck, I was once again overwhelmed by the urge to hide.

There were so many people. Most of whom I didn't know.

I started to turn back around to run inside when Lisa showed up and wrapped her arms around me in a squishing embrace, pinning my arms to my sides.

"I'm so glad Lillian decided to do this! I haven't seen some of these people in years! I wonder if Broddy is coming?" Lisa mused, almost to herself.

I had no clue who this Broddy person was, but Lisa was obviously familiar with them.

"Come on! They're going to light the fire pit soon!" She shouted, grabbing hold of my good hand and pulling me along behind her, leaving Ryder behind.

***

An hour or so later, I was actually having fun. I hadn't seen Ryder since Lisa dragged me away and I was dancing on the makeshift dance floor that had been created around the fire pit. Lisa had convinced me to let loose a little bit, despite being in unfamiliar territory—and being a terrible dancer. We had been dancing together for who knows how long.

My eyes had shut at some point, giving me more freedom to enjoy the music, but when I opened them again Lisa was gone. I knew she was more than capable of taking care of herself, but now I was alone surrounded by strange people I didn't know. Faces I didn't recognize.

I tried to not let her disappearing act bother me. I kept dancing, waving my arms around above my head and swaying my body to the beat. It was a party being held in my family's honor and I was going to do my best to enjoy it.

The moment didn't last.

I had closed my eyes again but snapped them back open again when I felt hands close around my hips and a hard chest press against my back. Stiffening, I stopped moving and lowered my arms to my sides. I tried to remove the unfamiliar hands from my body and turn around. The fingers held tight, holding me still.

"Don't you want to dance, love?" a cold, male voice asked, lips brushing the shell of my ear.

"No, I really don't," I gritted out through clenched teeth, still trying to pry his hands away from me.

"Are you sure?" he crooned. The sound of his voice and the feel of his mouth on my skin made me shudder in revulsion.

"Positive. Now get off me!" I said, putting more power behind my words. I was two seconds away from screaming.

The owner of the cold voice laughed at my attempts and only tightened his hold while he shifted his pelvis to line up with my bottom. "Now why would I do that, sweet cheeks? You're mine." I could hear the smirk in his voice. On top of his grotesque arrogance.

"She said 'get off,'" a tingly, deep voice growled out from somewhere behind me.

The hands gripping my hips tightened even more, to the point where I knew I would have bruises, before letting go with a shove, causing me to stumble directly into Lucas.

"Well, isn't that cute? Big, bad Alpha protecting the little she-wolf who can't even shift," the cold voice came again. The longer he spoke, the more he growled.

Turning away from Lucas, I got a good look at the man behind the voice.

He was cold.

He was big, about the same size as Ryder. He had dark black hair that shone in the light of the fire and cold blue eyes that somehow seemed to watch everyone in the yard. Especially me.

"You know exactly why I'm protecting her, Brendan. You have no claim to her and if you were smart, you would get the hell off my land and *never* come back," Ryder growled.

His eyes were shadowed, and I couldn't see them, but I knew they would be blazing with fury.

"Okay, Ryder. I'll leave if she comes with me. She is mine, after all," The cold voice—Brendan—said, smirking again.

He was taunting Ryder.

"She is *not* yours!" Ryder roared, taking a step forward.

"Oh, yes, Ryder. She is." Brendan lunged.

"No!" I screamed and shot forward.

An unexplainable protective urge clouded my senses as I ran toward the large men. Lucas reached for me, but I was already too far away.

Ryder and Brendan had already moved away from the fire pit.

By the time I reached them, they had already had time to exchange blows. Somehow, I wiggled myself between them. For a reason I didn't understand, I didn't want to see Ryder get hurt.

"Kaylee, no!" Ryder shouted, as I stood facing him with fists raining down on my back and sides as the man with cold eyes kept aiming for Ryder and missing.

I watched Ryder's face as he tried to get around me. His eyes shone with a pain that confused me and his brow was furrowed in concentration. Every time he moved, I mirrored him, and Brendan followed me. His fists never stopped flying.

Others approached but with how much we were moving, there was no way to get Brendan without risking hurting Ryder or me. Lucas and Blake were closest, along with another man who seemed to be the same age as the Beta.

I stood there for as long as I could, absorbing the blows that were meant for Ryder. But too soon it became more than I could bear and I fell to my knees with a cry.

Ryder finally got around me, but Brendan danced out of the way and I was now facing him instead of Ryder.

Bent over with my legs underneath me and my arms wrapped around myself, I had to look up to see his face. His blue eyes were gleaming with cruelty and something softer, more intimate, hidden under the surface. He smiled in a way I could only describe as malicious.

Reaching down to my face, Brendan wrapped one hand around the back of my neck and pinched my chin between the fingers of his other hand making me wince. He could have killed me right there with a flick of his wrist. I was no match for him. Luckily for me, the move was more of a warning than anything else.

Everyone around us backed off as soon as his hands were on me.

"You *will* be mine," he whispered, his face right in front of me and his breath cold on my cheek.

Next thing I knew, my cheek was throbbing and Brendan was running off. Blake, Lucas, and some others I didn't recognize chased after him. I was left face down in the grass, whimpering in pain.

"Kaylee!" I heard my name being called. Voices I recognized, and voices I didn't, erupted around me.

I tried to get up or roll over, but it hurt too much to move.

I felt hands on my lower back and groaned loudly, moving to curl into myself. I was rolled onto my back and Ryder was crouched above me, a worried frown marring his features. Lillian had settled on the other side of me, and I realized that the hands on my body were hers.

"We need to get her inside," Lillian said softly, while gently poking at my ribs.

"I'm going to kill him," Ryder growled, reaching out to touch my face but pulling back when he noticed the purple blooming on my cheek.

A bruise was forming above his eye, replacing the already faded one that Blake had given him before.

"I know, honey. But later. Right now, I need to check her out and I need for you to be there with her. But I also need you calm. 'No you' is better than an 'angry you.' But your presence will help her. You know that," Lillian soothed, stretching over me to rub his arm.

Ryder looked doubtful until Lillian said, "your Lady needs her Alpha." The strange words seemed to affect him more than everything else she had already told him.

Ryder nodded in agreement and lifted me into his arms, making me scream and stiffen, which only made my ribs throb more. Right before I lost consciousness, I heard my dad yelling at people to get the hell out, and Ryder whispering that everything would be okay.

Chapter 11
The Talk

Pine

It was the first thing I noticed as I regained consciousness. I was surrounded by pine. Enveloped in the scent of it.

Then there was the pain. It sliced through my whole body.

Flickering my eyes open, I quickly realized where I was. There was no question who the dark wood frame with green sheets and pillows belonged to. The same person who had green curtains and a dark wood dresser with a massive television hanging above it.

Panicking, I shot up and the room spun as pain spiked in my back and behind my eyes. Groaning, I fell back with a plop, my head cushioned by a mountain of fluffy pillows and my eyes closed on their own. I wanted to go back to dream world. There was no pain there.

"Kale? You awake, babe?" Lisa's voice came from somewhere to my left. I mumbled unintelligibly and waved uselessly, hoping she would go away and let me sleep. "Come on, Kale. You've been asleep for almost two days."

She groaned, slightly exasperated. But mostly she just sounded worried. My eyes popped back open and I instantly regretted it as pain spiked again. The light shining through the window was too much for my sore head, making me wince.

"*Two days*? How is that possible?" I choked out past a dry and achy throat, looking at my best friend.

Her hazel eyes shone with concern and there were dark circles forming underneath them. My vision was slightly off and my cheek throbbed, but I could still see the exhaustion on her face.

"Yeah, babe. Two days. Everyone's been worried sick. No one has really slept much. Especially your dad and Ryder. Do you remember at all what happened?"

I tried to readjust myself to sit up but Lisa came closer and sitting next to me, she gently eased me back down, shaking her head.

"Um, yeah," I rasped.

Lisa picked up two painkillers and a glass of water with a straw and I took small sips, closing my eyes as the cool liquid eased the scratch in my throat. "We were at Mayor Mansion," Lisa smiled slightly at my nickname for the house, "for a party that Lillian was throwing. *Somehow,* you convinced me to dance and I ended up by myself on the dance floor with people I didn't know. I was actually having fun." My brow creased as I went on. "Then some guy showed up and started touching me. His name was…Brendan, I think. I tried pulling his hands away and told him to back off, but he wouldn't listen. But then Ryder appeared. He came out of nowhere…and…and he got Brendan off me." I shook my head, staring at the ceiling, trying to shake away the memory of Brendan's hands on me.

"They fought and I shoved my way between them." I watched Lisa who was now sitting on the bed beside me. "What happened after that? I don't…I don't remember. Nothing but pain." The furrow between my brows made my headache worse. I forced myself to relax as Lisa explained the rest.

"Brendan hurt you, Kaylee. You wouldn't let him touch Ryder, you wouldn't even let him get close. And even though Ryder tried to move you out of the way, you ended up taking almost all of the blows from that asshole." She smiled sadly at me and took the glass out of my hands. "You've got a couple of cracked ribs, Kale. And Lillian is pretty sure you've got a concussion, though she's not totally sure. You've been unconscious, and we don't have the equipment here for brain scans or anything like that. Most wolves are too hard headed to get concussed so we've never really worried about it. But the asshole did hit you pretty hard, so Lillian's probably going to want to run a few tests."

"Isn't that just wonderful?" I breathed out sarcastically. I tried to make my words light, but I could barely finish my sentence without gasping from the pain. I truly felt as if I had been hit by a truck. Or an equally large *thing*.

I was about to ask for more water when the door burst open and Ryder rushed in, with his family and my parents hot on his heels.

"Kaylee! Oh, thank god, you're awake. Ryder's been insufferable! And your father hasn't been much better," Lillian exclaimed with a little giggle, her hands splayed above her heart.

I smiled and tried to sit up again, but when I winced at the throbbing in my ribs, Lisa did the same thing as before. She forced me back down onto the fluff of mattress and pillows.

I glanced at all the faces in the room, trying to ignore Ryder, but I couldn't. His eyes were burning holes in the side of my face as he stared at me with an intensity that sent chills up my spine and actually kind of scared me. His chocolate eyes had darkened and were focused on my left cheek.

Turning to my best friend, I whispered, "Do I have something on my face?" Lisa flinched at my words, keeping her eyes away from the same spot Ryder wouldn't stop staring at.

Mom heard my question and spoke up. "Oh, honey. You don't remember, do you?" she asked sadly. She sounded almost heartbroken.

I shook my head and immediately regretted it. I winced and responded. "I remember there was a fight and that I got involved. Lisa was giving me details when you all came in." My voice was still slightly raspy from having a dry throat, but nothing compared to what it had been only moments before.

Mom's face dropped at my response. "Lisa, honey. Where's your purse?"

I scrunched my face in confusion. While Mom spoke to Lisa, Lillian asked Lucas to fetch a glass of water for me.

Lisa pointed to the deep brown chair by the window and asked, "Why?"

Mom didn't reply. She simply walked to Lisa's purse and came back holding a compact mirror. She clicked it open and with Lisa's help, angled it properly so I could see myself.

As soon as my reflection came into view I gasped. The entire left side of my face was an angry purple and my eye was swollen. I reached up to gently prod my face but Lisa snatched my hand away. I had no idea how I hadn't felt it earlier. At least now I knew why my vision was messed up.

Then, like magic, I remembered *everything*. Brendan's hands on me. Brendan telling me I'm his. His fists raining down on me over and over again as he fought to get to Ryder. And finally, his hand wrapped around my neck in a silent threat to break it, before pounding my face in and running.

As the events of the evening came flooding back to me, silent tears rolled down my face before landing on the pillow beneath me. I heard Lucas return while I stared into nothingness, and then Ryder was approaching the bedside opposite Lisa and my mom.

Gently taking my chin between his fingers, he turned my head toward him. "Kaylee, look at me." I did as he asked, the tears running down my face in an endless stream. "You need to drink this, okay?"

I nodded minutely and Ryder placed the glass on the nightstand before gently helping me into a sitting position on the bed. While he helped, Lisa rearranged the pillows to prop me up. I didn't usually let him touch me; I didn't like or understand the tingles that always radiated from his touch, but I let him then. Strangely, I didn't feel the tingling. Or maybe I just didn't notice it.

I winced and whimpered a couple of times as we resituated me in the bed, and after what felt like forever I was leaning comfortably against the cushions.

Ryder handed me the glass of cold water with a look that told me I better finish it all. I didn't argue. Despite the water Lisa had already given me, I was parched. I had to consciously make an effort to drink slowly, knowing if I drank too fast I would only bring it back up. The cool water made it easier to think clearly and my heartrate slowed.

Lillian came and stood beside her eldest son.

"I need to ask you a couple questions, Kaylee. Are you okay with that?" she asked softly. Everyone in the room gestured encouragingly and I inclined my head once. "All right, what do you remember?"

I relayed the events of the night of the party, including the bit about Ryder finding me in his bathroom. As I talked, different people in the room would nod or make sounds of confirmation if they were there when it happened. When I finished, everyone seemed pleased with what I remembered.

Lillian smiled at me and pushed her son out of the way before sitting on the edge of his bed. She placed her hand right above my knee and shifted her gaze to Lisa. "Have you told her?"

Answering for her, I said, "she told me about my ribs and that I might have a concussion. But what I really want to know is why I'm in Ryder's *bedroom*?" I was sick of people talking *about* me in *front* of me.

The three women in the room laughed softly and Dad glowered. Ryder sort of grinned.

"Babe, you're here because Lil's the best doctor the pack has," Lisa answered as if it was obvious.

I huffed. "Lisa, that still doesn't explain why I'm in *Ryder's* room," I groaned, frustrated.

I threw my hands up in front of my body and realized my wrist was no longer wrapped.

"You're in my room because it's where I want you to be. You don't belong in the infirmary," Ryder rumbled. It was an amazing sound but that couldn't make up for the astounding arrogance of his words.

"Honey," Mom started. "You're in Ryder's room because this is where we wound up putting you the night of the party and your dad didn't want you moved until you woke up. Besides, we all know you deserve better than the infirmary." Mom smiled knowingly, her eyes gleaming with untold stories and hidden secrets.

At least Mom sort of knew how to explain things properly.

"Alright, cool, that's great. But why not a guest room?" I asked, slightly peeved.

"Like your mother said. You deserve better. And my bed is…better, Kaylee," Ryder answered.

His eyes darkening to that deep brown. His voice, as always, sent shivers across my skin. Shivers that were more than unwelcome.

Instead of responding to his arrogance, I moved to get up, Unfortunately, everyone in the room rushed to push me back.

"Woah, Kale. What're you doing?" Dad asked, his first words since I woke up. His arms were out, palms forward, reaching toward me, just like everyone else in the room.

"Guys, I just have to pee," I said, chuckling, a little exasperated at the worry that was so evident on all of their faces. It's not like I was dying.

Dad came around beside the bed, standing next to Lillian and shouldering Ryder out of the way. Ducking low, he took my wrist and slung my arm over his shoulder. I winced slightly when it pulled at my ribs.

"Be careful, Johnathyn," Lillian cautioned.

She was watching my face for signs of pain. Her attentive gaze made me slightly uncomfortable, as if I couldn't hide my feelings anymore. Dad grunted as he carefully helped me up. I had to bite my cheek to keep from whimpering.

Ryder walked on my other side, fingers brushing mine, and Lisa followed close behind. When we reached the bathroom, Lisa took my dad's place and he backed out. Ryder, however, lingered, standing in the doorway.

"Uh, Ryder?" I asked raising a brow expectantly. When he shot me a confused look, I sighed. "I'm not peeing with you in here," I explained, though I shouldn't have had to.

"Oh, right," he mumbled, shaking his head, before leaving and closing the door behind him.

Lisa helped me to the toilet and I did my thing. When I was finished and had my hands washed, she helped me back to Ryder's bed.

When I was once again settled, I rolled my wrist, testing it for pain. I was pleased when I didn't even feel a twinge.

"So, what's the plan? I mean, I'm awake. That means I can go home, right?" I asked hopefully and with a bit of snark. Being around Ryder always put me on edge.

"Well, Kale. As much as I want you to come home, and trust me, I do, I think you should stick around here for a little while. Just so you can start to heal."

"But, Daddy. I wanna come home! I wanna sleep in my bed," I whined, jutting my lower lip in that way I knew would help me get what I wanted.

"Kaylee, sweetheart. Your dad is right. I think you should stay here for now. At least until you can walk by yourself. Until then, it would be just too difficult to move you. You need to rest and heal," Lillian told me.

It made sense, but I didn't like it.

"Can I at least stay in a different room?" I huffed. *One that doesn't smell so deliciously of him?*

"No!" Ryder said loudly, not quite shouting.

Taken aback by his response, I glared.

"And why not?" I asked, mustering as much snark as I could manage.

"I already told you, my room is better," he responded with his arms crossed over his chest and his legs crossed in front of him. Why did he have to look so good leaning against a wall? A wall!

Ignoring him, I looked over to my parents. "Do I have to?"

They both nodded, Dad scowling and Mom grinning like she won the lottery, the secret gleam still in her eyes.

"Ugh!" I threw my hands in the air and winced when my ribs throbbed. "Fine," I hissed, wrapping my arms around my torso. "But only a couple days, right?"

Dad nodded, without shifting his glare from Ryder.

Lucas laughed at my crankiness. Lisa smiled, knowing I could throw one heck of a tantrum if I really wanted to. Mom and Lillian both grinned, a knowing look passing between them. And Dad glared at everyone except me.

When his eyes circled back to Ryder, I couldn't help but snort. If looks could kill.

Now that that was decided, Lillian ushered everyone out of the room so she could properly examine my injuries.

After a couple simple tests, she told me everything Lisa had as well as coming to the conclusion that I had a mild concussion and that I had to "rest my brain." I promised that I would, and she called everyone back in.

Blake came in first, though he wasn't there before, with a huge grin on his face.

"So, Kaylee managed to get herself beat up, huh? You've been here how long?" He walked over and patted my knee, and Ryder growled as he came through the door and went to lean against the wall again.

"Apparently," I snorted. "I guess I'm just that cool." I shrugged.

Ryder growled again and Blake backed off, going to stand at the window with Lucas, muttering, "Super cool, Kaylee," while he walked.

Lillian stood, shaking her head and mumbling under her breath.

"Do you want something to eat, baby?" Mom asked gently as she stroked my hair.

My stomach grumbled and I remembered that I hadn't eaten in more than two days.

"Yes, please."

"I'll be right back," she whispered, and bent to kiss my forehead before taking Dad's hand and leading him from the room.

Everyone else slowly dispersed, leaving me in Ryder's bed. Everyone except Ryder. As Lisa closed the door behind her, Ryder pushed himself off the wall and strode toward me, both confident and unsure.

"I'm really not so fragile, you know," I announced before he could say anything.

"We want to be careful with you, Kaylee. It's not often a werewolf doctor needs to tend to someone who is essentially human," he explained.

As much as I hated it, it made sense. I huffed a pouty breath of air and glowered.

"Now that you can't run, we really need to talk." His deep voice floated through the space and I remembered how he had said the same thing earlier and I had gotten myself lost in the process.

"About what?" I whispered passed the lump in my throat, wringing my hands together in my lap. Why did he so badly want to talk to me?

"About you, Kaylee. There are things you don't know, things you need to know so you can make an educated decision. And I want you to let *me* tell you. I know you'd much prefer to talk to Lisa about everything." I went to interrupt him, but he held up a hand, halting my words. "Please. I know you'd rather ask Lisa all of your questions, or probably anyone other than me for that matter. But please, let me tell you. Let *me* answer your questions." He was practically begging, sitting on his bed beside me and holding my hand with his head bowed.

For some reason, he craved the connection that answering my questions himself would form between us. I found myself wanting it, too.

"Okay." It came so quietly I wouldn't have been sure he heard me except for his head snapping up at the sound of my voice.

Ryder's eyes landed on me and the expression on his face made me think of my old neighbor when his parents bought him a puppy.

"Really? You'll talk to me?" he asked, disbelief and hope lighting his features.

I didn't understand why it was so important that he be the one to explain things to me, but obviously it was, so I nodded. He shifted closer to me, his hip pressed against my thigh.

"Do you have any questions?"

"Well, um. Yeah, actually," I started, more nervous than I probably should have been. "What's the Guard? Lucas mentioned it before."

It wasn't the question I wanted to ask, but it was a safer one.

"The Guard is sort of like the pack's military. Everyone in the pack takes self-defense, but the kids who aspire to join the Guard typically start sooner and then enter a more rigorous training program. At the end, they fight the Head Guard and, if they do well enough, they're allowed to join."

"That's really cool. Do you think I could watch sometime?" I asked hopeful. Ryder had completely rejected the idea of me learning to fight, but perhaps he would allow me to watch others.

"Of course, I think it could be good for you to see," he responded.

"Do you guys use guns?" I asked, my head to the side. They could transform into oversized wolves, so I couldn't see why they would need them, but it would still make sense to have them.

"The Guard has access to guns, but we mostly fight in wolf form."

A silence fell between us as I gathered the courage to ask what I really wanted to know. Finally, I was able to open my mouth. "Erm…what are mates, exactly? I mean, I have read a lot so I get the gist, but you were right before. This isn't a book." I knew I was rambling slightly, but hopefully it distracted from the blush staining my cheeks.

I couldn't believe I had asked Adonis what mates were. Ryder smiled and sat up straighter, preparing himself for a story.

"Hmmm, I'm glad you asked. Mates, essentially, are soulmates," he began, playing with my fingers. Oddly enough, I let him. "Your mate is the most important thing in the world. There's a connection that can't be broken in life. By anything. It's a connection that compares to nothing else. And when you meet, everything makes sense. You mirror each other perfectly. You fit together like pieces of a puzzle and your individual strengths make up for each other's weaknesses. It's not love at first sight, like they say in the stories, but things…shift. Your world changes, and even just thinking about being with anyone else makes you sick. Your skin tingles when they're around and just their presence can be comforting. Their voice is the most wonderful sound you have ever heard and you're attracted to them like you've never been attracted to anyone else. No one else compares, even remotely.

"There is a bit of a…let's call it a legend, that says when your mate's mother goes into labor you come down with a fever. It doesn't matter who is born first. That's just the way it is. Then when the babe is finally born, the fever breaks. Most wolves don't even realize it if this happens. But I know this happened with my mate." All of a sudden, his magically lulling voice became really intense and his eyes sharpened. "When I was four, I got sick and my parents were really worried. My mom wanted to stay with me but she had already promised to deliver a friend's baby." His voice faded into the background as he went on with the story.

I already knew how it ended. My parents had told me when Mom came back. Only they never told me what it meant. And there was no doubt in my mind that it had been completely intentional.

Ryder went on until I couldn't take it anymore.

"Stop." He looked at me, confused. "I know the story, Ryder. I was born and Lillian went to check on you, but when she got to your room, your fever had already broken."

Ryder's jaw hung slack and he stopped playing with my hand. His entire body froze as he stared at me. "You know? How?"

"About the fact that your fever broke when I was born? Yeah. Yeah, I know. My parents told me the story when we moved, but they didn't bother telling me how important it was," I spat out. How could no one tell me? "No one told me that we're," I took a deep breath, "that we're...mates," I breathed, struggling to get the words out.

Ryder was groaning, bent over with his elbows on his knees and his face in his hands.

"This is a mess. They should have told you everything a long time ago," he mumbled into his hands, running them over his face.

"Ryder, it's fine. At least people are *finally* telling me things. Even if it is taking a long-ass time," I told him in what I hoped was a soothing tone. But I couldn't keep the frustration from seeping into my voice.

"No, it's not fine." He raised his head. "I should have told you as soon as I knew that they hadn't. I should have pulled you aside the moment your family came back and told you every little detail. Because you deserve to know everything, Kaylee. You deserve to know that I'm your soulmate, that you're my Lady. You deserve to know how your gene gets triggered. No, you *need* to know how your gene gets triggered. Damn it, Kaylee. You deserve *everything*," Ryder growled, staring at me with a desperate fire in his eyes as he ran a hand through his hair in a frustrated gesture.

"What does being your Lady mean?" I asked curiously. Ryder was so tense, and I hoped answering my questions would help him calm down, maybe even relax.

"Only Alphas have Ladies. I know you read a lot, so you've probably heard of the term 'Luna.'" He looked at me for confirmation and I nodded. "We don't call it that. The Alpha's mate is called the Alpha Lady, and so you are my Lady." Answering that question had calmed him down some, but not nearly enough for me to be pleased.

Wanting to know more, I scooched forward, wincing when it jarred my ribs. I reached toward him and tentatively ran my hand over his shoulder, wanting to reassure him that everything was, in fact, fine.

"Why don't you tell me how to trigger my wolf gene?" I asked quietly, leaving my hand on him. "It seems really important to you that I know," I chuckled, trying to lighten the mood.

Ryder watched me with a scary intensity, effectively stopping my laughter.

"Does this mean you want to be a wolf?" he asked, turning and bringing his other leg up onto the bed so that his body faced mine completely.

"This means I want to know what my options are. Becoming a wolf isn't an option if I don't know how to make it happen," I explained calmly. Though calm was the last thing I was feeling. I didn't want him to get his hopes up.

Apprehensive about what the answer may be, I sat in a still silence.

Ryder spoke abashedly, so very out of character. I didn't understand why until his lips formed the words that nearly stopped my heart.

"You have to have sex with your mate, Kaylee. With me."

Chapter 12
Guilt

I couldn't breathe.

The air was going in and out of my lungs in short, random bursts and the world was going white, the room spinning. Getting light headed, I had to lay back down or risk falling off the bed.

"Kaylee? Kaylee, are you okay? Talk to me, sweetheart," Ryder sounded worried. No, he sounded scared.

Leaning over me, he cupped my cheeks with his hands as his chocolate eyes searched my face. I couldn't respond.

My chest rose sporadically as I tried to catch my breath, my ribs throbbing with the harsh movement. I knew the signs of a panic attack and I knew I had to calm down before I fell into the one rapidly seizing me.

"Kaylee, please, calm down," Ryder begged when I started to whimper from the pain assaulting my body.

He had started gently brushing my hair back from my forehead when Lisa, Lucas, and Blake rushed in.

"What happened?" Lisa screeched at Ryder, who had gone pale, and ran over to us. Lucas and Blake following closely behind her.

"I told her," Ryder whispered and Lisa shot him a murderous glare. "She knows we're mates. And she knows how to trigger her wolf gene."

He was still petting my head when Lisa shoved him away from me. "Great, Ryder. Completely ignore my plan and send my best friend into a panic attack!"

"I know you're her best friend, but you need to remember who you're talking to," he growled menacingly, but Lisa held her own and Ryder backed off.

"Kaylee, babe. You need to calm down." Lisa grabbed my face, one hand on each cheek, and she sat on my thighs, careful to keep her weight off my pained ribs. "Come on, hun, deep breaths." She stroked her thumbs soothingly along my cheekbones.

As my breaths began to slow, I became increasingly aware of all those in the room. Lucas and Blake were talking with Ryder, trying to calm him down, and my parents along with Lillian, all stood in the doorway, concern on each of their faces. Mom was running a hand over Dad's chest in a soothing manner and was whispering in his ear. His arm was around her waist and he looked ready to kill. I hoped that her words were calming ones.

Slowly, I reached up and put a hand over one of Lisa's.

"Thanks, Lis. I'm okay now." I tried to smile encouragingly, but it came out as more of a grimace.

I wasn't completely okay, but I was okay enough.

"You sure, hun? You were on the verge," she asked, unsure.

She knew how to handle my panic attacks, she was always the one to talk me down from them. But she also knew how easy it would be for me to fall over the edge and have it start all over.

I smiled reassuringly at her and she climbed off but stayed sitting beside me. Mom patted Dad's shoulder and approached us.

"Oh, honey. Are you okay?" she asked, voice higher than normal, eyes shining with unshed tears.

"Yeah, Mom, I'm fine. It was just a panic attack. No biggy," I gave her a small smile. I just wanted this to be dropped. It was embarrassing. If this conversation continued, details would be brought to light that would only make her feel like she was to blame.

"No biggy? Kaylee, you could barely breathe! I've never seen that happen to you before!" Her voice was raised, but I knew it was because she was concerned. "How long have you been getting these?" There it was—the question I had been dreading.

"Since I was twelve," I mumbled, hoping that she wouldn't connect the dots.

"Since you were twelve? You mean since I left?" Mom ask softly, shocked.

There were tears welling in her eyes. The same eyes that were glowing with pain and guilt. She figured it out. I guess it had been too much to hope she wouldn't. I nodded silently while Dad came up behind her and placed his hands on her shoulders, kneading his thumbs into her back.

"Don't blame yourself, Mom. You couldn't have known it would happen," I said gently.

She had to know I didn't blame her. No one could have seen it coming, and there's a good chance I would have gotten them anyway.

"You're right. But I should have known it was happening, Kaylee. I should have been *told*," Mom whispered, and I knew nothing I could say would convince her otherwise.

She shook off Dad's hands and wiped the tears off of her cheeks. It was obvious she was upset at being kept out of the loop and her self-guilt only made it worse.

I sent Dad a pleading look. He nodded and led her out of the room, running his hands up and down her arms. As Mom turned from me, I saw a single tear slide down her cheek. That single tear hurt me more than all the tears before it. If Dad couldn't convince her not to blame herself, then I would find a way no matter what.

Lillian followed my Dad. Mom was her friend, she would help as well.

Ryder was looking at me, his brown eyes dark with emotion. He watched me as I sat up against the headboard. Lisa helped me adjust when I groaned and wrapped an arm around myself.

"I'm sorry, Kaylee," he whispered from his place by the window, Lucas and Blake perched on either side of him.

"It's not your fault either, Ryder. You were just telling me what I need to know, what I *asked* you to tell me. Please don't blame yourself," I whispered back.

Mom was already taking enough blame on herself, I couldn't have him feeling guilty too.

Ryder stepped away from the window and sat on the edge of the bed beside me, opposite Lisa, with his hip against my thigh. Brushing my cheek with the back of his hand, he spoke.

"Are you sure you're okay?" He was so quiet that even with how close we were I could barely hear him.

"I am," I nodded, tears brimming at the shame and tenderness shining in his eyes.

The three of us sat there for a long time while Blake and Lucas stood at the window, speaking in hushed tones. Lisa stroked my hair and Ryder played with my hand the same way as before.

I was drifting off when Mom and Dad came back in the room. Mom was holding a small plate with a sandwich. She came to stand by Ryder, but wouldn't meet my gaze.

"It's peanut butter and honey, you always liked it when you were little." She reached past Ryder and handed me the plate. A small smile tainted with regret tugged at her lips.

"Thanks, Momma." Her head shot up and her eyes widened. I hadn't called her 'Momma' since she'd been back, but it had the effect I was hoping for. Meeting her gaze, I said, "It is *not* your fault, Momma."

She nodded, her eyes brimming with unshed tears once again. Mom bowed her head breaking away from my gaze, before saying, "I'm so sorry, baby, even if you say it's not my fault. Six years I didn't know you were having panic attacks. I'm so sorry." Mom's voice broke at the end and the tears started streaming down her face in a river that couldn't be dammed.

She shook her head back and forth and her knees gave out. She would have hit the ground if not for Dad catching her, arms wrapping around her waist.

"Come on, Helen," Dad whispered as he led her from the room once more.

"Mom," I choked out once they were gone. It came out at barely above a whisper.

Tears began streaming down my face in rivulets before I could stop them. Falling into wracking sobs was the last thing I needed. Lisa continued to stroke my hair, trying to sooth me. The sandwich was left forgotten on my lap and I covered my face with my hands, knowing it was getting red and blotchy.

Lisa's gentle stroking and soft murmuring weren't working. The sobs became more and more intense, wracking my sore body, until large, warm hands firmly, but gently, pulled my hands from my face and against a hard chest.

Ryder was holding my small hands in his much larger ones. His heart pulsed under my fingers and the rhythm of it became the only thing in the room. It was all I could focus on and I swear I could hear it drumming in my ears. I could feel it in my soul.

The beat of Ryder's heart became the center of my world and eventually, with him and Lisa sitting with me, my tears ebbed and the sobs plaguing my body slowed until only little hiccups escaped from between my lips. With Lisa to my right, stroking my hair, and Ryder holding my hands to his hard chest, stroking his thumbs over my knuckles, my eyelids quickly drooped. Too exhausted from pain and the roller coaster of emotion to stay awake any longer.

Later, when I woke up, Blake and Lucas were both gone, but Lisa remained next to me, and Ryder sat reading in a big chair he had pulled up so close to the bed that both pieces of furniture were touching. The sandwich had been moved from my lap and placed on the nightstand beside the bed. Seeing it sitting there reminded me once again that I hadn't eaten in days.

I didn't let myself think about the bombshell Ryder had dropped on me. Nor did I let my mind wander to my mother's guilt, or how I was the cause of it. All I let myself think about at that moment was sating my hunger.

My stomach growled and I reached for the sandwich but pulled back when my ribs twinged at the movement. Ryder's head shot up at my shuffling movements and one side of his mouth twitched. He silently reached over and handed me the plate.

I placed it beside me and sat up—having laid down in my sleep—wincing at the way it jarred my torso. Ryder frowned at me and stood before helping me rest against the headboard. When he asked if I was comfortable, I nodded, and he moved my sandwich to my lap.

Lisa watched us silently before excusing herself while I ate. Ryder's gaze never strayed from my face as I finished my sandwich, which had gotten a little dry, but the honeyed goodness made up for it.

My hands were slightly sticky by the time I was finished. I was licking the honey from my fingertips when Ryder sighed and went into the bathroom, coming back seconds later with a damp cloth. Sitting on the bed, he took my hands in his and gently wiped off the remaining sugary magic.

"You didn't have to do that," I told him softly as he dropped the cloth on the nightstand.

Ryder's lips twitched up in a barely there smile. "I know. But I want to take care of you," he spoke quietly, for my ears alone, even though we were the only ones in the room.

"Is that part of the whole mate thing? Wanting to take care of me, I mean?" I asked, and with one simple question, I was nervous again.

"It's…part of it," he nodded slowly, not letting go of my hands. Running the tips of his fingers over my knuckles and between my fingers, he continued. "But I also just want to take care of you because I want to. Believe it or not, Kaylee, I actually like you. I think I would even without the mate bond. Despite your obvious joy at seeing Blake hit me," he grinned.

I laughed at that, because he was right. I *had* enjoyed seeing Blake smack him around a bit. But I had learned that, for some reason, when there was a real threat, like Brendan, I couldn't stand to see him get hurt.

My laughter abruptly stopped when Brendan's cold blue eyes flashed in my mind and I remembered something he said. Sensing the shift in my mood, Ryder's laughter died as well.

"What is it? What's wrong?" he asked, fierce worry coloring his deep voice. My skin tingled, and now that I knew why it happened, the sensation had become soothing, reassuring even.

"What did Brendan mean? When he said I'm his?" I asked quietly. I wasn't sure I wanted to know the answer, but I was sure that I needed to.

Ryder stiffened, his body turning to stone and his expression hardening. For a moment after the words had left my lips I wished I could take them back, but only for a moment. No matter Ryder's reaction or his feelings on the matter, I needed to know. And he knew that.

"Brendan…Brendan is under the impression," Ryder's chest rose and fell as he took a deep breath, a muscle ticking in his jaw. "He's under the impression that you're his mate," he finished through clenched teeth. I could hear his teeth grinding together and he wouldn't meet my gaze.

"What? Why? Why would he think that? And if he thinks I'm his mate, why did he hit me? No, why did he *beat* me?" I asked loudly. My voice rising in pitch as the panic built up through my body, accumulating in my chest.

Cupping my face, Ryder leaned his forehead against mine. "Hey, hey, hey. It's okay. It doesn't matter why he thinks that. All that matters is that I won't let him have you. He won't get that close ever again. I promise. Besides, you're mine," He assured me, almost growling.

I could tell he was trying to control his anger and, when he made his promise, everything about him softened.

I nodded and the panic ebbed. Ryder was a big, strong Alpha. He would take care of me. As much as I wanted to say I could take care of myself, I was toast against a wolf. But maybe I could learn.

"Do you think I could learn how to fight now?" I asked nervously.

Last time I asked, he had all but laughed in my face. Different emotions crossed over Ryder's features as he considered my question. Slowly—very slowly—he began to nod.

"It might be a good idea for you to learn how to defend yourself."

I was shocked he had agreed to let me watch but, I did not expect him to agree so easily. I was overjoyed that he did.

"Thank you! When do we start?" I asked, more excited than I probably should have been at the idea of learning how to inflict pain.

"When you're better." He smiled, a happy glint in his chocolate brown eyes.

It was then that I realized how close we were. Ryder had both his legs on the bed and with my face still clasped in his hands, he was practically on top of me. His heat seeped into me, spreading through my bones. With his forehead still pressed to mine, I could see that there were little gold flecks in Ryder's irises. His presence calmed me like nothing else, but the proximity left me more nervous than anything I could remember.

"Go out with me, Kaylee. Let me take you on a date," Ryder said, surprising me. His warm breath blew across my face as he spoke and I gasped.

A date? An honest to god date?

I sat there flabbergasted, completely in my own little world until Ryder pulled away.

"Alright, that's fine. I just thought—"

I interrupted him before he could finish his disappointment speech. There was no use fighting it anymore.

"Okay," I said, slightly breathless. "I mean, it's a little out of nowhere, but I think it could be fun."

"No, really, Kaylee. It's o—" Ryder stopped himself short as my words sank in. "What did you say? Are you serious? You'll go out with me?" he asked, like a little boy getting ice cream for the first time in a long time.

Biting my lip to suppress a grin, I nodded. Ryder's smile lit up his face, and quite frankly, the room. He whooped, and Lucas came through the door.

"What's all the commotion about?" Lucas yawned, rubbing the sleep out of his eyes.

I glanced out the window in confusion and was struck when I saw it was dark out. Ryder's shout had woken Lucas. I hoped he was the only one.

"She said yes, Luke!" Ryder hollered. You'd think I agreed to marry him with how he was reacting.

"That's great, bro. Now can you shut up? Some of us are trying to sleep." Lucas glared, but gave us a sleepy thumbs up before turning and leaving, closing the door behind him.

Ryder laughed at his brother and turned back to me, grinning. Taking a good look at him, I saw there were circles under his eyes that I hadn't noticed before and he had scruff covering his jaw.

"Ryder, you kind of look like crap," I said sheepishly, knowing it was my fault.

"Ouch, sweetheart," he said, feigning offense.

I blushed at the nickname, actually liking it this time, as I giggled at his reaction.

Something occurred to me then. "Um, Ryder? Where have you been sleeping?"

"Oh, um, I haven't, really."

I was shocked to say the least, but I was too tired to care about the extent of the implications.

"You know, you can sleep here if you want. You look exhausted and I wouldn't mind." I flushed brighter when he raised a brown at me. "I mean, if you want to."

Ryder didn't say anything, he just strode to the door and flicked off the light. The room fell into darkness and I couldn't see a thing. But I heard a belt being undone and pants being dropped to the floor. My pulse quickened.

A drawer opened and fabric rustled. A few moments later the bed dipped and Ryder slid in next to me.

I scooched down onto my back, biting my cheek to keep from whimpering at the pain the movement caused. My hands were on either side of me, clenching and unclenching. Ryder was in the bed next to me. The smell of him was so much more intense with him so close.

I had just started to drift when one of Ryder's large hands wrapped around mine, threading our fingers together. My breath caught in my throat at the subtle intimacy of the gesture. I smiled. I fell asleep with Ryder's hand in mine and the comforting scent of pine hugging me.

Chapter 13
Stay

Days passed as I healed. Ryder and I talked, mostly about my life before returning to Redheart. He wanted to know about all of my old friends and what classes were like in the "human world." He asked about my old teachers and what I liked to do for fun. I didn't tell him about my relationship with Carter. Mom's reaction to the news a couple days earlier told me not to share that information with someone who was supposed to be my soulmate.

I told him about my "old lady side," as I liked to call it; the part of me that liked to sit on the couch all day crocheting blankets and weaving bracelets. I talked about how much I enjoyed hiking and all of the photography that came with it. And when I spoke of my love for reading, he snorted and told me I had horrible taste in literature, which reminded me of how he would to sit in my backyard with me as a wolf while I read. Before I knew it was him.

"Hey! There is nothing wrong with my choice of reading material." He opened his mouth, most likely to tell me I was crazy, but I held up my hand. "And there is nothing you can say to convince me otherwise."

Ryder choked on a laugh and shook his head.

I also reminded him about my learning how to fight. When I mentioned it, he sighed and ran a hand through his hair. "I know I said you could train when you get better, but I really don't want you fighting, Kaylee."

"Why? I think it's important that I learn how to defend myself. Especially after—"

"I don't want to see you get hurt." Ryder stood from his place beside me and began to pace.

"I think I'll get more hurt if I can't defend myself, Ryder."

He sighed again and agreed that I was right. He said that after I was healed, he would start me training with one of the smaller wolves. He said that, even though the small wolves had skill, it would be less dangerous for me.

My family came to Mayor Mansion every day to check up on me. Even though they knew Lillian would contact them if anything went wrong, they still came. I appreciated it more than they could ever know.

Something occurred to me one day when Mom and Dad came to see me.

"Dad? Did you actually expand the company?" I asked him, an hour or so after he and Mom had arrived.

His eyes appeared to nearly pop out of his head. He looked like a deer caught in the headlights.

"Um, not really," he muttered. "Darrel and I promoted William to CEO so we're just owners now. We no longer run it."

"But we're okay and everything, right? We aren't going to struggle?" I was sort of worried now. Dad had bought us this huge house. He had said it was all taken care of, but what if we couldn't afford it?

"We'll be completely fine, Kale. It's a successful company and Darrel and I still own it. We still make most of the money, William just got a raise. But even if money was going to be a problem, it's not something I want you worrying about."

"As long as you're sure," I said, slightly appeased.

"I'm sure, now rest." Mom and Dad both left after that.

Lisa spent a lot of time with me while I was bed ridden, but there were times that she would disappear for hours, saying nothing more than she's going out. I knew she couldn't be with her parents, but I also knew she could take care of herself.

Lucas came and bothered me a few times, calling me 'Spencer' just to get a rise out of me. More often than not, he brought Blake, who would mostly stand there and laugh at my expense. Darrel and Karen even visited once, two days after my panic attack.

Lillian would check on me every few hours—even at night—making sure I was taking deep breaths. Apparently, that's something you have to do when you have fractured ribs. On the fifth day of sitting around doing nothing, I was deemed well enough to go home if I could walk down the stairs by myself, which I did.

Despite being well enough to leave, Lillian insisted I stay for dinner. She said that she wanted to make up for what happened at the party, completely ignoring me when I told her that it was in no way her fault. My parents were coming, as well as Lisa's. It was to be a family affair, Lillian said. Plus Blake, who was turning out to be like an annoying cousin.

"It'll be just family. No one you don't know, so you don't have to be all uncomfortable," Lillian told me that morning while she prodded at my ribs. "There will be music and food and everything a party *should* be, but with a much more select guest list." She winked excitedly. But when she mentioned the guest list, her eyes darkened, and the shiny green became a murky hazel.

"I look forward to it Lillian," I smiled. And I actually did. With only people I knew in attendance, I would be able to enjoy myself without worry of a repeat incident. "And I thought Blake was coming?"

"I did say family, didn't I?" Lillian questioned.

"Yeah, you did. I know Blake is the Beta and all, but does that make him family?"

"Sweetie, Blake is my nephew," she explained. He really was an annoying cousin. "No one told you?"

Her fingers continued poking around and when she hit a particularly tender spot, I hissed between my teeth, sucking in a sharp breath of air.

I shook my head and she chuckled. "No one tells you anything around here, do they?" she asked, amused, but not without sympathy.

"Nope, not a damn thing," I mumbled, looking over her shoulder at the ceiling.

"Well, my dear, you're clear for dinner. And maybe a bit of dancing, if we drug you up first," Lillian laughed. Her eyes shone with sad humor.

"Sounds like fun, Lillian. But I don't think I'll be dancing again any time soon."

"That's fair, honey. Just promise me you'll try to have fun."

I agreed and she handed me a couple of tablets for pain, then left the room.

Later that day, Lisa barged in, interrupting my glorious dream about purple bunnies buying me ice cream. Startled by her shouting, I shot up from the bed, wincing when that especially sore spot in my ribs twinged.

"We're gonna part-*ay*!" Lisa shouted over excited, bouncing and dancing around the room.

"Lisa, calm down. It's literally just dinner with family." I rolled my eyes. She was insane.

"Doesn't matter! It's still a party and I'm excited!" She hopped—kind of like the bunnies in my dream—and her blond hair bounced around her face.

"Trust me, I am too. But honestly, I kind of want the day to be over already so I can get home and into my own bed."

"What, is Ryder's bed not good enough for you?" Lisa teased. She crossed her arms and popped her hip, staring at me expectantly.

"Ryder's bed is fine, Lis. But all of this is a little overwhelming, you know? It's a lot to take in and I think it would be a lot easier to deal with if I could just do it in my own space," I said softly.

The excitement that had been lighting up Lisa's features quickly dimmed, and she nodded in understanding.

"I'm sorry, Kale. I didn't even think about that," she apologized, understanding written all over her face.

"Don't worry about it. Look, can you do me a favor?" I asked, changing the subject completely, my mouth forming a sneaky grin.

"Of course, babe. What do you need?"

I told her what I wanted and her lips spread into a wide grin. I thought I was being clever and, evidently, Lisa did too.

"Think you can do that for me?"

"Hell yes! How'd you think of that?"

I gestured to the book I had placed on the nightstand earlier and Lisa burst out laughing.

Shaking her head, she walked to the door. "You and your romance books." Laughing, she left the room, walking past Ryder who stood in the doorway.

"What about your romance books?" Ryder was leaning against the door frame with his brow quirked. His lips twitched at the mention of my reading choices.

"Oh, nothing," I chirped with an over exaggerated shrug.

"Mhmm, sure," he said skeptically, drawing out his words.

"You already judge me for liking them. So you don't get to know!" I crossed my arms and stuck out my tongue like a big child.

Ryder laughed and walked toward me, sitting down on the bed, one leg on and one left hanging off the side. "How are you feeling?" he asked, placing his hand on my thigh, just above my knee.

"Good. Your mom cleared me this morning. So I can get out of your hair tonight." I smiled, and for the first time in weeks, I was legitimately excited about something.

"What if I don't want you 'out of my hair'?" Ryder asked nervously, not meeting my gaze.

"What do you mean?" He couldn't mean…

"I want you to stay, Kaylee. For just a little while longer. This past week has been amazing. Everything I've learned about you, everything you've told me about your old life. It all makes me want to know more."

I was utterly and completely astounded. I wanted so badly to go home, but the raw honesty in his voice and the vulnerable openness displayed on his face made me consider what he was saying—what he was offering.

"Let me think about it?" My heart was pounding in my chest, but I kept my voice even and calm.

"Of course. If you decide before dinner, come find me." Ryder stood left the room, leaving me alone with my thoughts.

It had been a long few weeks. I was still reeling over the fact that almost everyone around me was a werewolf. Not to mention the fact that I had a mate, that I *was* a mate. My life had turned into one of my books I loved to read and I wasn't sure how I felt about it. Werewolves, mates, werewolf fights had all entered my life and it was all a little…much. I enjoyed reading about situations like the one I had found myself in, but that didn't mean I wanted it to happen to me.

My thoughts were interrupted by the door being swung open with Lucas and Blake standing in the doorway.

"We need to talk to you," Lucas said in a serious and not at all Lucas-like tone.

"Okay, sure. Come on in, guys," I responded, wiggling to sit up straighter. They exchanged a look and came inside, closing the door behind them. "What's up?" I asked, as they both sat on the foot of the bed, facing me.

"It's about Ryder," Blake told me.

"What about Ryder? Did something happen?" I tried not to sound panicky, but when neither of them said anything, the panic took hold. "Guys?" He had barely been gone five minutes. How could something happen?

"Kaylee, Ryder's fine," Lucas told me after exchanging another look with Blake. My heart rate slowed at his assurance that Ryder was okay, and my breathing evened out. My reaction wasn't something I was expecting, but there were obviously more pressing matters than my feelings.

"Okay, so what is it?"

The boys looked at each other again and took deep breaths.

"Ryder told you that you guys are mates, right?" Lucas asked me, wringing his hands in his lap.

"Yeah, and he told me how to trigger my wolf gene, too." Raising my brows, I crossed my arms impatiently.

"Well, there is another Alpha who also thinks you're his," Lucas continued slowly.

"What do you mean, 'another Alpha?'" Lucas shot Blake a look at my question and he took the reins.

"The Alpha of another pack, Kaylee. His name is Brendan," Blake sighed.

"Wait, the same guy who showed up at the party and beat me is an *Alpha*?" My breath started coming faster and I had to consciously fight to slow it.

"Yeah, Kaylee. Brendan's an Alpha." Blake ran a hand through his hair. I could tell he didn't want to have this conversation with me, but obviously felt he had to. "But that's not what's important. Not right now anyway. What's important is that Brendan hates Ryder, and is almost as powerful as him."

"Okay, but why is that so important? And what does it have to do with me?"

Sighing, Blake continued. "It has to do with you because Brendan will use you to get to Ryder. There's no could or maybe, he *will* use you. It's bad enough that Brendan thinks you're his mate, but his desire to have you is only heightened by the fact that, in his mind, Ryder has stolen you from him."

"So, you're saying that Brendan will use me to get to Ryder?" I asked in disbelief. Most of what the Beta said didn't soak in, but when someone tells me I could be used as a tool to hurt someone I'm starting to care about? I notice.

"Yes, that's what we're saying," Blake answered while Lucas nodded. "On top of the fact that he wants you for his own twisted pleasure."

"But, why? Why does Brendan hate Ryder so much?" What possibly could have happened between them that would cause that kind of hate to fester?

"No one really knows. Not even Ryder. Or at least if he does, he's not saying anything," Lucas said softly. I could see the worry for his brother shining in his eyes.

I was just opening my mouth to ask what I could do when the door slammed open against the wall and Ryder strode in, seething. Blake and Lucas both jumped off the bed when they saw him.

"What the hell are you two doing in here?" he growled through clenched teeth. That aggravating muscle ticking in his jaw.

"Chatting," Lucas shrugged, trying for nonchalance, as he struggled to plant his signature grin on his face.

"Bullshit. What did you tell her?" Ryder's shoulders were shaking as he tried to control his anger.

Crawling to the end of the bed, I spoke up. "Ryder, we were just talking. Really."

"I *know* you were talking, Kaylee. I want to know what about." His eyes softened when they landed on me and the grimace covering my face, but there was no hiding the blazing anger in the chocolate pools.

Not wanting to lie, I shot the boys apologetic looks, hoping they understood, and opened my mouth. "They were telling me about Brendan." Ryder growled at the name. "They told me that he hates you and that he'll try to use me to get to you." I spoke quietly, calmly, thinking that maybe it would sooth Ryder and he would relax some.

No such luck.

"Get out." When no one moved, Ryder spoke again, louder. "Get out, both of you." Neither of them moved. "*Now*," Ryder roared.

Bowing their heads, Lucas and Blake left the room. They each sent me an apologetic glance before closing the door behind them. My eyes bugged with

I noticed the doorknob sized hole in the wall from when Ryder slammed the door open.

Ryder didn't speak as he approached the foot of the bed where I still sat on my knees.

"Ryder?"

No response. He didn't even blink.

"Ryder?" I tried again.

Still nothing.

"Ryder, please," I practically begged. I ached to know what was going through his mind.

"What do you want me to say, Kaylee?" His voice sounded tortured. Pained.

"I want you to tell me what you're thinking."

His eyes shot to mine. There was anger blazing, but behind that, there was fear.

"You want me to tell you what I'm thinking? Fine. I'm terrified, Kaylee. Terrified that he's going to get to you no matter how hard I try to keep him away. That despite every effort, somehow, he'll still sneak in and get to you. I'm scared that he'll steal you away before I even get the chance to know you." Ryder's shoulders slumped and he collapsed onto the side of the bed.

"I'm not going anywhere, Ryder. He won't get me, ever," I assured him, reaching out to rub his shoulder. I couldn't erase the nagging feeling in the pit of my stomach that told me this was a lie. But I ignored it.

"But what if he does? What if, even with the extra patrol I've put on since the party, he finds a way in?" he sounded so defeated. And I didn't like it.

"Then I'll protect myself, and so will my family…and…you," I stated matter-of-factly. "He *beat* me, Ryder. Nothing he can do could make me choose him." I shuffled forward until my knees were against his lower back and hugged him. I wrapped my arms around his shoulders and hugged him.

Ryder reached up and wrapped his hands around mine before tugging gently and bring my chest flush with his back, bringing us closer than we've ever been.

"Thank you," he whispered as he ran his thumbs along the backs of my hands.

"For what?" I asked, slightly breathless.

I felt him shrug underneath me. "I'm not entirely sure. For being you, I guess. I don't know, I just felt the need to say it."

There wasn't really anything to say after that. I held him while he lightly stroked my knuckles and I fell into the intimacy of the position.

"I want you to promise me something," Ryder said, breaking the silence that had settle on us.

"What is it?"

"Don't worry about Brendan. Let the Guard and me handle it," he requested.

I wanted to object, but then I thought about how the Guard was basically like the police and, if something like this was happening in the human world, I would let the police handle it.

"I promise." Ryder squeezed my hand and we fell into a comfortable silence once again.

Time passed as we sat like that, and eventually my ribs started to ache like nobody's business, but I ignored it. We stayed together until Lisa barged in with a bag in one hand and a shoebox in the other.

"Alright, Mr. Mate. Beat it. I have work to do," Lisa demanded, popping her hip. Ryder shot her a quizzical look but let go of my hands and stood. Turning around, he bent over and placed a gentle, lingering kiss on my forehead.

"Remember what I asked you earlier?" Goosebumps danced across my body as Ryder's lips brushed my skin and I nodded, though I couldn't for the life of me remember with his soft mouth on me. "Have you decided yet?"

He pulled his lips away from my forehead so he could look me in the eye. I quickly realized he was talking about me staying at Mayor Mansion and I shook my head.

"Not yet."

"Alright," he sighed. A sigh that held so much disappointment, I wanted to tell him that I would stay. But I couldn't.

Pressing his lips to my forehead once more, he whispered, "I'll see you at dinner," and left me alone with my best friend.

As soon as the door shut, Lisa's jaw dropped and she squealed. "*What* was that?"

She ran over to me and plopped on the bed, not even caring that she was holding one of my favorite outfits.

"He wants me to stay here for a little while longer," I told her quietly, not worried about her being unable to hear me.

"What do you mean, 'longer?'" she asked, her crazy energy fading.

"I don't know exactly," I shrugged. "All he said was a bit longer."

"And do you want to?" Lisa asked, but more for my benefit than her own. Sure, she wanted to know, but she knew sometimes I needed prompting to help me figure things out. She was crazy and bizarre, but she knew when to calm down, she knew when calm Lisa was needed.

"I really don't know Lis. I mean, I like being here, but it's not home. You know?" I peeked over at her face, quiet and thoughtful.

"I think you know what you want, babe," Lisa said softly. And she was right.

"I want to go home," I nodded.

A gentle smile softened Lisa's already breathtaking features. "Well then, my dear, let's get you ready for dinner so that you can." She stood and, very gently, removed the contents from the bag and lay it all out on the bed between us. She then opened the shoebox and grasped the heels by the straps before placing them next to the clothes.

"It's perfect. Thank you so much, Lisa!" I squeaked, sitting up to pull her into a hug.

"You are, of course, welcome!" She squeezed me back gently.

With dinner so close I could taste it; Lisa and I got my plan under way. Although with Ryder wanting me to stay, I wasn't sure I needed to go through with it anymore.

By the time we were done, dinner was ready and my dad was yelling at us from somewhere in the house.

On our way to the dining room, I couldn't help but feel a little nervous. I was wearing jeans that fit my legs like a second skin and a shirt that could be considered classy or trashy, depending on what you paired it with. In this case, it was a little bit of both. The red material crisscrossed over my torso with wide straps that almost covered my shoulders. It was short enough that it barely reached my pant line and kept riding up, showing off some skin, not to mention a tasteful amount of cleavage.

Lisa's outfit matched mine except for the colors. Lisa's shirt was a light turquoise. We were both wearing strappy, three-inch heels, but where hers were silver, mine were gold. We had bought the shirts together to celebrate both of our seventeenth birthdays. She turned seventeen four months before me, so a month after I did, we went out together and celebrated, just the two of us.

All I could think while we descended the staircase and strode toward the dining room, was that I really hoped Ryder was a guy who could appreciate the whole package. I had a sneaking suspicion that he was.

Chapter 14
Dinner

As Lisa and I came closer and closer to the dining room, the voices got louder and louder. We turned the corner and I saw Dad standing by the head of the table, laughing with Blake and Lucas. Mom and Lillian were standing a few feet away from the entrance with their heads close together. They gossiped more than teenage girls. The Perrys were there as well. Including…

"Carson!" Lisa shrieked and bounced over to where her brother stood by a door that presumably lead to the kitchen.

"Hey, Mothball," he said in his deep tenor as he enveloped his little sister into one of his famous bear hugs.

Just as I took a step toward them, strong arms snaked around my waist from behind, pressing me back against a solid, warm chest.

"You smell amazing, like coconuts," Ryder whispered, his lips brushing the shell of my ear.

Giggling, I placed my hands over his on my belly and unwrapped his arms from around my body. Turning to face him, he smiled. "Thanks, so do you, but like pine."

"Sit with me?" he asked with a boyish grin, offering his hand.

I stared at his outstretched hand for a moment. And this time, I took it. "Sure, but I want to say hi to Carson first." With Ryder's hand clasped in mine, we approached the Perry siblings. "Hey, Carson, I didn't know you were here!"

"Hey, Leelee," he chuckled, using my old nickname. "I came up a few days after my parents. Figured I'd spend the big nineteen with my buddies and then join everyone up here."

Carson seemed to be doing well. He had turned nineteen a few days after Lisa, Dad, and I had moved. It made sense for him to stay behind to celebrate.

"What about college?" I asked. He had been really excited about Europe.

"Put it off for another year. Figured it would be good to be home for a while. I've always loved this place. Besides, Europe will still be there next year," Carson shrugged. He was telling the truth, but also…not.

"As long as you're sure, Carson."

"Are you kidding? I'm thrilled!" He all but shouted, laughing loudly.

Shaking my head, I let Ryder lead me away to the very center of the table and took a seat. Ryder tugged me down to sit next to him while Lucas pulled himself away from the conversation with my dad. Lisa called dibs on the spot to my right before running off to do who knows what, and Carson took the chair opposite the one his sister had claimed, their identical eyes gleaming with excitement.

A bell dinged from somewhere behind the closed door, and everyone left on their feet took a seat, with Lillian at one end and my Dad at the other.

Lisa came scurrying back into the room just as the door to the kitchen swung open. Her face was lit up as she sat beside me. I raised a brow in question, but she shrugged with a wink and turned to catch up with her brother.

A dozen men and women came spilling out through the swinging door, carrying different drinks and appetizers. The people holding drinks walked around the table, offering whatever they were holding, and the people carrying trays of food set them down before retreating to the kitchen. My jaw dropped at the display and I leaned forward in my seat to glance at Lillian. I raised an eyebrow expectantly, and much like Lisa had before, she shrugged.

"I wanted to go all out. After what you've been through because of us— because of what we are—I figured you deserved a big, safe meal. So, I hired a catering company and had them use the big kitchen." She smiled.

The *big* kitchen? They had *two*?

I fell back against my chair with a gob-smacked look on my face. Ryder glanced down at me and barked out a laugh. Taking my hand, he squeezed it reassuringly. And didn't let go.

Everyone started digging into the appetizers, especially Lucas. I nibbled on a potato skin, distracted by Ryder's hand in mine, and tried to slip silently into the background.

"So, Leelee. You found yourself a mate, huh?" Carson smirked with a smug twinkle in his eyes. Of course, *he* would notice my attempt at invisibility. Not only did he call me out, he used that embarrassing nickname from when we were toddlers again.

"Um, yeah, He's actually going to take me on a date as soon as I'm well enough," I told him from across the table. As soon as the words left my lips, I wished they hadn't. A hushed silence fell over the room and all eyes were on me and Ryder.

"All right, I give. What's the big deal?" Leaning forward, I splayed my fingers on the tabletop.

"A date, Ryder?" Lillian asked skeptically, completely ignoring my question.

"She didn't grow up around us, Mom. Not to mention, she deserves it; she deserves to be dated," he answered, somehow soft and passionate at the same time.

"Wait, what do you mean I 'deserve it?'" I asked, using finger quotes. But once again, I was ignored. Everyone was talking about me like I wasn't even there. That happened far too often around these people, and I was seriously getting sick of it.

"You know that's not really how we do things, Ryder," Darrel spoke up, leaning forward to be better heard. "Not Alphas."

"Darrel, I appreciate your concern, but it's not necessary," Ryder assured him and stood, his chair scraping the ground as it moved back across the floor. "I know dating isn't conventional for Alphas, especially when their lady has a dormant gene, but she was raised apart from all this. Dating is what she knows. I won't force her into anything."

Lillian stood and rounded the table, walking toward her eldest son. He towered over her, yet she still managed to demand attention and respect without a word.

"You really feel the need to do this?" Ryder nodded. "Then I will support you." Lillian smiled up at him and returned to her place at the end of the table.

Ryder turned to face Blake who nodded in response to an unspoken question and Ryder let out a sigh of relief before sitting back down.

Dad released a breath and whispered, "Oh, thank god." Mom ran her hand up and down his arm and patted his hand.

The rest of dinner passed in relative silence, but by dessert, everyone was talking again. Everyone except me. I couldn't get this no dating thing out of my head. If Alphas didn't date, what did they do?

After the dating issue had been resolved to everyone else's satisfaction, the evening passed quickly. It was finally time for me to go home.

While dinner was being cleaned up by the catering crew, I headed to Ryder's room to collect my things. I smiled as I left the dining room. My plan had worked; Ryder kept sneaking glances at me all night. Although with him wanting me to stay at Mayor Mansion longer, he may have done it even without my slightly provocative clothing.

My smile quickly shifted to a wince as I began climbing the stairs. Out of nowhere, I was scooped up and cradled against a hard chest. "You're still in pain," Ryder said softly as he ascended the grand staircase with me in his arms. He didn't phrase it as a question, but I nodded anyway.

"It's only been a week, Ryder. It takes longer than that for us mere mortals to heal," I joked.

"But you're no mere human, Kaylee." His chocolate eyes bored into the dull flatness of mine.

I averted my gaze, uncomfortable with the reminder that I wasn't actually human.

We reached his room and he placed me gently on the bed. Stepping back, Ryder ran a hand through his hair. "You're not staying, are you?"

"No, Ryder. As wonderful as it's been, spending these last few days with you, this isn't home," I told him softly, playing with the comforter beneath my fingers.

"I understand. You don't have to explain yourself." Sighing, he sat down beside me and grasped one of my hands in his, halting my finger's journey along his blankets. "I'm sorry."

"For what?" I asked, scrunching my forehead.

"Dinner. It was supposed to be enjoyable, but instead you were stuck sitting there feeling awkward and confused." Ryder began playing with my fingers like he had been doing whenever we were alone together. I couldn't deny that I enjoyed it.

"About that, what did everyone mean about dating not being conventional?" I stared at our hands, engrossed by the differences. Large, small. Tan, pale. Rough, smooth. We were complete opposites, but we balanced anyway.

"It's an Alpha thing. Typically, when an Alpha or an heir finds their mate, he's expected to mate with her almost right away. Hormones generally shoot up upon meeting, so it never takes long." He paused and shook his head. "There have been times in Lycan history where an Alpha and his Soul have managed to resist temptation and…date. Sometimes the pack lets it happen, but more often than not, the Beta will set a vote. To allow the courting, or to lock the wolves up together until they have sex."

"Why would someone do that? Why not just let them take things at their own pace? I mean, if other wolves are allowed to date, why not the Alpha?" I stood, tearing my hand from his. I began pacing around the room in disbelief, ignoring the persistent ache in my side and back.

Locking people up together until they did the deed was wrong, barbaric even.

"An Alpha is always at his best when he is mated. The Beta's job is to not only be the second in command, but to make sure the Alpha is doing his job properly," Ryder explained. All I could think was that, if Blake did this to us, I would beat him. I would probably lose, but it wouldn't stop me from trying.

"It's not as bad as it sounds, Kaylee. The wolves are always comfortable and nothing is forced to happen. Just…encouraged?" he said slowly.

"Encouraged?" I stopped in front of him, my hands on my hips.

"It's been known to happen, where the pack gets impatient and they drug the food brought to the pair," Ryder explained cautiously, afraid of my reaction.

"You've *got* to be kidding," I fumed. He shook his head and I started pacing again. I was too angry to notice the little twinges in my body from stomping around.

Ryder stood from the bed and came to a stop directly in front of me.

"That's not going to happen to us," he whispered, cupping my face in his hands. "Mom has already given us her blessing. Not to mention Lucas." His thumbs were running along my cheekbones soothingly and I leaned into his hands, letting my eyes slide closed.

"What about Lucas?" I asked softly, distracted by the feeling of Ryder.

"He hates the rule. As heir and a member of the Alpha family, he would have to do it too," Ryder spoke gently. "In case something were to happen to me before we mated, or if something happened to both of us afterward."

I nodded, not able to form words with tingles skating across my cheeks.

"Kaylee?"

"Hmmm?"

"If you're not staying, you should probably pack your things. I'm sure your family wants to head home."

My eyes snapped open and I pulled away from Ryder's distracting touch.

"Oh my goodness, you're right." My cheeks were flushed as I ran the words together.

Rushing around the room, I ignored my aching body and gathered everything that had been brought over for me during my time at the Mansion. My arms overflowed with the items I could carry, and I turned to look at Ryder who had a crooked smirk tilting his lips. Without saying a word, he walked into his closet and came back out holding a small suitcase.

"Oh, thank goodness," I breathed and dropped my arm load onto his bed. He laughed and helped me pack the bag.

Our arms brushed as we moved over the suitcase, throwing things in haphazardly.

When we finished, Ryder pulled me to him, holding me tight. At least as tightly as he could without hurting me.

"Friday?" he whispered in my hair.

"Friday?" I asked, repeating his question.

"Date? Friday?" Ryder leaned back and studied my face.

"Oh, sure! Friday. Just not anything too active 'kay? I'm still a little broken," I laughed. I had agreed to the date and I wanted to go. But now we had a day set, I was kind of nervous.

"Do you have a phone?" he asked.

"Of course, I do. I am a teenager, after all," Ryder laughed at my lame quip and I wrote my number on a piece of paper he handed me. He slipped it into his pocket and wrapped an arm around my shoulders.

"Let's get you home."

Chapter 15
Sabotage

Mom and Dad had already climbed into the front of the car and I had just pulled my door shut from my seat behind Mom when Ryder appeared at the window.

"Can I see you tomorrow? Just for a movie or something?" he asked, leaning through the frame after I had rolled down the glass.

"What about Friday?" I buckled my seatbelt and tilted my head.

"This wouldn't be a date, Kaylee. I just want to see you." His words made me blush lightly and I nodded, biting back a smile. "Great, I'll be at your place at around noon." I smiled and Ryder leaned further into the car, planting a kiss on my cheek.

A small smile graced Ryder's lips as he backed away. Just as I was closing the window, Lisa popped into view with a grin lighting her features.

"I'm going to stay with my parents and Carson tonight. But I'll see you tomorrow, okay?" She bounced; her hands wrapped around the bottom of the window.

"Are we good to go, Kale?" my dad yawned from the driver's seat.

"Yeah, Dad." I turned back to Lisa to say goodbye, but she was already hopping away from the car and toward her family. Carson's arms were already open, waiting for her enthusiastic embrace. We pulled away from Mayor Mansion and I let out a sigh of relief. Finally. I was more than ready for my own bed. Even if it had only been mine for a short amount of time. I'd spent almost as much time in Ryder's bed as I had in my own.

After driving for a few minutes, the vehicle started to swerve. Shifting my view from the side window to the front, I saw Mom's hand on Dad's forearm, gently shaking it. And then harder.

"Johnathyn?" her voice sounded worried, but as she repeated his name her voice became tighter and more panicked.

The world rushed by outside the vehicle as Mom shook Dad to no avail.

When we flew by our house, I leaned forward, unbuckling, and shook his shoulder. "Dad?"

His chin was resting against his collarbones and I realized this was a lot worse than I ever could have guessed.

That's when the real panic set in.

Mom shot me a scared look and I tried to reach for the wheel from the back seat while she continued shaking Dad with more and more vigor and saying his name.

But it was too late.

I was directly behind the driver's seat, leaning over the shoulder, and just as the fingers of my right hand wrapped around the steering wheel, we crashed.

The impact threw me against the seat and I choked on a scream when my chest made contact with the headrest, knocking the breath from my lungs. My head bounced off the side of the vehicle, right where the seatbelt comes out. My brain knocked around inside my skull and my ears were ringing.

The pain was almost too much.

Trying to get my bearings, I looked to my parents, who were both unconscious.

"Mom?" I choked, rolling my head back and forth. "Dad?"

I hadn't even realized I was crying until I tasted the salt on my lips. I knew I needed to get help. I needed to *move*. But, god, I hurt so much. My chest was tight with the effort it took to breathe, my ears were ringing, and my vision was blurred.

Forcing myself, I opened the door and fell out of the car. Laying in a heap in the dirt, I rolled my head to see what we hit.

A tree.

"Ugh," I half groaned, half whimpered, trying to roll onto my belly. I attempted to get my hands underneath me, but they were shaking too hard and I couldn't lift myself.

I lay on the ground for what felt like hours, but what had probably only been a few minutes, wheezing out calls for help.

Crunch.

Rolling my head in the direction of the sound, I saw a large dark figure. Or was it two? Three? I couldn't tell. My vision was blurry, and I very well could have been seeing things. From my other side, I heard a growl, but I didn't have the strength to turn and see. Whoever it was made the approaching figure—figures—halt. He was familiar, but I couldn't figure out why.

"Of course, *you* had to meddle. I suppose I'll just have to take the girl's father instead." The figure shook his head and clucked its tongue, its voice deep and menacing.

I knew I should have been afraid of him, but I couldn't muster the strength to feel much of anything apart from the pain plaguing my body.

And then it registered.

"No," I cried, trying to roll closer to the front of the car—to where my dad was—but I couldn't make it more than an inch or two.

The dark figure closed in and opened the driver's door. He reached in and I knew he was unbuckling his victim, before pulling back with my dad over his shoulder.

"No," I groaned again, tears falling down my face, my temple stinging. Once again, I attempted to move, but a growl and hot breath on my cheek kept me still.

"Please," I whimpered, breathless. I could barely hear myself.

"I'll see you soon, my dear," the dark man said before shifting his eyes to the figure on my other side. "This is on you, child."

And then he bounded away with my dad over his shoulder.

"Dad." It was meant to be a scream, but it came out as barely anything at all. Black invaded the sides of my vision and my head lolled to the other side, the side that didn't hurt when pressed to the ground, and I saw the source of the growling.

On some level, I knew what I was seeing wasn't normal, but my brain wouldn't register the significance of shiny grey fur and lean, powerful muscle.

Just then, the silver wolf shifted into a strangely familiar looking man who quickly dressed in a pair of shorts from around his ankle and pulled out a cell phone.

He leaned over me and placed his fingers to my throat, right below my jaw. I blinked, and the silver man's voice rang out.

"Ryder?"

And the blackness consumed me.

***

"Kaylee? God, sweetheart. Can you hear me?"

The familiar voice that was pulling me out of the void was deep and alluring but strangely pained. I slowly blinked my eyes open and let out a groan that was quickly swallowed by a whimper.

"Kaylee, oh, thank god," Ryder gasped and wrapped his arms around my shoulders, lifting me against his chest. I screamed at the movement and Ryder swore. "Shit. I'm so sorry."

He eased me back down, laying me on the ground, whimpers escaping me the entire time. My head lolled to the side and I groaned, whimpered, and let out little screams when a tear would roll into the gash on the side of my head.

"You're okay, sweetheart. You have to be," Ryder whispered, worry coloring his voice. I couldn't tell if he had meant for me to hear the last part, but it made me feel warm and gave me something to concentrate on other than the pain.

"Mom?" I croaked, my voice pinched from the agony.

"She's okay, too." He nodded, stroking my hair from my face, but careful not to brush my bloody temple. "She's already awake and actually is in the better shape out of the two of you."

I let out a sigh of relief at the assurance that my mom was all right. And then I realized exactly what Ryder had said. *Two* of us.

"Dad?"

"He's gone, Kaylee. He was taken. Broddy didn't recognize the man who took him. Their scents had faded already by the time we got here. I'm so sorry." Ryder shook his head, looking down at the road.

Shame and guilt flashed over his face, clouding his gorgeous features. I wanted to assure him that this wasn't his fault. I was too weak. And with the news of my father, I couldn't mumble a single word. I couldn't even wonder who Broddy was, no matter how many bells were ringing at the name.

"We'll get him back, Kaylee. I swear it."

I couldn't respond, but the sentiment warmed me from the inside out and I knew he really meant it.

Someone shouted what sounded like garbled words, but Ryder shouted his understanding without moving his gaze off of me.

"We have to move you, okay?"

I made a sound in the back of my throat that I hoped he would interpret as confirmation. Two men that I didn't recognize approached us and sent Ryder a questioning look. He nodded and they came closer. One of them went to my feet while the other went to my thighs and Ryder stayed at my shoulders.

"Now," Ryder commanded, and they lifted me.

I screamed.

"I'm so sorry, Kaylee." The pain in his voice was only too apparent. I wanted his pain to stop. I wanted *all* of the pain to stop.

Whimpering as they shifted me onto a cot of some sort, it was all I could do not to scream again.

"Shh, just breathe, sweetheart. Take deep breaths."

I did as I was told and the pain intensified, leaving me gasping on the stretcher type object. The deeper the breaths, the more it hurt. As I breathed, Ryder strapped me in place, pulling straps over my legs and my hips, carefully avoiding my ribs.

When Ryder was sure I was secured onto the cot, the two men left us.

"Kaylee!" A high-pitched screech sounded from somewhere nearby and Lisa came to a sudden stop, hovering above me with tears streaking her cheeks. "Oh my gosh, babe. What the hell happened?"

"They crashed, Lisa," Ryder answered, with his teeth clenched. I whimpered at the memories his words conjured.

"Shit. That shouldn't be possible. Even with John being practically human, he still has our reflexes."

"I know that, Lisa. Someone wanted this to happen, and I sure as hell intend to find out who," Ryder growled. Lisa nodded and grasped my hand, her company lending some comfort.

As I was carried in the cot, my world began to once again grow dim. Until I heard her.

"Damn it! Where's my daughter?" her voice was tight and panicky as it floated through the space. "Kaylee!"

"Mom," I croaked, barely audible. "Please," I begged, looking at Ryder. Tears were a constant stream down my face and my temple stung with a vengeance, the pain never ebbing.

Ryder motioned with his head and we got closer and closer to the shrieks.

"Kaylee? Is that you, honey?"

"Mom," I croaked again, unable to say anything more.

"Oh, baby," her voice broke and tears began rolling down her face as my own tears came faster. "We'll get him back, honey. I promise."

I wanted to nod to somehow agree, but I couldn't move my head anymore and every time I opened my mouth to say something, all that came out was one pained sound or another.

I was loaded into a large SUV, my mom occupying a cot beside me. Ryder sat on a custom-made bench that ran along the side. Lisa climbed in after him and the doors slammed shut.

"Get us home, Blake," Ryder said, barely contained rage causing a tremor in his voice.

"As fast as I can," Blake said. And we took off.

A familiar man was speaking to Blake from the passenger seat, but before I could figure out why I recognized him, we hit a bump and the world faded away.

***

Mom screaming.
Dad unconscious.
Pain.

115

Shadow man.

Pain.

Silver wolf.

Dad.

Pain.

"Mmm," I groaned in the back of my throat, my face scrunched.

"Kaylee? Are you awake, sweetheart?" Ryder was here. I groaned again and slowly blinked my eyes open. I was in Ryder's room again.

"Kaylee!" He was next to me in an instant, barely sparing a moment to dash to the door, swing it open, and shout, "Mom!" through the doorway.

Ryder grasped my hand and sat on the edge of the bed, gently stroking the pad of his thumb over my knuckles. He reached up and brushed the hair off my forehead just as Lillian came rushing into the room, Lisa only one second behind her.

"Kaylee!" They screeched at the same time.

I tried to smile, but my lips were so cracked and dry that the slightest movement made my bottom lip split and bleed.

Lillian bustled toward me and, unlike the last time I was in this position, she let Ryder stay where he was and stood on my other side.

"How do you feel?" Lillian asked, lifting the bandage from my temple.

"Hurts," I croaked, choking.

Falling into a coughing fit was the worst thing I could have done at that moment, and it's exactly what I did.

Shit," Lillian swore.

If coughs hadn't been wracking my body, I might have laughed. It was the first time I could remember hearing her curse.

Helping me sit up with an IV in my arm and a killer ache in my chest, Lillian rubbed my back gently, being cautious of the breaks and bruises I knew were there, all the while soothing my cough. She jerked her head toward the nightstand and Ryder handed her a cup of water with a straw which she then held in front of me.

"Drink. Slowly."

I wrapped my lips around the straw and pulled. Sighing when the water slid down my throat, easing the ache.

"Thanks," I wheezed, although not quite as badly as before.

"Of course, darling." Lillian nodded and ran her hand over my head in a very maternal gesture as she eased me back down.

Just then, my mom came into the room. And she was okay. She had to lean on Lucas for support and there was bruising on the exposed skin of her face, neck, and arms, but she was okay.

"Mom," my voice broke on the one simple word, and she rushed to me, pushing away from Lucas despite his protests, and winced with every step.

She threw herself onto the bed next to me and hugged me gently, but somehow more fiercely than I could ever remember.

"Oh, honey," Mom sobbed.

"Careful, Helen. It's only been three days," Lillian whispered, but we paid her no mind as we cried together.

Eventually, she pulled away and I got a good look at her. Her face was practically a big purple mass from the airbag and her left arm was in a cast and sling. It took me a second to figure out why, but then I remembered that she had been shaking Dad when we crashed. Her arm would have been hit by the airbags from an odd angle.

"I'm so glad you're okay," she whispered, sitting up and, ever so gently, brushing away some hair that had fallen into my face. "When they wouldn't let me see you, I thought for sure that—never mind, you're alive and safe and that's what's important."

"What happened, Momma? Dad...passed out, but he...definitely...wasn't sleeping," I croaked. My throat still dry and my chest contracting painfully with every word as I struggled to force them out. But I cared more about what happened to Dad than the agony filling me.

"We think he was drugged, sweetie," Mom told me, taking my hand in hers. Her dark brown eyes shining with barely restrained tears.

"Drugged?" My jaw dropped, and at that moment something occurred to me. "Set up?" I asked. Using as few words as possible to keep my throat from hurting more than it already did and hoping she understood.

"Yes, we think so."

I had no words. Why would someone drug my dad and cause us to crash? And why would they take my dad? There was absolutely no doubt in my mind that the events were connected. Coincidences of that magnitude didn't exist.

I sat there with my thoughts stewing in my brain, my body throbbing, while worried looks were passed around the room.

Until Blake ran into the room with the same strangely familiar man as before following closely behind him.

"We know who drugged him."

Chapter 16
Investigation

We know who drugged him.

We. Know. Who. Drugged. Him.

Those words bounced around inside my head as we all stared at Blake. My eyes started to water. Mom's hand went to her throat and a sound of horror escaped her.

"Who?" Rage emanated from Ryder. He kept his eyes fixed on me, even though everyone else's were fixed on his cousin.

"It was one of the catering staff," the familiar man said. He was only an inch or two shorter than Blake—who was probably the tallest person I had ever seen, standing at about six-foot-five—and had piercing blue eyes. Eyes I recognized. "I talked to Julie and some of her staff yesterday and she said she had her new girl working the night of the dinner. Her name is Elizabeth Berri. Julie originally had her serving Ryder, but Elizabeth Berri told one of the other servers, a guy named Mark Howel, who was assigned to Johnathyn, that the Alpha scared her and asked if they could switch."

"Of course, Mark had no problem switching and so with Julie's okay, Elizabeth got access to John," Blake cut in. "We went to the address she put on her job application, but the house was empty. There was a cot in one corner of the main room and that was it." Blake swallowed before continuing. "She was a plant, Ryder. She was here to do a job, and she got it done."

"Oh my god. What are we going to do?" I panicked. My throat was hoarse, but the pain was worth being able to put a voice to my feelings.

"We'll find him, Kaylee. And the bastard who did this," Ryder growled out. It was a promise. Even though he didn't explicitly say the words, we both knew it. "But first, we need to know *why* someone would want to take Johnathyn. Blake, I want you to double the patrol. Everyone from the Guard is on duty. Twelve-hour shifts. Half during the day, half at night. No one gets through without Mom's, yours, or my okay. Got it?" Blake nodded to his Alpha and left the room to follow orders. "Broddy, go back to the site. See if you can pick up anything. I know you said you didn't recognize him or the scent, but maybe you can find something else that'll give us a lead." The familiar stranger, Broddy, nodded and went to leave.

"Wait!" He turned at the sound of my voice. "It was you that night, wasn't it?"

Broddy nodded. His face was tight with shame and regret.

"You're the silver wolf." Although I didn't phrase it as a question, he still nodded. "And…you chased Brendan away. The night of the party, didn't you?

Another nod.

"Thank you."

Tears I didn't know I had left began forming in my eyes. I had no doubt that without the wolf standing in front of me, I would be the one missing. And who knows what else Brendan would have done that night, if it weren't for Broddy and the others.

"You have no reason to thank me, Kaylee. Because of me, your dad was taken." He bowed his head, his shaggy dirty-blonde hair falling over his face, but not before I saw the guilt and shame reflected in his sea blue eyes. "Because I wasn't strong enough."

"Ryder, help me up." I reached out and grabbed his hand. He opened his mouth to argue, but he wisely shut it a second later.

Ryder helped me stand and Lucas supported my other side while Lisa came up behind me as a third pillar of support. All three of them walked me to Broddy, despite my pained whimpers. I knew Ryder wanted to force me back into bed, but he also knew that what I was doing was important to me even though he didn't know exactly what that was. That gave me the strength to do what needed doing.

"Broddy, look at me," I ordered, slightly surprised by the strength and command in my voice. I sounded sure, steady.

Broddy lifted his chin away from his chest and looked directly at my face, wincing when his gaze travelled to the bandage on my left temple.

"I am here because of you. You protected me at the crash. That man wanted me and you made him leave me alone. Who knows what he would have done with me." I was shocked that I could think so clearly, through the torture of being upright, but this Broddy guy needed to hear what I had to say.

Lisa came out from behind me and placed her hands on either side of Broddy's face. "It's not your fault, baby," she whispered, before placing a chaste kiss on his lips.

Baby?

Broddy wrapped his arms around her waist and whispered, "Thank you, Lisa." She leaned into him and he kissed her forehead. "And you, Kaylee."

He bowed his head in a show of respect I wasn't sure I deserved, but I nodded my acceptance anyway.

Confused, I glanced between my rescuer and my best friend before turning to Ryder who had a small smile on his face.

He saw my questioning look and leaned down to whisper in my ear. "Let's get you back to bed."

I nodded minutely, trying to minimize my movements and trying even harder to ignore the pain ricocheting through my body.

When I was back in bed beside my mother, my breath was labored and I hurt all over. Lisa unwrapped herself from Broddy's embrace and walked back to the bed.

Gently kissing me on the cheek, she whispered. "I'll explain later, but right now he needs me."

I smiled at her, knowing she would be true to her word. "I need to rest anyway, Lis. Go."

She smiled at me and kissed my cheek again before going back to Broddy, taking his hand, and leading him from the room.

"Broddy has a hard story," Ryder said softly from his chair beside the bed. I looked over at Ryder, not really knowing what to say.

Lillian came back to the bed, having moved when I got up, and sat down on the edge by my thigh.

"You can't move around like that, Kaylee. You're in no state," she scolded, her brow crinkling.

"I had to, Lillian. He saved me," I defended myself, but I wasn't even worried about me at that point. Just Broddy and everyone else around me. Above everyone else, my dad.

"Just please don't do it again. Not until I clear you," She requested, sounding defeated and worried.

"I can't make any promises, but I'll try."

Lillian sighed, knowing that was the best she was going to get and got to work. She checked the bandage on my temple again and told me I had five stitches.

While she was prodding my torso, she asked how the pain was.

"Worse than before. More in my sternum now," I told her. She nodded at my answer like it made complete sense. I quirked a brow.

Huffing, she said, "You have a cracked sternum and a bruised lung. But there's not much I can do for it. Same thing as with your ribs, Kaylee. You'll be down for a couple days. Frankly, I'm surprised your injuries are as light as they are. Your lung should have collapsed."

"Alright," I winced as she prodded.

Something occurred to me and I couldn't help but chuckle.

"What's so funny?" Ryder asked quizzically.

"Oh, I was just thinking how I'm staying here a little longer after all."

A small smile pulled at Ryder's lips and he bent around Lillian to place a gentle kiss on my forehead, careful to avoid my temple.

"I guess so, sweetheart. Although I do wish it was under better circumstances," he sighed.

"Me too," I whispered.

"Everyone out," Lillian clapped abruptly. "My patients need rest and you're all in the way."

Ryder leaned down and brushed his lips to my forehead once more and whispered, "We need to talk later," before obeying his mother and leaving the room. Lucas followed right behind his brother.

"You two sleep. There will be food ready when you wake up," Lillian ordered, but she was out of steam and there wasn't much command in her words. We both agreed and she left, flicking off the ceiling lamp and closing the door behind her.

"Momma?"

"Yes, honey?"

"Is Lillian okay?"

"She blames herself, Kaylee. She hired the company, so, in her mind, this is all her fault," Mom explained.

Damn it. What was with everyone blaming themselves for things that couldn't possibly be their fault?

"I don't know, honey. I really don't know."

I was confused for a moment about why Mom was saying that, but then I realized I spoke out loud. There was absolutely no way anyone could have seen what would come from the dinner.

"Goodnight, Momma."

"Goodnight, my darling girl."

***

"I'm so sorry."

I woke up to the sound of Lillian sniffling from the chair Ryder had occupied the day before. She was leaning forward with her elbows on her knees and her face in her hands.

"Lillian?" My throat was horse again, but this time it wasn't only from the damage. Her head shot up at the sound of my voice, her red eyes welling with tears, alabaster skin glowing in the dark. "This isn't your fault. You know that, right?"

"How can you say that? Your dad is gone…because of me. And we have no idea who took him."

Her voice broke on every other word as the tears spilled over, streaming down her cheeks. Her shoulders were shaking with her sobs. She was well and truly a mess.

"Did you take him? Did you drug him? Did you hire the woman who did? Unless you can answer yes to any of these questions, you are blameless and have absolutely nothing to feel guilty for." I was as quiet as I could be while still making my point. I didn't want to wake my mom, but I had to get my point across and I had to convince Lillian to believe me.

"I hired the company—"

"That's not the same thing, Lillian. You hired this Julie woman, and her team. You did *not* hire Elizabeth Berri." I forced myself to sit up, gritting my teeth through the pain. I didn't realize I was getting louder until Mom stirred beside me.

Lillian didn't say anything as I watched her, she just cried and wallowed.

"Lillian, look at me." She lifted her head, eyes gleaming and cheeks wet. "Do you get what I'm saying? You can't blame yourself. For any of it."

She nodded and stood from the chair before hugging me close, but carefully. She knew better than anyone the extent of my injuries—even better than I did—and where she could safely touch me.

"Thank you, Kaylee. For believing in me." Lillian pulled back and smiled down at me. She had one hand cupping my cheek while her thumb ran soothingly over my cheekbone. "I will do everything in my power to help get your father back."

"Thank *you*, Lillian. For taking care of Mom all these years. For taking care of me because apparently I can't stop getting hurt." I joked and reached up to the hand cupping my cheek, squeezing it once.

With tears in her eyes, Lillian bent over, kissed my cheek, and left the room. But not before whispering, "*She* took care of *me*, darling."

I don't think I was meant to hear her, but I was oddly glad that I did.

"You did good, honey," Mom spoke quietly from beside me.

I turned and slowly and carefully lay myself down, propping my head up against the stack of pillows.

We lay there like that, neither of us speaking, both of us lost in thought. I was zoned out when I felt my mum's thumb brushing my cheek, sweeping a tear away. I hadn't even noticed it fall.

"It'll be okay, sweetie."

I nodded my head and rolled into her, wincing at the pain shooting up my sternum. I buried my face in her neck and inhaled, breathing in the scent that was uniquely Mom, cinnamon, and vanilla.

And I finally let the tears fall.

Even when I had first woken up after the crash and couldn't move without my body screaming at me, I didn't cry. Even when I remembered that my Dad, my rock, had been taken from me and my mom, and that he was most likely being tortured, my eyes stayed dry. But with everything adding up so painfully and my head feeling like it was going to explode, I finally cried.

I cried for my dad because of his absence and the pain he was surely feeling. I cried for my mom and the absence of her mate. Tears fell for Lillian and Broddy's guilt ridden minds and for Lisa having to see the man who was obviously her mate in pain. I cried for Ryder for not having a wolf mate, but I also cried for me. For not being good enough to protect my dad, or myself for that matter. I don't care that it made me a hypocrite. It was just how I felt. I cried because I missed my dad and because I *had* missed my mom. I cried for everything.

Mom stroked my head as I broke apart, murmuring soothing words. The tears kept falling as I sobbed in her arms.

Eventually, I dozed off, and I'd like to think that she did too, but when I awoke later that day, she was gone and I was alone.

With space to think, I was finally able to take inventory of my body. My ribs and back hurt from before, but now my sternum and something on my insides did too. Lillian had told me that I had a bruised lung, I just didn't think it would hurt so much. My neck was stiff and my head throbbed, most intensely at the temple on the left side of my head. When I lifted the blankets, I noticed a myriad of cuts and bruises scattered over my bare legs.

I was wearing nothing but a large black t-shirt and wondered who it belonged to. I caught myself hoping it belonged to Ryder and groaned quietly. It shouldn't have mattered who it belonged to.

The room spun when I sat up, and I had to hold still or risk retching over the side of Ryder's bed and all over his floor. When everything stopped moving, I forced myself out of bed, wincing and biting my lip to hold back all the sounds that were trying to slip through. The last thing I wanted at that moment was someone rushing into the room when all I was wearing was a big t-shirt on my way to go pee.

I padded into the bathroom as careful and as quietly as I could manage, flinching when I stepped on a loose floorboard. Moving made my body ache with a vengeance, but I couldn't not go to the bathroom. I refused to rely on everyone else *again*. Definitely not for something as simple as going to the bathroom.

I had just situated myself on the toilet when the bedroom door slammed open and I froze.

"Kaylee?" I heard Ryder shout.

Moments later he came into view through the open bathroom doorway, a panicked expression on his face. He stared at me, eyes wide with worry and chest heaving, while I sat dumbly on the toilet, not able to speak and barely able to breath.

Lucas came up behind Ryder and I saw his eyes go wide before he quickly turned around. I thought I saw his cheeks tinge pink, but he moved so fast that I couldn't be sure. Lucas leaned toward Ryder and said something that was too quiet for me to hear. Ryder nodded in response and Lucas left.

With Ryder's attention back on me, I realized I was still on the toilet with my underwear around my ankles and blushed ferociously. The man who was supposedly my soul mate and his little brother—the Alpha and his heir—had just caught me out of bed, when I'm sure I wasn't supposed to be, and in the bathroom in a very embarrassing position.

"Um," Ryder cleared his throat, "I'll let you finish."

I flushed an even deeper crimson as Ryder turned and took a couple steps away from the bathroom.

When I finished, I flushed and hobbled to the bathroom sink and washed my hands. Ryder walked in the room just as I was drying my hands on a green towel that was hanging from a loop on the wall. He took the towel from my hands, hooking it through the loop, before bending gracefully and sweeping me into his arms as gently as he could. But even with how gentle he was, a whimper escaped my lips when my feet left the ground.

Ryder flinched at the sound but didn't say anything as he carried me back to bed. He lay me down and I landed more softly than should have been possible. It hurt, but I was able to hold back the pained gasp that waited to be let out. Tears brimmed as I tried to keep my breathing steady through the pain. Ryder stayed silent and sat in what I was quickly starting to think of as *his* chair. Even though everything in the room was technically his.

"Why didn't you call for help?" Ryder asked softly. He was frustrated but trying not to let me see it.

"I needed some time by myself before everyone rushed in here worried."

Ryder wasn't appeased by my answer, but it was the best one I had.

"I get that, I really do. But you're injured, Kaylee. You can have as much alone time as you want while you're in bed. But if you have to get up, you have to call for help," he insisted, brown eyes glowing with worry and frustration.

"It was just the bathroom, Ryder." I rolled my eyes and winced when I felt a twinge.

"You could have seriously hurt yourself, Kaylee. That's why," Ryder growled, his voice bordering on a shout. He was worried about me, but I still flinched at his tone.

"I'm fine." We both knew I wasn't, but I couldn't have people breathing down my neck at every second of every day.

Ryder opened his mouth to say something, probably to berate me some more, but the bedroom door opened and Broddy and Lisa strode in, hands joined.

Broddy bowed his head toward Ryder in a respectful gesture and quietly said, "Alpha."

Lisa released her grip on Broddy's hand and sat on the foot of the bed while Broddy approached the big, bad Alpha.

"How you doing, babe?" Lisa asked me, a frown creasing her brow as she rubbed her thumb along my ankle in an oddly soothing gesture.

"I've been better," I answered honestly.

Lisa's lower lip pushed out in an exaggerated pout, and I couldn't help but laugh. I giggled and Ryder paused whatever he was saying and watched me with a deep heat burning in his eyes.

"Sir, we found traces of ebony silk and black hair in the trees at the crash site. Blake has the hair and is running DNA analysis. Hopefully, we'll have the bastard in our system, and we can go get John," Broddy said.

I could still feel Ryder's eyes burning holes in the side of my head when I switched my gaze to Broddy, but even though his eyes were on me, I knew he was listening. This was too important for him not to.

"Good work, Broddy. Keep me posted," Ryder acknowledged Broddy's work with a nod and shifted his full attention back to me. "We'll find him."

A small smile tugged at my lips. I believed him. How could I not? With all the effort the pack was putting in, there was no way we wouldn't bring Dad home.

Chapter 17
Broddy

I spent the next week much like the last.

Healing.

During this week, the investigation into my father's kidnapping continued as well as the search for Elizabeth Berri. Not much progress had been made with either, but I was hopeful.

I repeatedly relayed the events of the night of the crash to the best of my ability. But no matter how many times I went over it with Ryder, I still felt like I was forgetting something. Or missing something. I hadn't really been able to describe the man who stole my father, though something about him was frustratingly familiar. Almost like I had met him before.

Every time I was by myself and would get up to go to the bathroom, Ryder would race up the stairs with Lisa in tow, demanding I let her help me. To which I would roll my eyes and wince because I kept stupidly forgetting that it hurt to roll my eyes.

Ryder would also ask me if I remembered anything else, and my answer was always the same. If somehow, they didn't hear me and I managed to make it to the bathroom on my own, they would come check on me and ask the same questions.

On the second day after I woke up, Lisa came and told me how she and Broddy were mates. I couldn't believe that it took her so long to tell me, even after I'd found out about wolves. I told her so and she apologized, claiming that she didn't want to pour more information into my already-full brain. Lisa talked about how he consoled her while I was unconscious—which turns out was another three days—and she spent that time trying to convince Broddy that he was blameless. Which apparently was quite a challenge. Lisa's glowed when she talked about Broddy, and I was glad she had someone who made her so happy.

There was one day where Ryder carried me downstairs—ignoring my assurances that I was fine—and I was finally able to watch a training session.

Ryder had told me it was just a self-defense class, as the Guard trained deeper in the woods, but I was ecstatic regardless of who I was watching. It was fascinating seeing the ways the wolves of different ages and sizes moved—in wolf and human form. They came in all colors and I loved watching. It only made me more excited about eventually being able to do it too.

At the end of the week—when I was finally allowed to do things on my own and rolling my eyes no longer hurt—Broddy came to see me by himself. And he told me his story.

I was reading when Broddy stopped by to visit. I watched him curiously as he closed the door behind him and slowly approached the bed, not saying a word. When he reached the footboard, he sat with a weighted sigh and ran a hand nervously through his hair.

"I need to be straight with you, Kaylee," he huffed nervously.

I sat there quietly, unmoving, hoping it would be easier for him to jump right into it without my interrupting. I wasn't sure I wanted to know what he had to say, but it seemed like it was something I had to know. And it was.

Avoiding my gaze, Broddy groaned. "Brendan's my brother."

My blood froze in my veins and my skin grew cold, almost as if there was a layer of frost crawling across my body. For the first time since meeting Broddy the night of the crash, I took a good look at him. He was tall with broad shoulders and muscles that seemed to go hand in hand with being a wolf—even Lisa was toned, and I had never seen her work out a day in her life. He had shaggy dirty blonde hair, and deep blue eyes—familiar eyes…Brendan's eyes.

With a sharp gasp, I threw myself away from him, to the farthest side of the bed, crying out when my whole body screamed with pain at the abrupt movement.

"I won't hurt you," Broddy said, raising his hands in a motion of surrender.

Something in his voice told me he was telling the truth. Looking at his eyes again, I found that even though they were the *exact* same color as his brother's, that was the only quality that they shared. Broddy's were like a calm ocean when you take a walk on the beach, nothing like Brendan's icy stare.

"Why are you telling me this?" I asked, voice wavering.

"Because it's something I believe you should know." He sighed again. "I want to tell you my story, if you'll let me. But I need you to understand that my past in no way defines me. It may have helped shape who I am, but it's not *me*."

I realized then that there was really no reason for me not to hear him out, so I settled into the far side of bed—still wary—and Broddy let out a relieved breath of air.

"When I was born, I smelled human. Completely, one-hundred-percent human. My parents thought there was something wrong with me, so they left me on the side of the highway, swaddled in a quilt."

I raised my hand to my mouth, trying to cover the gasp that slipped out. Broddy smiled sadly at me, resigned to what had happened to him.

"When I was found by the RCMP, they called my birth parents." Noticing the blank expression on my face, Broddy explained. "The Royal Canadian Mountain Police. They're the police outside of city borders."

I nodded my understanding, and he continued.

"They called my parents because my father was Alpha at the time, or Mayor to the humans, of the closest pack, but they denied anyone having had a baby recently. So the police called George and Lillian next and they said no one had had a baby, but they decided to take me in anyway. They found a home for me with a couple who was having trouble conceiving and they raised me as their own.

"I had a happy childhood. I even ended up with a little sister name Maya. Our parents treated us equally, regardless of the fact that I'm not biologically theirs. The four of us were happy and completely oblivious to my past, until Brendan found me and told me exactly who I was." Broddy noticeably flinched at the sound of his "brother's" name. "No one knew before then. I'm sure Lillian and George had suspicions, but no one knew for sure."

I felt tears welling in my eyes and bit my lip in an attempt to hold them back. Broddy didn't need to see me lose it, not when he'd been through so much.

"My birth parents told Brendan about me right before they died. As the only family he had left, he decided to hunt me down. It wasn't hard for him to find me, and when he did, he told me everything. Why they gave me up, and how he thought they made the right decision. He said I was obviously damaged and didn't belong with them. I was sixteen years old. But you see, Kaylee, most wolves don't shift until they're fourteen or fifteen. I was eleven when it happened. So the thing that made my parents abandon me was actually a sign that I was different in a good way. Gifted, some would say." Broddy paused to let this sink in.

"Do you still smell human?"

He nodded in response. I understood why Brendan *thought* he was 'damaged.' Although that's definitely not a word I would use to describe Broddy. He had saved me more than once and, as far as I could tell, he was nothing but kind.

"Why are you telling me this?" my voice wavered as the question left my tongue.

"Because you deserve to know. Brendan is a danger to you and I need you to know that I'm not. You can trust me." Broddy's eyes begged me to understand, even as guilt shone in them.

They were the same as Brendan's...but not. His desperation for me to believe him opened a perfect window.

"I'll believe you on one condition," I told him from my place in Ryder's bed. Broddy didn't say anything, so I went on. "Don't you dare blame yourself for any part in the crash."

I couldn't call it an accident because that was the furthest thing from the truth. Broddy automatically flinched at my words, and I knew I had hit the nail on the head about where his guilt was coming from.

When again he didn't respond, I rose a brow, waiting, until finally he conceded. "Alright, consider me guilt free." I smiled at him and one corner of his mouth quirked up in return.

We were sort of smiling awkwardly at each other when there was a soft knock on the door.

"Come in," I called and Lisa's head popped out from behind the door. Broddy's face lit up when he saw her, and he stood to meet her halfway. She reached up and planted a kiss on his cheek causing him to flush the lightest shade of pink.

"I'm still mad at you, Lis." I mock glared and crossed my arms when they came to sit on the bed at my feet.

"Why?" Lisa's jaw fell open.

"Because you kept this wonderful person from me." I winked and she giggled, while one side of Broddy's mouth cocked up in what I was beginning to think was his only smile.

"I don't have competition now, do I? Besides, I didn't totally keep him from you, he *was* at the party," Lisa laughed, her eyes sparkling with joy.

I opened my mouth to reply when a growl came from the doorway and I shifted my gaze from the happy couple to see Ryder standing there.

"Absolutely not," he growled.

"Oh, *relax*, Ryder. She was only joking." I laughed, not realizing how big of a mistake *that* was until later.

"Relax? You're *mine*, Kaylee," Ryder bit out through clenched teeth, a muscled ticking in his jaw. "No one jokes about even the possibility of you belonging to anyone else, understood?" He shifted his piercing gaze to Lisa who shrank into Broddy.

No one treats my best friend that way.

"Knock it off, Ryder." I started slowly sliding out of bed. "We might be mates, but that does *not* give you the right to yell at my best friend. And I definitely don't *belong* to anyone. I am my own person and that's that." I stood in front of him, repeatedly poking his hard chest, wincing slightly when it pulled at my injuries.

Everyone in the room looked shocked by my outburst, but Ryder appeared more hurt than surprised.

Lisa's soft voice rose from behind me, but I cut her off before she could get more than my name passed her lips.

"No, Lisa. I don't care that he's my mate. I don't even care that he's the Alpha. If he can't take a good-natured joke without fuming like a steam engine and yelling at the woman I consider my sister, then he's probably not someone I want in my life."

Ryder was shocked into silence, standing there blinking at me as I glared.

"I'll just leave you to your jokes then." Ryder blinked at me, the hurt was washed from his face and his voice was empty of any and all emotion. He blinked again before bowing his head and leaving the room.

"Kaylee," Lisa repeated before walking up behind me and resting her hand on my shoulder. "Let's get you back to bed. Apparently, I need to explain a few things."

I quirked a brow in confusion, but let her lead me back into Ryder's bed, wincing and biting back the groans that were rising to the surface.

When I was once again settled, leaning against the headboard, Lisa perched by my thigh, patting the comforter around me. Despite the fact that it was sitting comfortably on top of me.

"Lisa," I coaxed. She kept silent. "Out with it, Lis. What do you need to explain to me?"

"*Apparently*, I need to explain mates to you," Lisa sighed, slightly exasperated.

"What do you mean? Ryder already told me about mates." My brow furrowed and my eyes flickered back and forth between the pair sitting in the room with me.

"Obviously not well enough," Lisa growled under her breath, and I'm sure I wasn't supposed to hear her.

"Look, Kaylee. What Lisa is trying to say, is that Ryder had every right to be angry. Any other wolf would have reacted exactly the same way. Alpha or not. And considering what's going on with Brendan…" Broddy let the sentence hang, standing behind Lisa with his arm around her shoulders.

"But why? Why do wolves get all angry like that? And why does it make them think that they can just yell at whoever-the-hell they want?" I asked, trying and failing to keep the frustration out of my voice.

"It's just genetics. We're protective and slightly possessive creatures," Broddy paused and rose an eyebrow when Lisa snorted. "What?" he asked, sounding almost offended.

"*Slightly* possessive?" Lisa laughed and I couldn't help but smile at the mischievous glint in her hazel eyes.

"Okay, fine. Some of us can be very possessive," Broddy admitted, sending Lisa a look that said she was going to get it later. I so did not want to know what *it* was. "Based on what just happened, Ryder is one of those very possessive wolves. Of course, it doesn't help that he's an Alpha," Broddy tapered off, squeezing Lisa into his side.

"What does him being an Alpha have to do with it?" I questioned, feeling a pang of jealousy in my stomach at the show of affection when Lisa reached up and squeezed Broddy's hand.

"Alpha's are notoriously dominant, Kaylee, and with that dominance comes possessiveness," Lisa explained.

"Oh," I said dumbly.

Lisa smiled gently at me and nodded. "Yeah, oh," she laughed softly.

I decided then that I needed to do something about the mess I had unknowingly created. So, I pushed at Lisa's leg and she stood, taking a couple steps away from the bed and pulling Broddy along with her. Standing, I went to the suitcase that had found a home on the corner chair of Ryder's room. Lisa had brought it for me the day after I woke up.

"Kale? What are you doing?" Lisa's voice sounded from close behind me. Ignoring her, I continued rummaging through the bag until I found what I was looking for. My navy-blue leggings and white hoodie with a big fighter jet printed on the front.

"Kale?" Lisa said again.

Turing around with the clothes in my hands, I faced Lisa and her mate. Her Soul. "I have something I have to do. Please don't try to stop me."

"Kaylee. You really should be resting," Lisa said softly. It was obvious she meant well, but this was something I needed to do. Besides, I'd been resting long enough.

I shot Broddy a pleading look and he spoke up. "Babe, if she says she has to do this, then she has to do this."

When Lisa turned her back to me in order to face Broddy, I snuck to the bathroom and changed into the fresh clothing. It felt amazing to be in actual clothes again after spending a week in pajama bottoms and baggy t-shirts.

Opening the bathroom door, I stepped out and Lisa stood from where she had been sitting on Broddy's lap. She strode over to where I stood, hugging me as tightly as she could without causing me pain.

"Be careful," she whispered. "His protective instincts are essentially on steroids and he's worried about losing you enough as it is already."

I hugged her just as fiercely, not having to ask to know she was talking about Ryder. Although Lisa appeared to be, I wasn't worried about Ryder hurting me. No matter how upset he was, he always seemed to know my limits better than I did.

"Of course, I'll be careful," I whispered back.

As I was leaving, Broddy's voice drifted through the doorway, making me pause outside the room. "He won't hurt her."

"I know that, I'm just worried about her, Broddy. More now than ever," Lisa sighed sadly.

"I know, baby. I am, too."

Chapter 18
The Date

I found Ryder at the tree line behind his house. It had taken me forever to get there—thank you stairs—but the moment I saw his tense stance I knew it had been the right thing to do. The pain was more than worth it.

"What do you want, Kaylee?"

I jumped at the sound of his voice and realized he must have heard my approach. Damn wolf senses.

"I, uh," I paused, clearing my throat. "I wanted to talk to you."

"About what? You have more jokes or something?"

I blinked stupidly at the flatness of Ryder's voice and stopped walking. I stood only about five feet away. That five-foot gap was far too wide.

"I actually came to apologize, but if you're going to be like that then I guess I'll just go." Ignoring every instinct inside my body that was saying to stay and talk, to get closer to Ryder and to hold him, I turned around and started the trek back to the house.

"Wait," Ryder said abruptly, his large hand wrapping around my upper arm and spinning me to face him. I released a surprised breath of air at his speed, at how quickly he reached me. "I'm sorry. I'm being a dick."

He released his grip on my arm when I winced and ran his hand through his hair. Something he does whenever he's stressed or confused.

"Yeah, you kind of are," I agreed, crossing my arms carefully in front of me.

"I guess I deserved that," Ryder chuckled derisively at himself.

Instead of responding—although I agreed wholeheartedly—I stood in front of him waiting.

"Are you up for a walk?" he asked finally, offering his hand.

I shrugged, utterly astounded that he was suggesting something that, in his mind, was too much for my injured body. Ignoring his outstretched arm, I walked straight into the tree line with him following close behind me. I must have been going the right way, because he didn't say anything or direct me at all.

We walked for a while, neither of us saying a word, until we came to a clearing. A clearing with a blanket spread out on the ground and a wicker picnic basket resting on top of it.

Eyes bugging from my head and my eyebrows hiding in my hair, I asked, "What's this?"

"It's Friday," Ryder shrugged as a sheepish smile spread across his face. His answer coaxed a giggle from deep in my belly and passed my lips. Ryder grinned the way he had when I had first agreed to go out on a date with him and held his hand out. Grasping his offered hand, he led me to the blanket, and that's when I noticed there was also a big stack of throw pillows.

I lifted my free hand to my mouth to stifle another giggle as we walked. We reached the cozy picnic set-up and Ryder helped me ease myself down onto what I realized was a comforter. A very fluffy one at that. Ryder set himself down beside me and began rummaging through the wicker basket, pulling out all sorts of assorted fruits and a couple of sandwiches. The entire time he was removing the items from the basket, I was grinning ear to ear. I was paying very little attention to what was coming and going from Ryder's hands, so I was pleasantly surprised when I looked down at the spread before me to see that there were strawberries and pineapple. My favorite fruits.

Ryder noticed my appreciative gaze and smiled, seemingly embarrassed. "I asked your mom what you liked to eat. She said that you always liked these, so that's what I got." I nodded emphatically when he shot me a hopeful, yet slightly scared look and he sighed in relief. "She also said you were always more of a turkey girl than a ham girl, but she wasn't sure if that had changed," he said, holding up the two sandwiches. "So, I made both."

I burst out laughing at the play of emotions running across his face. It felt so good to laugh. It hurt, but the joy was so worth the pain.

"It's so good to hear you laugh," Ryder said, surprising me.

Gently reaching up a hand, he gently brushed away the hair that had fallen in front of my eyes. My laughter ceased and my cheeks flushed as I bowed my head.

Ryder cleared his throat and waved the sandwiches in front of my face with his eyebrows raised.

"Um, turkey, please," I sputtered, loving the fact that Ryder put this together.

He handed me the sandwich and I eagerly unwrapped it.

"I'm sorry for joking around earlier."

Ryder's gaze turned serious as he watched me. "I know. I'm sorry too, I overreacted."

I smiled at his words and went back to my sandwich.

I moaned at the first bite, never having tasted such an amazing sandwich. Most likely it was the lack of any real food that made it taste so good, but whatever the reason, it was delicious. Ryder's head snapped toward me at the sound, his chocolate brown eyes darkening to almost black.

"Good?" he asked, voice gruff.

"Amazing," I moaned again, having taken another bite. It was too tasty for me to be embarrassed by the sounds I was making. "Lillian's had me on a mostly liquid and mush diet because it puts less strain on my body or something. So, this? Is amazing." Ryder raised a singular brow at me as I bit down again. "What?"

"Nothing," he smiled secretly to himself.

I raised a brow in turn, but he just kept smiling around bites of his sandwich.

"Sure," I said, drawing out the word. Ryder laughed at me and shook his head.

"It's good to hear you laugh too, you know," I told him with a big grin plastered on my face. Ryder didn't say anything, and we sat in a comfortable silence, just eating our food.

Ryder finished his sandwich way before I did, and had practically demolished the strawberries by the time I got to them.

"The rest of those better be for me."

"Really, now?" He quirked a brow and one side of his lips tugged up.

"Really, really," I responded, reaching for the container and wincing when it pulled at my injured sternum.

Ryder noticed and automatically went into panicky, over protective mode. "Are you okay?" he blurted. "Maybe this was a bad idea," he continued before I even had the chance to answer his question.

"Ryder, I'm fine. It was just a twinge," I said in a voice that I hoped was soothing and cheerful. The pain was there, but it was easily manageable.

"Are you sure?" he asked, brow creased and hands cupping my face.

"Positive. Besides, Lillian said I need to return to life as normal otherwise I won't heal properly," I assured him with a comforting smile.

She hadn't actually said that, but it had the desired result. Ryder nodded his assent and slowly removed his hands from my skin. I tried to keep the disappointed look off my face, but I must have failed miserably because Ryder smirked at me before moving on to the pineapple.

It took us a few moments to relax and get back to the comfortable place we had been in before, but we got there. When the strawberries and pineapples were finished, Ryder returned the now empty containers to the picnic basket. As his hands came back into view, I was overjoyed to see a jar filled with the best surprise of all.

"Pickles!" I squealed, launching myself into his arms, trying to ignore the ache in my bones. I wasn't successful enough to prevent a groan from escaping. Then again, I didn't really care.

Ryder caught me without dropping the pickle jar and wrapped one arm around my waist. He fell backwards onto some of the pillows, and I fell on top of him. Our eyes met and we broke down laughing. Placing the jar down beside his thigh, Ryder moved his hands to my hips, helping me sit.

It didn't take long for me to notice the intimacy of the position we were in; Ryder was leaning back on some pillows with me straddling his lap and his hands on my hips. I tried to get up, but he held me where I was. The look in his eyes was all heat and intensity as they darkened to almost black once again.

Then he leaned up and kissed me. Sparks ignited and my eyes closed.

His lips were warm and soft, yet still somehow firm. The kiss started slow and easy, almost polite, as Ryder gave me plenty of time to pull away. It wasn't necessary. The moment his lips touched mine I was putty in his hands, and pulling away wasn't a possibility.

Ryder leaned back, taking me with him until I was completely on top of him, his hard chest under my much softer one. His hands tightened on my hips and I heard a strange little sound of pleasure, which I quickly realized came from me.

Ryder must have heard it too, because the next thing I knew, I was gently rolled onto my back and he was above me, keeping all of his weight off of my body with his hands braced on either side of my head.

I wrapped my arms around him and he brushed his tongue along my bottom lip before running it along the seam, asking to be let in. I hesitantly let him through and didn't regret it for a moment. His tongue tangled with mine as they brushed together. He tasted like strawberries, pineapple, and something that was distinctively Ryder.

We kissed like this until we couldn't breathe. Only then did we pull away.

We stared at each other, chests heaving. Breathing as hard as we were was painful, but I couldn't bring myself to care. Somehow, it was a good pain. Ryder had just given me the most passionate and intense kiss of my entire life. I was glad it came from him.

Ryder recovered more quickly than I did and sat back on his butt, resting between my calves. I hadn't even realized my legs were spread. Which means he must have been laying between them. Which means we were pressed...

My cheeks flamed and I threw my hands up to cover my face, completely incapable of finishing the thought. My cheeks were hot to the touch, and the fact that Ryder was *still* between my legs made them hotter. I groaned and felt Ryder's hands wrap around my own, gently tugging them away from the horror that was my crimson face.

"Hey. What's the matter?" he asked, concerned.

"Nothing," I replied, probably way too quickly, because he sent me a look that was entirely unconvinced. He stared at me until I gave in. "It's just that, um, you're. Well, you were," I broke off, laughing nervously. "We were, you know, pressed together. *There*," I whispered, like it was some big secret.

My cheeks had been cooling, but flamed even hotter than before when Ryder barked out a laugh that could probably be heard from the house. He had to gasp for breath and his face quickly turned as red as mine.

"You're laughing at me," I stated plainly. "Why are you laughing at me?"

"I–I'm sor–sorry," Ryder said, holding his stomach and trying to calm himself.

I sat up and smacked him in the chest—his very hard chest—before saying, "I repeat. Why. Are. You. Laughing at me?"

"Because you're innocent and adorable?" he suggested, though it came out as more of a question than an answer.

I glared at him. A glare I'm sure, if he were anyone else, would have put him six feet under.

It was then I remembered that I never got my pickles. I held out my hand expectantly and Ryder sent me a confused look. I sat there waiting with my hand out until understanding finally dawned on my mate.

Woah.

What?

That was the first time I had thought of him that way, and it kind of frustrated me.

I made an impatient motion with my fingers, and Ryder handed me the jar of pickles. Still closed. I raised a brow in a 'what is this' look, and Ryder huffed in an over-exaggerated show of exasperation before taking it back and popping the lid off. He once again handed it to me before turning to the basket and rummaging around.

When he found what he was searching for, he turned to me with a fork in his hand, but I was already crunching happily away on a pickle. Ryder rolled his eyes and dropped the fork into my lap.

All of a sudden there was a crunch that did not come from me and my pickles and I stopped moving. Ryder turned to face the source of the sound while I froze. Another crunch, and then three large figures stepped out from the tree line. Blake, Lucas and Broddy.

I sighed in relief and felt the tension leave my body at the friendly faces. When the three of them got closer, it became apparent that something was wrong. Very, very wrong.

Ryder stood to meet them, but when I tried to follow his lead, he said, "Stay here; you're still injured."

I rolled my eyes at the command. I stood anyway, ignoring the exasperated glare he sent my way.

All three boys wore strained expressions and dirt covered Broddy's face. He was bleeding. It was only as they got closer that I noticed he was leaning on the other two for support, and the rigidness of his face was akin to agony. Every muscle in my body stiffened and tension returned to my bones.

"What happened?" Ryder's voice boomed from behind me as adrenaline kicked in and I ran to the trio. I hadn't even realized I was moving until I reached them.

"He was jumped, Ryder," the Alpha's brother answered, voice tight with barely restrained fury.

"Where?" Ryder asked in what I was starting to think of as his 'Alpha voice.' I gestured for Blake and Lucas to follow me, leading Broddy to the mound of pillows Ryder had set up for our date.

"Crash site," Blake grunted as he and his younger cousin eased Broddy down onto the cushy blanket.

Broddy groaned on impact and I rushed to his side, gently moving his hair away from the gash on his head. There was too much blood on him for that to be his only wound. Not wanting to risk agitating anything else by searching, I started at his head. I hoped the red covering his body wasn't all his.

"What was he doing there?" Ryder growled behind me as I peeled off my hoodie and pressed it against Broddy's head, ignoring the blood staining the white fabric and seeping into the rest of my clothes from various places on his body. This left me in nothing but a little grey tank top and my leggings. It was a good thing it was June and warm out.

"Trying to find clues, I guess," Lucas said. "But he was ambushed. Whoever did this was waiting for him."

"Ryder, I need your phone," I demanded, interrupting their conversation. I had left mine at the house. Turning toward me, his eyes blazed when he saw what I was wearing, but he reached into his pocket and handed me his phone. I unlocked it—it didn't have a passcode—and went into the contacts, searching for Lillian. I scrolled and pressed call when I found the number listed as 'Mom.'

"Ryder? Is everything okay? Did she like the picnic?" Lillian's loving voice came through the phone.

"Lillian? It's Kaylee."

"Kaylee? What is it? What happened?" Lillian asked, worried, after hearing the tight panic in my voice.

"We're in the clearing behind the house. Ryder's fine, but Broddy's hurt," I said, tears welling in my eyes, my throat tightening.

"I'll be right there," she said, doctoring up. She ended the call.

"Lillian's coming," I told Broddy softly when he groaned again. I kept constant pressure on the wound on his head, wishing I could do more.

"How many?" Ryder asked.

"Four. They probably got sick of him spending so much time at the site, poking around where they didn't want him," Blake answered morosely.

I couldn't imagine how they were feeling. I hated seeing Broddy this way, and I had only known him for one short week.

"Why so many? He's small." Ryder sounded confused and worried.

"He's also gifted; we both know that," Blake answered.

"But no one outside of this pack should, Blake! That shouldn't matter to them, because they shouldn't know!" Ryder shouted, frustrated and concerned. "Did you recognize any of them?"

When neither Blake nor Lucas responded, Broddy piped up.

"Brendan's. Men." He was clutching his midsection as he forced words passed his lips.

I wondered if the others didn't respond because they didn't know, or because they didn't want to be the one to tell their Alpha.

"What?" Ryder snarled and, sounding more animalistic than I had ever heard him before, turned to face me and Broddy.

Broddy nodded, gasping, confirming for Ryder that he had heard correctly.

"Damn it!" He roared, along with a string of other curses that would turn a sailor's ears red.

The boys were all seething quietly as I continued pressing on Broddy's head, trying to process this new information.

If Brendan's wolves ambushed Broddy at the site of the wreck, that meant he was behind it all.

Chapter 19
Infirmary

Lillian arrived not long after Broddy announced he was ambushed by Brendan's wolves. Lisa was with her and rushed, to Broddy's side the second she crossed into the clearing.

Lillian quickly patched Broddy's various wounds—most importantly the tear-like gash in his side—before ushering us all back to Mayor Mansion. Blake and Lucas carried Broddy, Lisa right behind them whispering that he would be all right, while Ryder carried me. He claimed that I had put too much strain on my injuries, despite my assurances that I was fine, and insisted on carrying me the whole way back to the house. Apparently walking to the clearing and rushing to help Broddy constitutes as over exertion on an already-battered body.

We reached the mansion and the boys followed Lillian deep into the house while Ryder carried me up the stairs and to his room.

"Really, Ryder, I'm fine," I insisted as he finally put me down on the edge of the bed.

"Until you stop wincing every five minutes, you aren't fine," he grumbled kneeling on the ground in front of me.

He wrapped his fingers around one of my ankles and slipped off my flip-flop before repeating the process with the other shoe. Sitting next to me on the bed, he did the same thing with his shoes, and then sat back against the headboard with his legs out in front of him. He tipped his head back against the dark wood, closed his eyes, and let out a heavy sigh.

Peeking one eye open, his lip quirked. "Quit staring and come here."

I silently obeyed, unsure of what else to do other than continue staring dumbly. I carefully crawled across the bed to sit beside him, copying his position. Ryder let out a huff and gently wrapped his arms around my waist, settling me between his spread legs and holding me against his chest, back to front. With his arms loosely wrapped around me, he nuzzled the crook of my neck, running his nose from ear to shoulder and back again. I tried to suppress the shiver that ran through me, but with the adrenaline still pumping in my veins and my emotions scattered, it was a futile effort.

Feeling me tremble against him, Ryder tightened his arms around my waist—being careful as not to hurt me, somehow knowing my limit without me having to tell him—and began slowly peppering soft kisses along the column of my throat. I sighed in contentment at the tingles his lips left in their wake and tilted my head to the side, giving him more access.

Until I remembered myself.

"Ryder," I protested, "stop." My voice came out much breathier than I had intended, but the moment that word left my lips, his left my skin. I sighed again, only this time I wasn't sure if it was in relief or disappointment.

"This isn't right," I said, pulling free of his embrace and turning to face him, my legs crossed in front of me while I remained between his open thighs.

"You're right," he agreed, but I didn't really hear him. Or, at least, I didn't process what he had said.

"I mean, with Broddy. And my dad—wait, what?" I stopped dead in my tracks, my eyes popping and my jaw dropping.

"You're right. Your dad's missing, Broddy got attacked by someone who *should* love him, and you're still a target. So, you're right. There are more important things to focus on. But, please, for now, just let me hold you."

To say I was stunned would be an understatement. I nodded dumbly and crawled back into his outstretched arms, taking solace in his embrace.

Sitting in Ryder's arms was a new experience. I was essentially in his lap…and I was happy there. It was different than kissing him, different than sleeping next to him. In a way, it was even more intimate than either of those things. We were both awake and aware, sitting with our thoughts, instead of being distracted by each other's lips. But we were together and there was a vulnerability in that that I hadn't experience before. Not even with Carter, who I had believed I loved.

Sometime later, when the blood on my clothes had completely dried and grown crusty and my muscles had tightened, I realized that I should probably get cleaned up.

"Hey, Ryder?" I started, not really wanting to get up, but knowing I had to get out of those clothes and bathe.

"Yes, sweetheart?" he murmured, running his fingers through my hair, which also had blood in it.

"I'm kind of covered in blood." I felt Ryder's body stiffen and jerk behind me at my words.

"Shit, Kaylee, I'm so sorry. I wasn't even thinking. I just needed to hold you and didn't think about how uncomfortable you would be, laying covered in our friend's blood and all. I'm so sorry, sweetheart." He was rambling and I shifted in his arms so I was facing him.

"It's fine, Ryder. I just need a shower," I assured him, brushing a lock of dark brown hair out of his eyes.

"'Kay." He nodded and carefully lifted me off of his lap. "I'll go run a bath for you." He shifted off the bed and started toward the bathroom.

"Ryder, I'm covered in blood. A shower would probably be a better idea," I said.

"Are you strong enough for that?" Ryder asked, worried.

"Of course I am," I insisted indignantly, although I wasn't completely sure.

"If you say so," he said, laughing, but his heart wasn't in it. Ryder disappeared into the en suite for a few moments with the door closed. When it reopened, he had a mischievous glint in his eyes. "It's ready."

Walking into the bathroom hand in hand, I couldn't help but roll my eyes, even as a giggle slipped out. He had drawn a bath for me. With bubbles.

"A bubble bath?" I couldn't hold back the smile that graced my lips as I looked up at him with my eyebrows way higher than they normally are.

"I know you said a shower would be better, but I thought this could be nice. Maybe make up a bit for the crappy ending to our date. Besides, you can still take a quick shower first." He shrugged, looking every bit as sheepish as he had in the clearing when I first saw the picnic.

"Okay. One, our date was wonderful, despite the ending. Even if it was a week late," I teased. "And two. Thank you."

"Do you need any help?" Ryder asked, and I couldn't tell if he was being a cocky guy or if he was being completely genuine and actually wanted to know.

I stared at him for a few moments before he spoke again. "I mean, I know Lisa and Mom have been helping you bathe. So, I was just wondering…"

"No, that's okay. I think I can manage," I said calmly, hopefully easing his confusing nerves.

"I'll, um, leave you to it then." Ryder turned and left the room, letting the door swing shut behind him.

I gingerly stripped off my clothes, careful to keep the crusted blood from touching my skin. I took a quick shower as Ryder suggested, if only to wash away the blood before stepping into the tub. I eased myself down and sighed the moment I was seated, the heat massaging my muscles and the bubbles tickling my skin. I rested my head on the rim of the tub and my eyes slid shut of their own accord.

I lay in the bath until the water cooled and the bubbles dissipated. When I was finished, the water was tinged pink with the little blood that was left on me before I got in and my skin was pruned. Standing, I stepped out of the bath, my foot going out from under me.

My feet slid forward and my hands went down in an attempt to prevent my body from hitting the ground. But when my hands touched the floor, they slid as well and a small scream escaped me when my head hit the edge of the tub.

Groaning, I reached back to cradle my head while also trying to keep my ribs from falling apart. The door flew open revealing a panicked Ryder. Noticing my position on the floor holding my pounding skull, his eyes widen and darken in the same second. His expression reminded me that I was wet and naked on the floor of his bathroom.

We stared at each other for a moment before I quickly turned, moving the arm from around my middle to cover my breasts, and peeked over my shoulder to look at Ryder expectantly. He cleared his throat and shook his head. He reached for a fluffy towel from the shelves by the sink and I watched him as he approached me, towel in hand. Gently wrapping the towel around my shoulders, Ryder covered me from my shoulder blades to just under my backside. With my back turned to my mate, I wrapped the towel all the way around myself, tucking the end under my armpit.

Embarrassed, I turned back around. Ryder's hand was extended out in front of him and I took it with the hand not holding my towel. Tugging me to his chest, he held me against him and nuzzled his nose into my hair. In his arms, the pain was all but forgotten.

"Are you okay?" His voice was muffled against my head, but I could still hear the worry.

"Just slipped."

I hid my face in his chest, horrified at myself for my obvious klutziness. There was no way he would have fallen the way I had, or at all, with his inhuman grace. Ryder began to chuckle I felt his laughter more than I heard it, but that didn't stop me from smacking him lightly on the chest.

"It's not funny. I hit my head," I pouted.

"I'm sorry, you're right," he admitted.

I could really get used to him agreeing with me.

Ryder held me for a moment longer before letting go, mumbling something about grabbing clothes for me. I followed close behind and stood behind him while he rummaged through my suitcase. He turned suddenly, holding some of my clothes, and stopped short when he noticed how close we were.

"Here," he said, holding the items out.

"Thanks," I took the clothes from him, grinning. Not wanting to trudge back to the bathroom, I turned and slipped the underwear and leggings on under my towel before dropping it, giving Ryder the bare skin of my shoulders and back. I heard his sharp intake of breath behind me the moment the towel left my skin. I snapped on the bra Ryder had chosen—which just so happened to match the underwear—and pulled the purple tank top carefully over my head. Turning around again to face Ryder, I threw on the gray, off-the-shoulder sweatshirt he had handed me.

I stood on the tips of my toes and kissed his cheek. "I have some questions," I said, looking down at our feet.

"Okay." He lifted me against his chest before he settled us on the bed in the same position as before, with me between his legs. "Ask away."

"Before, what you said about Broddy being smaller? And gifted? What did you mean?"

Ryder's chest expanded against my back as he took a deep breath.

"Technically," Ryder started, "you're not a wolf yet so I shouldn't tell you. But you're my mate, and have enough wolf in you that I think it should be okay. Plus, I'm Alpha." His voice was teasing but cautious at the same time. He took another deep breath and started drawing shapes and patterns on my thigh with his fingers before continuing.

"I don't know how much Broddy told you about his past, or even about himself, but if he told you anything at all you know it was complicated." I nodded. "Broddy shifted early and smells human; he always has. But for some reason, when he shifted, he shifted small. He's still smaller than your average nineteen-year-old wolf. He's smaller than most all wolves, actually. He's about the same size as a first shift pup. For some reason, one that none of us can figure out, he still, to this day, smells human. None of us even know why he smelled human in the first place, and none of us can figure out why he's so small."

Ryder spoke slowly, measuring his words as they came out of his mouth. I was getting antsy—impatient really—wanting to know more, to understand more about this world I had unexpectedly found myself in.

"As for him being gifted," Ryder sighed, ruffling my hair with his breath, and shaking his head behind me. "It's kind of complicated. The basics of it is that he has heightened senses. More heightened than your regular, every day wolf. They're more…acute, I guess? There's more to it than that, but I don't really know how to explain it. It's almost as if he's just more tuned into the world around him or something."

I sat silently as Ryder spoke, finding peace in his arms, which I think surprised me more than the news about Broddy. With my dad missing and everyone getting attacked all the time, peace wasn't something I expected to feel.

"Has this happened before?" I asked, both curious and wanting to coax understanding from my mate.

"Not that I've been able to find. In *any* of our history books. And all of the Elders are just as clueless as I am," he huffed, frustrated. "Even human mythologies don't hint at anything like it. Ever since I turned twenty and became Alpha, I've had access to more resources, but even with those I'm clueless."

I knew he cared about Broddy regardless of him being different, but I could also tell that it really bothered him not knowing *why* Broddy was different. It probably bothered Broddy too. I'd be shocked if it didn't.

"Elders?" I asked, leaning to the side and twisting my neck to see Ryder's face, effectively halting his finger's movements on my thigh.

"They're the oldest members of the pack. They aren't all powerful or anything, like I'm sure it says in your books, but they do keep our history. The ones who are able anyway. There are also Lycan Circle Elders who attempt to keep the history of all of the packs around the world, but I don't imagine they've had total success," he explained patiently, and I made a sound of understanding.

"What's the Lycan Circle?" I asked.

"Short version; they're a large pack that sort of acts as an overseeing government for all of the packs."

"Ah, okay."

Ryder went on after repositioning me the way I was before and resting his chin on the top of my head.

"Both the Elders and our history books mention cases of wolves who smell human when they are born and eventually shift, but it's usually late and under extreme duress. Not only that, but they always smell like a wolf after they shift—always. There have also been cases of wolves with more acute senses and these wolves are usually early shifters like Broddy, but there has never been a case, at least a documented case, of someone like Broddy who has both…abnormalities." He resumed running his fingers along my thighs in strange patterns as we sat in comfortable silence, both of us mulling over the words that had just been voiced. "It's my job to figure out things like this. Broddy shouldn't be left in the dark about who he is because I fail as Alpha. Or as his friend."

I turned sharply in his lap—ignoring the sharp twinge in my sternum—and sent him the glare of all glares. "You are *not* a failure as Alpha, and you sure as hell are not a failure as a friend. Get me?"

Ryder looked shocked at my outburst, and, frankly, I was too. "I got you," he said quietly.

I cozied back into his lap.

Ryder and I sat on his bed, his fingers playing over my thighs and his nose nuzzling my neck, until the door cracked open and Lisa's head popped in.

At the sight of her tear stained cheeks, I shot up and out of Ryder's lap and ran to her. Throwing the door the rest of the way open, I pulled her to me. The moment my arms were around her, she broke down sobbing. She was a few inches taller than me and had to lean over to rest her head on my shoulder. I led her to the bed and we sat on the edge.

I could feel Ryder's gaze on us, but I ignored it, as well as the pain running through my body from jumping off the bed so suddenly.

I held Lisa until her shoulder-wracking sobs turned into little hiccups, and even then I still held her. For her sake or my own, I wasn't sure.

"Sorry, Kale. I was just so worried about him, you know?" Lisa hiccupped against my shoulder and sniffled.

"Yeah, I know. You don't need to apologize, though," I murmured soothingly. I ran my hand over her hair, not saying anything else until her breathing evened out a little more. "What happened, Lis? I mean, when I left the two of you were all snuggly and a couple hours later he was hurt and could barely walk."

"He left pretty much right after you did," she told me, her voice slightly muffled until she pulled away slightly. Lisa sat up, no longer leaning against me, but she held my hand as she spoke. "No matter how much I tell him not to worry about it, he still feels guilty over your dad being taken. After you left, he said he had to fix this. To find a way to make it up to you or something. I guess he thought if he could find a clue, then maybe everything would be okay. Thank god Blake and Lucas found him when they did. Otherwise…I don't even want to think about what could have happened." Lisa looked up at me through her lashes, head bowed and voice choked.

"I'm so sorry, Lisa." I hugged her again. "Where is he now?"

"The infirmary," she sniffled, looking down at her lap, biting her lip, and fighting the sobs I knew were just beneath the surface.

I thought about this for a moment and knew I had to go see him. And possibly give him hell for making my best friend cry, regardless of his good—more than good—intentions.

"I'll go get you some water, 'kay?" She nodded with a little sniffle. "And maybe something to eat?" Another nod.

I motioned to the door with my head after getting Ryder's attention by poking his foot, and he followed me out of the room.

"I need to go see Broddy, but I don't know how to get to the infirmary."

"I'll take you."

And so we went to the infirmary to see Lisa's mate, and maybe raise a little hell.

When we got there, Lillian was putting supplies away in the big main room. It was massive and circular and there were doors spaced out every ten-ish feet.

Lillian glanced up when she heard us come in and, before either of us could utter a word, she assured us that Broddy was fine. Or at least he would be in a day or two.

"I threw your hoodie in the trash, Kaylee. I hope that's okay," Lillian told me from behind a desk that sat in the center of the large room, her brow furrowed.

I flinched at her words, but nodded. I had loved that hoodie. My dad had gotten it for me on one of his "business trips" when I was fifteen.

"That's fine, Lillian. Thanks." I smiled at her. I knew the last few weeks had to have been hard for her and they were likely to get worse before they got any better.

"Can we see him?" Ryder asked, practically reading my mind.

He reached his hand down and laced his fingers through mine when his mom gave us the go-ahead and pointed us in the direction of Broddy's room.

When we crossed the threshold into the room, I froze, gaping. Broddy lay in a large version of a hospital bed, a sheet tucked up under his arms, pulled tautly around his bare chest. He was pale and so, so still. I moved slowly to his bedside, sliding my hand out of Ryder's and holding Broddy's between both of mine.

"Why did you have to go and be a hero? You stupid boy."

I was surprised when his fingers tightened around mine and I got an answer. I thought for sure he had been sleeping.

"I was trying to find answers," he groaned with a pained smile. He sat up in the bed without taking his hand back, and clutched at his side, hissing through his teeth. "You deserve at least that much," he gasped. "Brendan won't stop until he gets what he wants. And he wants you. I figured if I could find a lead, I could help protect you." Broddy groaned in pain and clutched at his side again.

"Damn it, Broddy." I shook my head and used the voice my dad did when he was disappointed in me, although disappointment was the last thing I was feeling. Suddenly overcome by a rage I hadn't known I was capable of, I tore my hands away from his and started pacing. "You've protected me enough!" I barely recognized my voice as the words spewed out of me. "You do realize you could have been killed today? You could have died! And where would that leave Lisa? Huh?" I didn't wait for an answer, I kept going. "Mateless and depressed! That's where!"

I threw my arms up and stormed out, ignoring the shocked expressions of both Broddy and Ryder. I stalked passed Lillian without glancing back and made my way to the kitchen—which was on the opposite side of the house—to get Lisa the water and food I had promised her. I took a couple of wrong turns but eventually made it.

I knew my outburst had come out of nowhere—literally nowhere—but something inside me had broken. It wasn't Broddy's job to protect me. As far as I was concerned, that was my job, and mine alone.

When I arrived back at Ryder's room, I found Lisa sleeping across the foot of the bed with her knees tucked up against her chest and her hands under her head, acting as a pillow. I hadn't realized how late it was until I saw her lying there. I placed the glass of water and the sandwich I had made onto the nightstand, shuffled a real pillow under her hands and draped a blanket over her sleeping form before crawling in next to her with a blanket and pillow of my own.

I was asleep before Ryder made it to the room.

Chapter 20
The Plan

The next morning was a flurry of action.

Lisa had disappeared before I woke up. Assumedly, she had gone to see Broddy. Ryder wasn't in the room like he so often was first thing in the morning, and it was a little disorienting. And, I realized, disappointing. I didn't like the empty feeling waking up alone had given me, so I went searching for company. Still in a pair of boxers and one of Ryder's t-shirts, I wandered the house, but it was void of life, eerily silent.

At least, until I reached the infirmary where everyone was huddled together in Broddy's room. Without me.

I stood in the open doorway, tapping my foot, as my friends and family discussed different ways to take Brendan down and get *my* dad back.

"Use me as bait."

The room became so quiet, so still, that you could have heard a pin drop.

"*What?*" Ryder asked, incredulous. Anger churned in the depths of his chocolate brown eyes.

"Use me as bait," I repeated, stepping further into the room. Mom and Lisa both gaped at me as if I had lost my marbles, and Lillian looked appalled that I could even suggest such a thing.

"Don't even say that," Ryder growled, seething. He stepped toward me and I looked around the room for support but found none. Lucas wouldn't meet my gaze and I was almost certain that he approved of my idea. Blake's face was an emotionless mask as he leaned against the wall behind his younger cousin. I worried that I had put him back in the ice cube he had hidden in when I first arrived in Redheart. And Broddy watched me with something like approval in his eyes, the rest of his face schooled to match his mate's.

"Fine, but I want in on whatever you're planning," I demanded.

My first suggestion was still echoing in everyone's minds; I knew this seemed a lot more reasonable.

"All right," Ryder agreed, though the fury at my words continued to roll off of him in waves. "If it'll get you to stop making fatal suggestions."

I rolled my eyes at him half-heartedly. I was honestly just glad that they weren't excluding me anymore.

"So? What's the plan?" I asked, when no one offered any information.

Blake stepped forward and glanced at Ryder, silently asking for permission. Anger bubbled inside me at the obvious display of someone needing *Ryder's* permission to tell *me* something, but I pushed it down, knowing it was a fight for another day. Maybe when I truly became Ryder's mate, and he truly became mine.

"At this point, we're thinking of storming the Coldmoon Pack House. We don't have definitive proof that it was Brendan who was behind your father being taken, but with his men being the ones who jumped Broddy, it's enough evidence to go after him," Blake told me, standing tall and intimidating with his arms crossed.

"I'd call that definite proof," I grumbled, before more loudly saying, "Storming his house? Is that really the best idea? I mean, won't he be expecting that?" My brows furrowed as I crossed my arms, shaking my head. "No, that's not good enough. I've seen how you wolves work. You trespass and beat each other. You no doubt kill, too. Probably without a thought. So, we need a plan that ends with as few people dying as possible. As little bloodshed as possible. On *both* sides."

"She's right," Lisa said from her perch on the edge of Broddy's bed. "As a species, we kill far too readily." Her brow furrowed much like mine had before. "And, what if, what if Brendan isn't the mastermind? I mean, Broddy and I have been talking and neither of us think he is smart enough, or conniving enough, I guess, to pull this off. What if someone else is pulling the strings?"

"You mean like—" Lucas was cut off by his brother.

"No. There's no way. He's dead," Ryder growled, more animalistic than I had ever seen him. Even more so than the day before in the clearing.

"Ryder, what if he's not?" Lisa said softly.

"No, it's not possible," he snarled in that Alpha voice of his, and Lisa bowed her head.

Every time I saw her do that, it made me livid. Lisa never bowed to anyone in her whole life.

"We don't know that for sure," Lucas said, but before Ryder could get mad at him too, I butted in.

"Alright. Who the hell are you talking about?" I snapped, sick of being left out of the loop.

"No one," Ryder growled again, but less aggressively. He was trying to control himself.

"Bullshit." I walked closer toward him and poked him in the chest. "If I'm going to be your mate, or whatever, you need to tell me these things. You need to *include* me."

Ryder didn't say anything. He stared at me for a moment, mouth slightly agape, before stomping away from me and out of the room, slamming the door behind him.

I flinched at the sound and turned to face everyone in the room. "Anyone want to tell me? Lucas?"

When no one said anything, I rushed out of the room, much like Ryder had, and went searching for him.

I found him in the backyard, and it wasn't at all how I was expecting. I figured he'd be waiting for me much the same way he had been the day before, I was wrong. Ryder was a wolf. I hadn't seen him in wolf form since the day I found out about werewolves, three weeks before. He was still as gorgeous as he was then—lying in my backyard with me. His dark brown fur smattered with sandy highlights and his chocolate brown eyes somehow softer in this form. Not as aggressive and angry.

He was staring out into the trees like he had been the previous day, only this time he was sitting back on his haunches instead of standing on his feet. His ears twitched at the sound of my approach but I was left otherwise unacknowledged. Without warning, Ryder stood and bounded into the trees. I followed. I needed to talk to him regardless of whether or not he wanted to talk to me.

I chased him until we reached the clearing. He had gotten too far ahead a couple of times, escaping my line of sight, but I always found him again. It was like he stopped to wait for me whenever he knew I was too far back. Even angry at me, he was still protecting me.

He reached the clearing before me. When I cut through the tree line, Ryder was back and Wolfy was gone. He was in a pair of shorts and nothing else, giving me a glimpse of the body I had only ever seen clothed or felt pressed against me. It was better than I had imagined and I longed to feel the smoothness of his skin over his hard muscles.

Ryder was sculpted beautifully. I was once again reminded of Adonis come to life. His chest was solid and beautiful and his stomach put the saying 'washboard abs' to shame. My mouth dried when he crossed his arms over his chest, making his muscles bulge.

Embarrassment rose in my throat as he swiveled his head in my direction and he cocked a brow. Bowing my head, I flushed more deeply than I ever had.

He approached me and let his arms fall to his sides. Just then, I realized where he had been standing.

Ryder had been facing the part in the trees where Blake and Lucas had pulled Broddy through only a day before.

"It's my fault, you know."

I jumped at how close his voice was, having not seen or heard him approach.

"What do you mean? What's your fault?"

"The crash. Your father. Broddy," Ryder spoke with so much remorse that he didn't sound like himself. His voice was thick with a mixture of regret and pain instead of the confidence and surety I was so used to hearing from him.

"In what possible way is any of this your fault?" I asked, crossing the last few feet between us. I was really getting tired of everyone's misplaced guilt. I knew it all came from a good place, but these people needed to realize that the only ones at fault were Brendan and those helping him. And possibly those controlling him.

"Brendan is doing this because of me, Kaylee," Ryder sighed, completely resigned to his guilt.

"That doesn't make it your fault, Ryder!" I all but shouted, reaching to place my hands on his shoulders before remembering that he was half naked. And I was in boxers and a baggy t-shirt.

"Say it again," he whispered, closing the last few inches separating us, wrapping his hand around my wrist. I smiled.

"It's not your fault," I repeated, placing my hands on his arms, my finger gripping his biceps.

I no longer cared about our lack of clothing, I only cared that he was hurting, and I wanted to fix it. The strength of emotions I was feeling at the moment kind of scared me, but easing Ryder's pain was more important to me than easing my fears.

"No, my name. Say my name again." He leaned down, nuzzling his nose into my neck, sending all too familiar tingles coursing along my skin.

"Ryder," I whispered, slightly breathless from having him so close to me, not to mention shirtless.

He groaned against my skin and pulled me more tightly against him.

"I love the way my name sounds when you say it. I don't hear it often enough."

My heart thudded loudly at *the* four-letter word. It was so loud I worried Ryder could hear it. His arms were completely looped around my waist and his lips brushed the juncture between my neck and shoulder as he spoke.

"I'll remember to say it more often, then," I sighed as he started laying little kisses along the skin of my neck and shoulder. My arms swung up around his neck while I tilted my head, giving him better access.

Ryder hands moved to grip my hips as his lips ran along my jaw up to my ear. When his warm lips met a particularly sensitive spot behind my ear, a little sound of pleasure escaped me, shocking me into reality.

I pulled away, breathing hard. I wrapped my hands around Ryder's and peeled them off of my hips.

"Stop," I gasped out. It didn't sound like I wanted him to listen to me.

Ryder made a disappointed sound in the back of his throat, and said, "Yeah, okay," just as breathlessly as I had.

I released his hands and realized something.

"You distracted me!" I shouted. "Why?"

"Because I knew there was no way I was going to change your mind." Ryder shrugged with a smirk. "It was a pretty good distraction though, don't you think?"

"Ryder!" I flushed again and he laughed. "No matter how…how nice it was, you shouldn't have changed the subject! Everyone is on this stupid guilt trip and I hate it!" I yelled, throwing my hands up and turning around.

Just as I stepped away from Ryder, his hand wrapped around my upper arm and drew me back to him,

"You're right, I'm sorry. I shouldn't have changed the topic. But," he trailed off and his lips met mine. Firm and soft at the same time. His hands returned to my waist and mine went back around his neck. His lips coaxed mine open and his tongue slid in. He was so amazingly Ryder.

I moaned into his mouth and his fingers slipped under my shirt, playing with the bare skin underneath. Ryder's fingers ran along my belly. When he reached my navel, he wiggled his finger inside and tickled me, making me giggle.

I tore my lips away from Ryder's, laughing so hard it hurt—not that it took much in my condition—but I'm sure even if I had been healthy, my belly would have gotten sore. With a big grin on his face, he tickled me gently until I fell over, landing safely thanks to Ryder's help easing me down.

"Ah! Stop!" I laughed tears forming in my eyes. "Stop! Please!" I gasped, kicking and laughing, trying to dislodge his torturous fingers from my body.

"I'll stop…" he grinned, slowing his fingers and in return my kicking eased. "…if you go shopping with Lisa tomorrow."

"Shopping? Why shop—" He tickled me more. "Okay! Ah! Okay!" I screeched. He finally let me go and I gasped, taking in as much air as I could manage.

When I finally caught my breath, I became increasingly aware of Ryder's position on top of me. His leg was between mine and one of his hands was tracing my navel under my shirt, while the other was splayed beside my head keeping his weight off of me. I nervously cleared my throat and Ryder sat up. Swinging his leg out from between mine and sitting beside me, his legs casually brought him in front of him and his arms draped over his knees.

I mirrored his position, facing him, and smiled. I was really starting to like him. Like, *really.* And then I got mad at myself for spending time with Ryder, my mate—someone I felt I could love—when my father was still missing.

"Why do you want me to go shopping with Lisa?" I asked, sober after my tickly, kissy high.

"You deserve a day out without worry about all of our wolf drama." He shrugged before reaching out and brushing a strand of my dark hair out of my eyes.

"I already promised, so I'll go, but I don't want or need a day away from the 'wolf drama,'" I told him using finger quotes. Ryder smiled sadly at me. That smile told me a lot.

"Thank you for agreeing to go." His voice was as sad as his smile and it nearly broke my heart. I knew he had other reasons for sending me out with Lisa, but they were his and his alone. No matter how badly I wanted to know.

"You didn't really give me much of a choice." I winked, smiling.

Not many people could get away with tickling me. Unharmed, anyway. Even Lisa had come away with a few cuts and bruises over the years. Ryder laughed and shook his head, his shaggy hair swaying in front of his eyes.

"True enough," he smiled. "But now I know your weakness."

He returned my wink and stood, offering his hand and helping me up. He wrapped his arm around my shoulders and I wrapped mine around his waist, and we slowly made our way back to Mayor Mansion. Enjoying each other's company too much to move quickly.

"Hey, Ryder?" I asked, nervously. He peeked down at me in way of acknowledgement. "When this is all over, can I see you as Wolfy more often?"

Ryder burst out laughing at my request and shook his head, making my heart drop.

"Sure, sweetheart," he chuckled. "Sure."

***

The next day, I went shopping with Lisa as promised. Lisa was thoroughly enjoying herself, knowing Broddy was healthy and safe, but with everything going on, I just couldn't.

Lisa made me buy a new pair of sandals, using the argument that they'd go with everything. Especially a cute pair of shorts she convinced me to buy. The summer was half over and so summer clearance sales had already started.

It was nearing lunchtime and I was complaining to Lisa about my rumbling stomach, but she just laughed and shrieked, "One more store!" before pulling me into said store behind her.

I rolled my eyes, groaning, but Lisa just kept tugging. She dragged me along the shelves and clothing racks with her until she had a pile of things to try on. She continued to drag me through the store until we reached the changing rooms so she could go through the pile she had amassed.

An hour later, I sat outside the dressing room, waiting for Lisa to come out wearing *another* outfit. I stood and knocked on the door, getting impatient and cranky.

"Lisa," I whined, drawing out the '*a*,' "I'm hungry."

"Oh, be patient, babe," she laughed through the door right before it swung open. She was wearing a pair of dark denim booty shorts and a white sleeveless blouse.

"Cute," I said curtly. Every outfit she'd tried on had looked amazing. "Now let's go," I groaned.

She laughed at me again and shook her head, going back to the change room and closing the door behind her.

I sat down on the stool across from the stall she was in, trying very hard to be patient.

"Li—" my voice was cut off by a hand covering my mouth.

I shrieked against the hand and struggled to dislodge it as well as its owner, but it was to no avail. I couldn't see my attacker, nor were they saying anything. I reached up to pull the hand off my mouth, but the next thing I knew there was a pinch in my neck and my body went limp, my world beginning to fade. I was slung over a hard shoulder.

The last thing I heard, before the darkness consumed me, was Lisa screaming my name.

Chapter 21

The Theory

My eyelids fluttered. As I regained consciousness, the feeling in my body returned. First in my fingertips and toes before eventually awareness flooded through my entire being, leaving a tingling sensation in its wake. I wiggled my fingers and tried to lift my hand to my face—to see if my fingers were actually moving.

I couldn't.

Lifting my head, I realized my wrists were cuffed and chained to metal bedposts above me. Thank god, I was still fully clothed. I couldn't imagine what I would do if I wasn't. I was still dressed in the outfit I had been wearing when I went shopping with...

"Lisa!" I gasped, struggling against my restraints.

There was a dark chuckle from one corner of the room. "Your friend is fine, my dear."

When the words left the hidden figures lips, my mind flashed back to a time where another shadowed figure had used the same endearment, in much the same way.

"You!" I rasped, and cringed.

Aside from being groggy and chained to a bed, I was utterly no worse for wear than before I was taken, but I did have a skull-splitting headache. I wondered how long I had been unconscious.

"Yes. Me." The man smiled, stepping out of the corner and into the little circle of light provided by a small lamp on the bedside table.

"What do you want? Who are you?" I kept my voice as even as I could manage, but there was nothing I could do about the waiver that slipped through.

"I want *you*, my dear," he laughed at my stricken expression and shook his head. "You misunderstand me. You're a little...young for my tastes." The strange man approached the bed.

I shrunk back as far as humanly possible with my wrists bound above me. His lips tilted up in amusement and he sat on the edge of the narrow bed.

"I have a theory that I need you to help me prove. And I've waited a long time to do so." The tilt of his lips was part sneer, part smirk. And extremely unsettling. I couldn't possibly imagine what I could prove for a man who was more than twice my age and obviously unhinged.

"Why do you need me?" my voice, tight with fear, wavered, no matter how much effort I put in to keep it strong and steady.

The smirk on his face grew as he leaned toward me.

"Why? Because you're half human of course!" He exclaimed, sounding way too excited. I half expected for him to start clapping right there. "Oh, and because you're my nephew's mate," he sneered.

The delight in his eyes vanished as contempt took its place.

"*Nephew?*"

"Yes, nephew," he replied. I hadn't even realized that I had spoken until he answered.

"You're Ryder's…?" I hadn't known Ryder *had* an uncle.

"Uncle, yes. My name is Samuel." His sneer once again took on smirk like qualities. He leaned closer, laying one palm flat on the other side of my legs. "Heard of me?"

"But, Brendan…" I trailed off, not quite understanding *Samuel's* role in any of the horrible events that had taken place since the day of the party aside from the obvious. He must have been behind everything.

"Ah, yes. Brendan!" Samuel's voice had grown louder as he said Brendan's name.

His smirk grew to an evil grin as the door swung open, revealing the man who had haunted my dreams for weeks. I couldn't stop seeing his eyes, how cold they were. Nor could I stop feeling his bruising grip on my hips.

"How are you feeling, *mate*?"

I shuddered at the word.

When I didn't respond, the grin fell off Brendan's face and he growled. "Bring him."

My stomach dropped to my feet at the two simple words. Samuel backed away so I could see the door. The blood drained from my face and I was almost sick when they brought *him* in.

My father

"Dad!" I shouted, pulling at the chains binding me to the bed with a renewed strength.

They knocked together, clanging from my efforts. But it was futile. He stumbled as they forced him into the room. Dad looked horrible. His cheeks were sunken in and there were dark smudges under his eyes from a mixture of exhaustion and abuse. He was frail and noticeably weak. He had bruises covering every inch of his exposed skin and his lip was split. My heart wept at the sight of him.

At the sound of my voice, his bruised face shot up and hope shone in his bloodshot, dark brown eyes. Unfortunately, he wasn't the only one affected by the sound.

The two large men holding his arms roughly shoved him further into the room to where Brendan was standing at the foot of the small bed. My father stumbled again but managed to keep upright. All four wolves had the same evil smirk on their faces.

When they reached the cruel Alpha, Brendan let his fist fly into my father's stomach. Dad's cry of pain echoed my cry of horror and brought tears to my eyes as if it was my own body being abused.

"Daddy," I whispered, hoping no one would hear.

But Samuel turned his eyes back to me after watching what I'm sure was his form of entertainment and cocked a brow, disgustingly amused.

The men holding my dad let him drop to the ground, where he clutched his torso, groaning on his knees. It killed me to see him like this. I almost didn't hear Samuel's next words.

"That's your incentive to behave. Understood?"

"Yes, I understand."

Samuel grinned at my agreement and motioned with his hand. Any urge to fight left me when the two men dragged Dad away. Brendan, however, stayed. An expectant expression shaping his features.

"Not yet, Brendan. I need to finish first. You know that."

Brendan nodded, but the way he pursed his lips made him look like he was pouting. Like a child.

The room fell into silence as both men stared at me. Brendan with lust and desire, Samuel with a crazy sort of wonder, almost as if I were a science project.

And then I realized that very well could be *exactly* what I was.

"What do you need me to do?" I asked, resigned to my fate. I had to do everything in my power to keep my father safe.

Samuel's dark eyes—Ryder's eyes—lit up in victory. He had won and he knew it.

"Don't fight." The eyes that only seconds before had shone with an inner glory, took on a more sinister edge as they gleamed crazily. I was confused by what he meant by 'fight.'

Until I saw the knife.

The knife—dagger—in Samuel's hand was at least nine inches long, not including the handle. It gleamed in the same terrifying way that his eyes did. My breath caught in my throat when Samuel turned more fully toward me, mimicking his own movements with the knife. Brendan strode closer and sat across from Samuel.

Panic seized me. I knew there was no way I was getting out of there. Not as long as I was chained to a bed with two large, male wolves trapping me further. But even if I could leave, they still had my dad. I was stuck.

Samuel leaned closer above me, readying the blade in his hand, when Brendan's hand shot out to grab his wrist and, silly as it was, hope rose inside me.

"Have you told her yet?" His voice was softer than I had ever heard, softer than I had thought he was capable of.

"Whoops." Samuel shrugged, shook off Brendan's hold, and swiped the edge of the blade along the outside of my calf.

I screamed.

Brendan roared.

"You're supposed to tell her why we have to do this!" He tore the knife out of Samuel's hand and crouched above me, in a stance I could only describe as protective.

I couldn't decide what to focus on; the searing throbbing of my leg or the utter shock of Brendan defending me.

"Fine, I'll tell her, but you need to leave. We both know you won't be able to handle this," Samuel conceded, sending Brendan a meaningful look.

Brendan nodded at the agreement, though I could see resentment burning in his eyes, and handed the knife back. The shock faded and the pain returned to the front of my mind. My jeans were getting wet where Samuel had cut me.

Samuel stood and began to pace. Sheathing the weapon in a piece of leather on his belt, he steepled his fingers under his chin as he walked, his demeanor completely dismissive. Brendan took the hint and walked out. Samuel smiled.

"Story time," he sang. "I was the youngest child in my family. When I was little, I was the favorite. I was doted on and adored by my parents. By the whole pack, really. But as I grew older, all of that attention shifted to my perfect brother," Samuel sneered.

It was easy to see where this was going, and I didn't like it. Not one bit.

"George was trained to be Alpha from the moment he shifted. He found his mate and they had two adorable little boys. Of course, him having two boys meant that *I* would never be Alpha, so I devised a plan. I started a war and when I was set to be executed, faked my own death. There were Packless wolves in the area who were all too happy to assist me. And when I told

Coldmoon that my dear old dad was planning an attack, they jumped at the chance to strike first. So, five days after you were born, we attacked. We were after *you*. Because what is an Alpha without his Lady? But the rest of the pack was too focused on protecting the precious little baby for us to get anywhere near you. Your parents fled with you. So, I settled for killing my family along with the rest of yours. Did you know you had an uncle?" he sneered.

The hatred in his words was palpable in the air. I could practically taste it. It hurt that this man knew more about my family than I did.

"Of course, you didn't! We killed him! Redheart saw him as a warrior, and yet we took him out only too easily," Samuel laughed manically. I think that scared me the most.

"Ever since then, I have been here, trying to find a way to get back at the Redheart wolves for so quickly and blindly choosing my brainless older brother," Samuel stopped pacing and looked me dead in the eye. "You're the perfect tool." He began pacing again and that evil smirk was back. "You see, I started the war just a few short years after Ryder was born. Of course, faking my death and killing my wife meant I had to leave my own son to be raised by my brother, but it was necessary."

Understanding hit me then. I wasn't sure why it had taken so long in the first place.

"You're Blake's father," I gasped. I finally understood why Blake was the way he was.

"Yes, my dear. I am. Now, don't interrupt," he scolded, flashing the dagger threateningly, turning it in his hand. "My son went on to be Head Guard, as well as a Beta. If I had my way, I would have been Alpha and my boy would have taken after me. The power belongs to my family, not yours. Your mate hasn't even triggered your gene yet. He's too weak to be Alpha."

"No—" I went to protest, but cut myself short when Samuel sent me withering glare.

"Now, I've gotten off track." He shook his head and sighed. "Oh, yes. Brendan's parents were killed only a couple years after my own brother's untimely death. Of course, you understand it was all necessary."

"You killed them?" I asked in disbelief. "All of them?"

"I *told* you not to interrupt," he snapped. "But yes, I did. I poisoned my brother. Slowly, to make his suffering last just like mine has. And then there's Brendan. Brendan was to be a tool, just like you. I killed his mate not long after she was born and convinced him that it was actually you he belonged with and there was an issue with your bond. So, mating would never bring out your wolf and we would have to do it a different way. Which is how I convinced him to let me do what I'm about to do. Two birds with one stone, so to speak." Samuel grinned evilly. He was going to enjoy whatever he had planned.

"What are you going to do?" I pushed the words passed the fearful lump in my throat. *After* I was sure he was done talking. He'd already used the knife on me once, and threatened me with it if I interrupted. I couldn't risk having him make good on his threat.

"Ah, yes. I have a theory, you see. A theory that I need you to help me prove."

I began to ask why, because he still hadn't told me what—apart from aid him in his revenge—I could possibly do. He shot me a look over his shoulder that quickly silenced me. "You're a second generation Dormant, and, in Brendan's mind your mate bond is…broken, shall we say. Which makes you the perfect candidate."

He knew perfectly well that there was nothing wrong with my bond.

"My mate bond is fine and you know it."

Samuel's head snapped toward me and anger flashed on his face before Brendan threw open the door and obscured my vision, becoming the only thing that I could see by sitting right in front of me. He'd been listening. At least to the last part.

His hand reached out to cup my cheek and I recoiled, causing him to frown. "Don't you see? It is broken. If it weren't, you'd allow me to touch you. You'd feel the pull too," Brendan said, sounding sad, but not at all surprised. As if he'd known this information his entire life.

"But Ryder's my ma—" My words were cut off by a large hand striking my cheek.

I hissed at the contact, my head snapping to the side, and moved to hold my cheek, only to be stopped once again by the shackles holding my wrists.

"Do *not* say that name in my presence," Brendan growled in a tone achingly similar to Ryder's 'Alpha voice.'

I nodded as tears stung my eyes and my lip trembled. Brendan pulled away and I could once again see Samuel, who seemed frightfully amused.

"Anyway, now that we've established your mate bond is well and truly broken, I can continue." He began to pace again, still steepling his fingers. "Remember what I said about sex not triggering your wolf gene?" Not waiting for an answer, he continued. "*That* is why having a broken mate bond makes you the perfect subject."

My heart stopped at his words and fear gripped me. I would rather die than do *that* with Brendan.

"Because it won't trigger your gene, your mate has no other option if he wants a wolf by his side."

My heart began beating again and I relaxed slightly. I didn't know what Samuel was getting at, but at least it wasn't *that*.

"So, you see, I believe that there is another way to bring forth the wolf inside you," he paused for what I can only assume he thought was dramatic effect.

I was finally going to get the answer I was waiting for.

"And that is to cause you so much stress and pain, that the gene triggers itself as a form of protection."

The words took a moment to sink it, but when they did, I began struggling in earnest and protesting loudly. The evil grin was back.

"Ah-ah. Remember, child, you father's life depends on whether or not you behave yourself." Samuel smirked, his eye shining with unbridled glee. He didn't truly want me to behave.

"Please. Don't," my voice broke.

I knew I could struggle all I wanted, but it wouldn't change anything. I was chained down and weak. I was useless.

"Oh, but I must. It is necessary if you ever want to be with your mate." Samuel's eyes gleamed wickedly. I knew he meant Ryder, but Brendan thought he meant himself.

Brendan bounced slightly with a boyish excitement and Samuel rolled his eyes.

"It's time to begin."

"Please. Don't," I begged again, and my kidnapper sighed.

"Bring the other," he called.

The door flew open once again, and I had no idea what to expect. Maybe they had Lisa. Samuel said she was fine, he never said where she was. The person who was shoved through the doorway was the last person I expected to be there. It was a face I never thought I would see again.

"Carter." The word tumbled out, breathy with disbelief.

His head slowly lifted from his place kneeling on the floor.

"Kaylee," he cried, but was cut off with a strike to the back of his head. His breath left him in an *oomph* and his body visibly tensed, waiting for more.

"Shut up, human," Brendan growled, standing behind my ex-boyfriend and tugging his head back, pulling his hair and straining his neck painfully.

"You see, my dear? If you don't behave, not only will your father die, but your boyfriend as well," Samuel spoke in an almost soothing manner, but his words were anything but.

He must have seen what he wanted in my eyes. The next thing I knew, Carter was being shoved out through the doorway and the wicked blade had returned to Samuel's hand. Brendan was back on the bed beside my legs, holding my ankles to the mattress.

"Please don't let him do this," I begged, trying to use Brendan's mating instincts against him.

If he thought we were mates, I may as well try to swing it in my direction. He shouldn't want to see me hurt. However, based on my past experiences with him, it obviously wasn't a high priority.

"Not too deep, Samuel," Brendan warned. It was obvious that Brendan thought he was the one in control. Samuel and I both knew otherwise. It was my *true* mate's uncle that was in charge.

"Of course. I wouldn't want to scar your mate, now would I?"

The light from the bedside lamp reflected off the blade, and the blade's reflection shone in Samuel's eyes. Scarring me was exactly what he wanted. The knife was simply a tool Samuel was using. If he could, he would be cutting directly into my skin with nothing in the way. No tool, no made up reasons, just him and his insanity.

The blade came down on my leg once more, barely an inch away from the previous wound and I screamed.

Chapter 22

Rescue

The knife sliced through my clothes and skin repeatedly. Until my pants and shirt were torn and ratty, and my skin was coated with blood and flayed open. I couldn't imagine what I looked like. I didn't want to.

At Samuel's orders, Brendan had left after the first sweep of the blade. They had cuffed my ankles to the bed so Brendan's restraining grip had no longer been necessary. My screams had ceased early in the torture, my throat unable to handle screaming for long. Pathetic whimpers quickly sounded instead.

I felt pathetic for not being able to handle it longer. I was weak.

Samuel seemed to be enjoying himself, taunting me with the promise of freedom if I would shift. I wanted to—God, I wanted to—but I didn't know how to make it happen. I didn't know if it *could* happen.

Samuel continued until I didn't think there was any skin on the front of my body left unmarred. The worst part was that the wounds weren't very deep, so he could cut and cut and cut, and I wouldn't pass out. They were just deep enough to bleed, but not nearly deep enough for me to bleed out. Every time I would start to zone out, he would dig his fingers into one of my wounds, forcing me back to the present.

"This isn't working," Samuel grumbled, frustrated, when I was completely covered in blood. "I think we need to try harder, child."

I whimpered at his words as fear gripped me. I didn't want to know what he was thinking, nor did I want to find out, but I knew I was about to.

Samuel's grip on the blade changed, going from relaxed and fluid in his fingers to stiff and hard in his fist. He smiled, a wicked idea glowing from behind his eyes, and he plunged the knife into my shoulder.

Releasing a scream I didn't think I was capable of, I struggled with energy I no longer thought I had. Samuel tutted at me, clicking his tongue and shaking his head. "What did I say about fighting, my dear?"

"Please," I whimpered breathlessly, thrashing my head from side to side. "No more." I needed the pain to end.

Samuel hemmed and hawed, but I knew he wasn't about to change his mind. He was enjoying this too much. And he had a point to prove. I wasn't the perfect tool just because of my genetics, it was because of the pain this would cause Ryder, I knew that.

The evil grin was back, and Samuel twisted the blade sharply before tearing it from my shoulder, drawing a cry from my chapped lips and weighing the knife in his hands.

He moved so fast I didn't even see him stab the dagger into my other shoulder until it was already buried to the hilt, making me scream again.

And then it happened.

I started shaking, my stomach clenched as a wave of nausea crashed over me. My stomach clenched again and again and my pulse thrummed in my head, throbbing behind my eyes and in my ears. My head flew back and my back bowed. Samuel's eyes flashed in victory and I screamed again. This time, there was a strangely guttural quality to it that I didn't recognize. It terrified me.

The door flew open again, but I was too wrapped up in the hot agony burning through my body to notice who it was.

"It worked?" Brendan shouted excitedly. Panic bubbled inside me at the sound of his voice, but it was overrun by the burn coursing through me.

"It worked," Samuel's voice confirmed. He sounded awed, slightly mystified. As if he couldn't believe whatever had worked.

Then it registered—I was shifting.

My body jerked and, all of a sudden, a bone in my arm snapped. I screamed again and, if possible, my back arched further off the bed. The process repeated in my other arm and then my legs. Bones continued to break until my screams turned into snarls and, even then, it continued. The snarls swiftly changed to canine whimpers, and I was no longer human.

My eyes had closed while I shifted. I opened them and was taken aback by the view. Samuel and Brendan were crouched in front of my shivering form, gaping at me.

"She's beautiful," Brendan whispered in awe, his eyes wide with appreciation.

He reached a hand forward to stroke me and I let out a growl. It sounded so strange, coming from me.

Samuel's expression mirrored the Alpha's, but his eyes were wide for a completely different reason.

"It worked." His words left him in a breathy sigh, colored with disbelief.

At some point during the change, Samuel had unchained me. And my clothes had slipped beneath me, shredded. I tried to stand but was only successful in whimpering. I wished I could see myself. It wouldn't change anything, it wouldn't save me, but I wanted—no, needed—to know if being a wolf was at all worth what I had just gone through. Especially when I knew there was a far less painful way to achieve what had just been forced upon me.

I tried lifting my head, but I couldn't even manage that. I was spent.

"We can be together now, Kaylee. Isn't that wonderful?" Brendan smiled, unadulterated joy shaping his features.

I just lay whimpering, unable to respond—not sure that I would bother even if I were able. I wanted Ryder. It was then, laying on a dirty mattress and burning from the inside out, that I realized I loved Ryder. We hadn't known each other all that long, but love doesn't have a timeline. I loved him with everything in me. I only hoped I would get the chance to tell him.

Both men sat staring at me as I whimpered. Brendan's hand stroked the top of my head and, as much as I hated him, I couldn't deny that it felt good, relaxing even. They watched me until shouts and other sounds erupted from somewhere in the house.

Samuel shot Brendan a meaningful look and Brendan bolted from the room, shouting at whoever was in the hall, barking orders and demanding someone tell him what was going on.

Samuel remained in front of me, balancing the blood covered knife between his fingers. The sharp point poking the index finger of one hand and the handle doing the same in the other hand—he must have taken it out of my shoulder while I was shifting. He stood and started poking me the way Lillian did when she was checking whatever wounds I had managed to acquire, examining my Lycan form.

It hurt. The blood seeping from my wounds was slowly soaking into my fur causing it to stick to my body. I flinched and whimpered at his touch, wishing I had the energy to pull away. He did this until the shouts drew closer, coming from right outside the door which Brendan had shut when he left.

The wood splintered apart when a body was thrown through it and against the far wall. Lucas came striding through, looking fierce and much older than he actually was.

My heart soared. If he was here, so was his brother. I was worried he wouldn't recognize me as a wolf, but when his sad eyes landed on me, they widened and his face paled.

He only looked at me for a second before shifting his gaze to land on something behind me. Finding strength in his presence, I turned my head to see Samuel clenching the knife in his fist the way he had moments before he had plunged it into my shoulder.

"Ryder," Lucas said quietly, his sad eyes on me once again as he raised his hand.

In it was a gun.

Samuel's eyes widened, but he schooled his features so quickly that I couldn't tell if it was from fear or shock. Lucas held his gun aimed at my tormentor. A couple of moments later, my Soul rushed through the door, breathing hard. His eyes darted around the room, quickly took in his surroundings before stopping on me.

Ryder's eyes held so much anguish that I cried out. It came out as a yip that shocked me and the brothers. The distraction gave Samuel the perfect opening, as the next thing I knew his blade was against my jugular.

"Don't. Move," he growled, putting the slightest bit of pressure against my fur covered skin.

Not knowing if he was talking to me or to the men in front of me, I froze.

"Let her go, Samuel. Your fight is with me," Ryder growled lowly. His words only made the man behind me grin, I could hear it in his taunting voice.

"You're right, nephew. But that's why she's so perfect." Samuel laughed manically, pressing the blade harder against my throat.

"What do you want?" my mate asked, slowly inching closer. His eyes were glued to the knife at my neck.

While staying at Mayor Mansion, I had seen some sparring and had picked up a few moves—although being damaged all the time meant I wasn't able to actually try any of them so I would most likely fail if I *did* try—but in wolf form, I was worse than useless. Not to mention I was still too weak to even move more than my head. I quickly became aware that I had two options. I could do nothing and hope that the men before me had impeccable aim as Samuel was hiding behind me and the bed, or I could figure out how to shift into human form and try to fight back.

I chose the latter, although in the state I was in I wasn't sure what good it would do. If nothing else, it would surprise Samuel enough to give the Mason boys an advantage.

I closed my eyes and tried every trick I had ever read about. Spending the longest on picturing myself human when a tingle ran along my spine. After a few long moments, I still didn't shift back.

Disappointment swept over me before a true want consumed me, and the tingle was back, but more intense than before.

My bones once again started breaking and rearranging themselves.

Samuel jumped in surprise before tightening his grip on me and yelling at Ryder.

"What do I want? What. Do. I. Want?" He was one step away from completely losing it. "I want what was stolen from me the moment you were born! You stole my title from me! And because of you I lost my family! My son!"

Understanding slowly fell over Ryder's face and he raised his hands, dropping the gun he had been holding. "You want to be Alpha? Fine, be Alpha, but let Kaylee go. This has nothing to do with her," Ryder said, and I gasped in horror.

My life was not worth the pack. Ryder couldn't let Samuel's slimy paws anywhere near Redheart. I'd only been there for two months, but it already felt like home. Everyone was like family.

"I don't believe you for a moment, you insolent wretch!" His blade nicked my now furless skin, making me hiss, and Ryder growled.

"Careful, Samuel. If you want to be Alpha, you better not spill one more drop of Kaylee's blood."

"Is that any way to speak to your uncle?" I could see Samuel's face from where I lay on my back with his knife pressed against my neck.

I saw the decision flash in his eyes seconds before the pressure increased.

Ryder roared, lunging forward.

I flinched, knowing there was nothing I could do to change my fate.

A gunshot rang out across the room.

For a moment, I thought Lucas had fired the bullet, but he was looking behind him. Blake was standing in the doorway with his gun raised and an unreadable expression on his face. He looked in control, but there was pain in his eyes. I couldn't imagine how Blake felt, but at least this had come to an end.

Relief flooded through me and my entire body relaxed. The torture was over.

I hadn't realized I had closed my eyes until a gentle hand grasped mine. Crouching in front of me was Ryder, my mate, and behind him was Lucas, still holding his gun at the ready. Even though I knew he wouldn't need it, I couldn't blame him for not being ready to relax. Brendan's minions were still in the house.

Reaching behind his neck, Ryder pulled his shirt off, his gaze sweeping over my naked body. Anguish and regret were so glaringly obvious in his eyes it hurt to look at him. He gently helped me sit up before slipping his shirt over me. I whimpered with every little movement.

Ryder eased me forward to lean against him, cautious of the gashes covering my skin; most importantly, the wounds in my shoulders which were still bleeding profusely. When I had to lift my arms into the holes of the shirt, I almost blacked out. The pain was unbearable.

Ryder still hadn't said anything apart from his attempt to negotiate with his uncle, and I ached to hear his voice. I glanced at Lucas from my place leaning against his brother as I was dressed, but his eyes were averted. I was grateful, but also couldn't bring myself to care about my nudity for more than a second.

"How?" I choked past the pain ravaging my body. The word came out hoarse and low.

Lucas turned and Ryder stiffened against me.

"Lisa called as soon as you were taken," Lucas told me, his eyes filled with remorse. Why, I wasn't sure. "But she called me, not Ryder. Which is why we took so long. I'm so sorry, Kaylee. I should have told Ryder right away..." Lucas trailed off, self-disgust and shame coloring his tone as he bowed his head. I couldn't remember a time where Lucas had called me by my first name instead of 'Spencer.' I hated that he did it in that moment.

Before anyone could say anything more, Broddy came crashing through what was left of the door, coming to a standstill next to Blake right inside the doorway. Ryder startled at the sound and glanced over at them. I was glad to see Broddy moving around and looking as healthy as ever. Wolves really did heal quickly.

"We found him. And a human," Broddy said, glancing at me.

My heart rate accelerated at the news. He meant my dad and Carter. They were safe.

"Good," Ryder nodded. The sound of his voice sent chills down my spine and tingles danced across my skin. The same way they did when I first met him. Just the sound of his voice made me feel a little better. "Lucas. Shorts."

Lucas shed his shorts and shifted. He was beautiful, but nowhere near as perfect as his brother. They were similar in coloring, but Ryder was mesmerizing in a way Lucas wasn't. Ryder motioned with his head and the other two men in the room approached us. They sat on either side of me, supporting my weak body as Ryder slid the shorts over my shredded skin, but not allowing himself to actually touch me.

He wouldn't even meet my gaze.

He was disgusted with me.

I hadn't cried since Samuel stabbed me for the first time, but Ryder's disgust brought tears to my eyes like nothing else. I couldn't even blame him for being repulsed.

"Baby, please don't cry. I can't take it," Ryder begged, tears pooling in his own eyes.

I couldn't respond. The pain was too severe and my energy was completely gone. My breaths started coming in pained gasps and I couldn't get enough oxygen.

"Where's Mom?" Lillian was here?

"Right here." Her sweet, comforting voice rang through the room as she came into view with a syringe in hand. "Lisa told me how they got you, so I know you don't have a great past with these things, but this one will ease your pain until we can get you home, okay?"

I wanted to nod, to make some sort of physical acknowledgement, but I couldn't. I just groaned.

Her bright green eyes shone with such honesty and love I knew I could trust her with just about anything. Not to mention she had been taking care of me practically since I arrived in Redheart.

Lillian must have seen the acknowledgement she was looking for reflected on my face, as she came closer and gently took my hand. Broddy gently held my arm still and Lillian stuck the needle into the fleshy part of my arm. Before, I might have winced, but after what Ryder's uncle put me through, the pinch didn't even phase me. I was surprised she found any skin to put the needle in.

The drug worked quickly. The pain in my body soon dulled and I felt myself relax to the point where I was no longer aware of the world around me. Words were exchanged quietly, but through the haze of the medication, I couldn't understand any of it.

Ryder's face came into view once more and his lips moved. I could have sworn they shaped the words 'I love you,' but before I could think anything of it, the drugs pulled at me and I finally fell away into nothingness.

***

I awoke to the sound of a heart monitor.

My eyes were closed as the effort to open them was still too much, but I was awake. I felt my pinky twitch of its own accord and I heard a rustle before a large hand enveloped mine. It was shockingly warm against my cold skin.

"Kaylee? Sweetheart? Can you hear me?" It was Ryder. My heartbeat accelerated, made evident by the monitor beeping more quickly. "Please, baby, open your eyes."

I wanted to do as he asked, but it was so…hard.

Ryder kept murmuring until eventually I found the strength and opened my eyes. They fluttered slowly at first, attempting to adjust to the bright light in the room.

"Oh, thank god" Ryder breathed, dropping his forehead to rest on top of our joined hands.

With my eyes open, I could tell that I was once again in Ryder's room. Only now it had been transformed into my own private hospital room. There was a heart monitor with a little clip on the tip of my finger, reading my pulse. Looking at myself, I realized I was covered in bandages almost head to toe apart for where an IV was poking me in the arm. The strangest part was that I wasn't in any pain. My mind was muddled, thoughts blurry, and my body felt heavy, but there was no pain.

"What happened?" I asked—croaked really. Ryder's silhouette was slightly blurry and I blinked, trying to clear my vision.

"You don't remember?" Ryder asked, alarmed. It was so soothing having him sitting with me. Just hearing his voice, as tense as it was, made me feel better about what happened.

"I remember what happened while I, while I was...*there*. But how did—how did you find me?"

"Lisa called Lucas the moment you were taken. They didn't tell me until that night—when you both were supposed to come back—that you had been taken that afternoon. I lost it, Kaylee." Ryder paused, taking deep breaths and running his hand through his hair. "I started tearing everything apart and it took Blake, Broddy *and* Lucas to convince me not to storm Brendan's house looking for you. You were gone for two days before we finally came up with a plan that would end up with the fewest people getting killed. Although, to tell you the truth, I didn't really care about that. But everyone else reminded me that you would." Ryder took another deep breath, shaking his head. "But it was *Samuel*. The entire time it was my *uncle*. My own flesh and blood. Behind all of it. I'm sorry. Lucas tried to suggest it could be Samuel, but I refused to believe it. He was supposed to be dead."

Ryder stood and began to pace.

"Ryder." He turned his head, but he wouldn't look at me. "I'm okay. I can't feel a thing." I hoped he believed me, because I wasn't sure I believed myself. Tears welled in my eyes and I knew even though I wasn't okay, I would be. Because I had him.

"No, Kaylee. You're not. You've been unconscious for five days. Five! And the only reason you're not in *agony* right now is because Mom has you on really strong meds." Ryder took a deep breath. "I saw what he did to you." Ryder finally brought his eyes up to meet mine and he flinched.

"I disgust you. Don't I?" I wasn't sure I wanted to know the answer, but I needed to.

Ryder seemed to be appalled by my question and rushed to my side.

Grasping my hand, he quickly eased my worries. "What? Oh my god, no! You're perfect. Nothing they did changes that. Even if every single one of those wounds' scars, you'll still be the most beautiful woman I have ever seen. Wolf and human."

His words made the brimming tears spill over.

"Oh, baby. Please don't cry."

"I'm sorry. I just thought…" I trailed off, unable to finish my sentence as I choked on a sob. I thought he wouldn't ever love me. Not only because of what they did, but because I was weak. Ryder deserved someone who was as strong as he was. He deserved someone who would match and compliment him perfectly.

"You're perfect, okay? You're strong, and beautiful, and perfect," he said, leaving no room for argument. "God. This is all my fault," Ryder sighed and there was a pang in my chest. "You wouldn't have been taken if I hadn't insisted you go shopping."

I couldn't believe my ears. I went to deny his claims, but he spoke again before I could get a word in.

"And you know what the worst part is? I sent you out so we could plan without you knowing, so you wouldn't be involved, and you wouldn't get hurt. And then you get taken anyway!" Ryder sounded so pained.

I must have been on some really strong pain medication, because all I wanted in that moment was for him to be happy. I wanted his pain to go away.

I gingerly reached up with a bandaged hand and cupped his jaw. My shoulder throbbed slightly at the movement, but the medication kept the worst of it at bay.

"Ryder, none of this is your fault," I whispered, crying the entire time. I gently ran my thumb over his cheekbone.

"How can you say that, Kaylee? If it weren't for me, you wouldn't be hurt and bedridden. Again." Ryder appeared to be on the brink of tears and it broke my heart.

"It's because of you I'm home. Don't you get that? If you guys hadn't found me, I'd either still be trapped in that horrible room, stuck as Brendan's pretend mate, or quite possibly dead. So, don't you dare blame yourself for any of this! Got me?" I demanded.

I was sick and tired of everyone's guilt trips. The only people to blame for what happened were Samuel and Brendan. I couldn't even *really* blame

Brendan, because he had been manipulated his entire life. Samuel had been preparing him for a moment just like this one.

When Ryder still didn't respond, I raised my brows and whispered, "Okay?"

He nodded. "Okay. But you have to know that I could never find you disgusting or anything other than beautiful. Okay?"

I nodded in return, my heart hammering in my chest, as I sniffled, "Okay."

He seemed pleased by my acceptance of his words. I was so relieved that Ryder wasn't disgusted by me, I probably would have agreed to anything he wanted.

Abruptly, Ryder stood and went into his closet. He was only in there for a few moments before coming back out with a small smile on his face and one hand behind his back.

"Ryder?"

"I have something for you," he announced, sitting back down in his chair.

Silently, I waited. Ryder brought is hand out from behind his back, it was fisted. I raised a brow and waited for him to open his hand. When he finally did, all of the breath in my lungs left me.

"My necklace," I gasped, tears in my eyes.

"I found it on the floor of that room. It must have popped off when you shifted or something," Ryder said with a shrug.

"Oh, Ryder," I sniffed happily.

"Here, let me put it on you," he slid to the edge of his seat and, very carefully, clasped the necklace behind my neck.

We sat in silence for a time, Ryder just holding my hand, playing with my fingers the way he did. I had to tell him before something else happened and I lost my chance.

"Hey, Ryder?" my voice cracked nervously as I broke the silence. "Can I tell you something?"

"Anything," he promised, and I could tell he meant it.

Before I could say anything though, Ryder moved around the bed to sit next to me in the empty side of the bed, as there wasn't room where he had been kneeling. He gently cupped my face and leaned down, placing a soft kiss against my lips. My eyes closed as his mouth moved slowly against mine and I happily kissed him back. He teased my lips open and his tongue slid in, coaxing mine into a dance. This kiss wasn't like the past ones we had shared. Those had been full of passion and lust. This one was slow and completely filled with love.

"I love you," I blurted, no longer able to hold it in. I pulled back, shocked at my abrupt admission. I had wanted to ease into it, but I was more surprised that I didn't regret it.

Ryder pulled back to gaze down at me. His eyes were huge, reflecting the shock I felt. All of a sudden, I feared that I had made a huge mistake.

He leaned down and pressed his lips to mine in another sweet kiss. "I love you too, sweetheart."

My heart thudded erratically at his words and my lips split wide across my face into what was possibly the largest smile ever.

Ryder kissed me again, like I was the most perfect person to him. And I think I finally believed him.

Chapter 23
Family

I awoke with a cry, shooting up in bed, whimpering when my body ached and burned.

It was only a dream.

Samuel had been standing above me with the knife in his hand. Brendan had been holding me down, but this time I wasn't clothed. I couldn't breathe. I knew Samuel was dead and Brendan was being taken care of somehow, but that knowledge didn't help in my nightmares where I was chained down and tortured, unable to move or even try to defend myself.

"Kaylee?" Ryder groaned softly beside me.

His sleepy voice triggering my guilt. I had been staying in his bed again and, every time I had a nightmare, I would end up waking him. I had tried to convince him to let me stay in another room, but he would have none of it. He wanted me close. And if for some reason he couldn't be with me for even a moment, he would call someone in to keep an eye on me.

At my request, Lillian had kept me in a drugged stupor for four days after I woke up. The pain had been too much for me to handle without medication, and a zombie-like state seemed like a better option. But nine days after the rescue, Lillian said she couldn't risk me getting addicted, so I was stuck being awake and living on *Advil*.

I couldn't decide what was worse, being stuck in my dreams where Samuel haunted me or being forced to look at the still healing scars marring my skin. Without the stronger medication, I was stuck with both.

My bones ached ever since Samuel forced me to shift, and my skin was on fire. I had yet to move my shoulders without crying.

"Kaylee? Are you okay, sweetheart?" Ryder sat up beside me, a concerned frown creating a furrow between his brows.

"Yeah," I whispered. "I'm okay."

Ryder huffed at my lie and sat up straighter. He hated that I refused to tell him when it was too much.

"You're still dreaming about it, aren't you?" he sounded disappointed.

He asked me the same question every time I had woken up screaming for the past three days. His disappointment wasn't at me, like I had worried the first night I had woken him with my screams; he was disappointed with himself for not being able to chase the ghosts away. No matter how many times I told him there was nothing he could do, he was adamant that he should be able to help.

"I'm sorry, Ryder. He just won't go away," I choked on a sob. I wanted Ryder to hold me, but I knew he couldn't yet—wouldn't let himself. Not until my skin healed more. For some reason, I was healing slower than I should have been, even for a human.

"Don't you dare apologize, sweetheart? I think I'd be more scared if what happened *didn't* affect you. I'm just worried." Ryder ran his hand through his shaggy black hair. "What I don't understand is why you're healing so slowly. You should be healing like a wolf by now."

"Your mom said it would take time for my body to adjust completely. You know, to take on all the attributes of being a werewolf," I repeated the words Lillian had told me after forcing me from my medically induced haze.

She had been confused too. Even though it was just a theory, having some sort of reason still made me feel better.

"I know, I just hate seeing you like this, Kaylee. I hate not being able to hold you." Ryder's face echoed the pain I felt in my whole body—in my very soul.

"Maybe, um, maybe we could try?" I swallowed hard. Lillian would freak if she found out, but I needed my mate's arms around me.

Ryder's head snapped toward me. "Are you sure?"

I nodded slowly, biting my lip. I was scared it would make something worse, but I was more scared of the damage to my heart if I couldn't have the love of my life hold me. It had been far too long since I'd felt his arms around me. And I'd been through too much.

"Lay down, sweetheart."

Tears sprung to my eyes as he helped me ease myself back down onto the mound of pillows behind us. The only way I could lay down comfortably was on my back; any other way and there was too much pressure on my wounds.

Ryder lay back down on his side and told me to lift my head slightly. He carefully slid his arm behind my head and draped the other over my belly. A hiss escaped from between my teeth when his arm came around my waist. He went to pull his arm back but I stopped him.

"Don't. I'm okay," I whispered. I would have grabbed his arm and held it there myself, but it hurt too much to move anymore.

"I'm hurting you," Ryder objected and went to pull away again.

"It hurts more being away from you." I felt the tears start to roll down the side of my face. "Please, Ryder. I need this."

His brown eyes glowed with uncertainty. He wanted—no, needed—this as badly as I did, but hated the pain he was causing me. He was far more selfless than I was.

"I can handle it."

Ryder sighed. "Alright. But the moment it becomes too much, you *have* to tell me."

"I promise." I'm sure he heard the lie in my voice, but he let it go.

Appeased, my mate snuggled closer. It hurt, but I kept the whimpers at bay. I couldn't let him pull away. He nuzzled the side of my head and I felt his breath through my hair. His even breathing was incredibly soothing, and I soon felt myself drifting off.

"I love you, Kaylee," Ryder whispered against my temple. His breathing deepened almost immediately.

"And I love you, Ryder. Always."

There were people from my old life who would have said I was too young to love so completely. That's the nice thing about being in Redheart, surrounded by other wolves; age was just a number. Love was what mattered.

***

Ryder's arms chased the dreams away for the rest of the night. Somehow, even asleep, my mind knew I was safe with him. It just needed the physical reminder that he was there.

I woke up to my mate staring down at me.

"You slept for the rest of the night." He was laying on his side with his head propped up on his hand. His voice was full of awe.

"Apparently, you're what I needed to keep the ghosts away." I smiled sheepishly up at him.

For some reason, I felt slightly embarrassed that I had to rely on him in this way. Even so, I never wanted to spend another night without his arms around me.

"I'll do anything to keep you safe, Kaylee." He leaned down and placed a gentle kiss against my forehead.

"I love you." I smiled up at him again.

"I love you, too. Always."

I gaped at him when the final word left his lips. He smirked and kissed my cheek, laughing when he saw the blush rise behind my skin.

"I thought you were asleep." He chuckled at my obvious embarrassment.

"Nope, but I love that you think about our future."

Pure love shone in his eyes. I blushed more fiercely at his words. He had a knack for making me flush the most humiliating shade of red.

"Do you?" I asked nervously. I wasn't completely sure that I wanted to know the answer.

"Do I what?" His brow furrowed as he rolled over onto his back. Not wanting to lose eye contact, I struggled to sit up.

"You know. Think about our future?" I said softly.

"Of course, I do. I want to marry you someday, Kaylee. I want to put babies in your belly and raise them together. I want *everything* with you."

Ryder's words brought tears to my eyes, but for the first time in days they weren't caused by my pain.

"I love you so much," I choked. Ignoring all of my hurts, I reached over and wrapped my hands around the back of his neck, pulling him in for a kiss.

When his lips met mine, I melted and now I was flushing for a completely different reason. With every brush of his mouth against mine, I fell in love with him a little bit more.

When I started playing with the hair at the nape of his neck, Ryder pulled away and groaned, resting his forehead against mine. "You need to hurry up and get better."

I knew exactly where his mind was. I laughed at his impatience even though I was on the same page.

"Soon. I hope," I added quickly, giggling. After a week of pain and frustrating sleep patterns, it felt really good to laugh again.

I leaned up for another kiss when there was a knock on the door. Before either of us could respond, the door opened a crack and my mom poked her head in.

Everyone had come to visit me over the past few days. Everyone except Dad, Blake, and Carter.

Whenever Mom came to see me, I would ask about Dad. I wanted to know what Samuel and his minions had done to my father, but more importantly, I needed to know he was okay. Every time I asked about him, though, she would say the same thing; he was adjusting. No one would tell me what that meant exactly, but I had my suspicions.

"Hi, Momma."

"Hi, my sweet girl. How are you feeling today?" She smiled at me with all the love of a mom. She visited me at least once a day, whether I was doped up on painkillers or not.

"I slept for most of the night."

I exchanged a secret look with the man beside me, and he grinned. We both knew no one was supposed to touch me in any way that could hurt me, except for Lillian when she was checking my injuries, but we had both needed last night. So as long as Lillian didn't find out, then everything was golden.

"That's so great, honey! I actually have a surprise for you, though."

Mom pushed the door open the rest of the way and stepped into Ryder's room.

"Daddy!" I shouted the moment I saw him standing behind her.

He grinned at me and hobbled into the room behind his wife. He was limping.

"Are you okay?" I asked, worried. I knew he had been through a lot in that damn house. I didn't know what, exactly, but his appearance was all the evidence I needed.

"I should be asking you that question, Kale." He smiled at me. As he came closer to my side of the bed, I noticed the cast on his leg and the splint keeping the first two fingers of his left hand straight.

"I'm fine, Dad. Just sore. You, on the other hand, have broken bones and a limp."

He didn't need to see what had been done to me. I was trying to joke around, but seeing him in front of me, and relatively healthy, brought tears of relief to my eyes. I had been so worried about him. Especially when no one would give me any information about his condition, or what had happened to him while he was in that god forsaken house. I knew he had been relentlessly beaten, but that's only because I had seen it firsthand. It was something I wished I could have saved him from. And something I never wanted to see again.

"*I* may have a limp, but *you're* still stuck in bed." Dad was trying to joke with me too, but I knew seeing me stuck in bed again with bandages covering every visible inch of me was a lot for him to handle. "Kale," he breathed. "What did they do to you?"

I wasn't the only one kept uninformed, apparently.

When I glanced at Ryder, he grimaced. "It wasn't my place to say. For either of you." I nodded.

I finally understood everyone's motives for keeping me in the dark. I didn't, however, understand why nobody told me that in the first place.

"Can we talk alone? Please?" I asked, nearly choking on my words. I needed my dad.

Ryder nodded and smiled sadly at me before leading my mom out of the room. When the door shut behind them, Dad joined me on the bed, sitting on the edge of the mattress near my knees. We stared at each other for a few moments, both of us too afraid to voice our thoughts, our worries. Until Dad broke the silence.

"Are you sure you're okay?" When he spoke, I took a good look at him.

He had aged since he was taken. Underneath the purple covering his face were deep wrinkles that hadn't been there before. The grey that was in his hair was now noticeable, whereas before I would have had to actively comb through his hair piece-by-piece, to find it. His jaw was covered in a scruff that told me he hadn't shaved in days. And his cheeks were slightly hallowed in. He had been starved.

"Kale?" he spoke again when I didn't respond to his question.

"Yeah, Dad, I'm okay." I smiled sadly at him.

We both knew I was lying. Even though he obviously didn't know the details of what Samuel and Brendan had done to me, he had seen me chained to that bed.

"They wouldn't tell me what they were doing to you. Brendan came down to the cells a couple times after I was taken to gloat about how they were following you around. He thought you were his mate, Kale. Why would he think that?"

I had never heard my father sounds so anguished. His eyes shone with tears. I couldn't remember ever seeing him cry before.

"Samuel set it up, Dad. All of it. He had this planned the minute I was born. Everything since that party seventeen years ago. He manipulated Brendan since he was a kid. Dad, he killed so many people," I paused, unable to continue passed the bump in my throat. Until I remembered something Samuel had said. "Daddy, did I have an uncle?"

My father flinched at my words. Samuel had been telling the truth.

"Yeah, Kale. You had an uncle." He smiled sadly at me as one lone tear slid down his cheek. Instead of wiping it away like I had expected, he let it fall. "His name was Kenneth. He was my older brother, and he died saving my life."

I gasped and raised a hand to cover my mouth, despite the agony in my shoulder.

Growing up, it had always been so strange seeing my friends and classmates with aunts and uncles and even grandparents. I had never had any so I never understood the dynamic of it.

Mom and Dad had never talked about their families. In fact, they outright refused to. I had come home from school one day in the second grade after doing a family chart and I realized I didn't have grandparents. So, when I got home from school and asked Mom and Dad about it, they had simply said that

I didn't have any. When I asked why, they explained that not all kids have grandparents or aunts and uncles and I had let it go.

I finally knew the truth.

"Your grandfather was one of the strongest men I've had the pleasure of knowing. He was head of self-defense in the pack. He trained Kenneth and me to be the best we could be. As a teenager, I was one of the best. I could take down almost anyone, no matter what form they were in—even though I had never shifted. But when your mom and I were attacked on her seventeenth birthday, I was severely injured. From that day forward, I stopped training with the rest of the pack. I wanted to train harder, but everyone else said it would only put me in more danger. I decided they were probably right, and I stopped fighting. When my father retired, Kenneth went on to be head of self-defense. Has Ryder told you anything about the Guard?"

I shrugged, tilting my head back and forth. "A little, but I wouldn't call myself an expert or anything."

"They're the most elite fighters in the pack. In order to be head of self-defense, you have to be just as good as them if not better. Kenneth was better." Dad shook his head, taking a deep breath. A sad little smile formed on his lips as he reminisced about his family.

"The day of the attack, my father found me trying to fight. He told me to get you and your mom and get you out of town. To get you safe. You were on the opposite side of the field from me.

"On my way to reach you, I was pushed to the ground and right when the wolf pinning me was about to kill me, Ken threw her off. Everything was going fine then—for us anyway. There were wolves dying left, right, and center, but *we were fine*. Until we were about ten feet away from you and your mom. I was tackled again. Kenneth got the wolf off me and, just as he was about to win that fight too, he was gutted. So I snapped the bastard's neck."

I had never seen such rage in my father's gaze. Or sorrow. The day Mom had left was hard, but looking back, Dad had been far more guilty than sad. Even on his worst days, he always refrained from cursing. It was a bit of a shock hearing it now.

"Jenny, his mate, saw the whole thing. She threw herself into the battle and died as well. It wasn't until later that we found out she had been four months pregnant."

"Dad," I whispered, shaking my head in disbelief. I didn't have the strength for anything more.

Samuel had been messing with our family for years and I had never known about any of it.

"Your grandparents died that day, too. It was a massacre. That's why we never told you why they weren't in your life. Lying about how they died would have been dishonoring their memories."

Dad began to cry. Well and truly. I had never seen him so broken before. It was then that I realized he wasn't crying because of the memories, he was crying because he had never let himself mourn.

"What were their names?"

Dad chuckled softly at my question, sniffling. He looked up at me, having dipped his head during his story.

"Your grandfather's name was Luther and your grandma's name was Anabelle. You look a lot like her, actually." Something inside me clicked and somehow, I knew, in that moment, that if I ever had a daughter she would be named after her great-grandmother. Anabelle.

"I wish I could have known them."

Samuel had taken so much from our family. I took comfort in knowing that he would never be able to touch us, or anyone else, again.

Dad leaned over and went to put his hand on my arm but stopped himself when he remembered the bandages. "Me too, sweetie. Me too."

We sat in silence again until it occurred to me that I still didn't know what had been done to him.

"What did they do to you, Dad?" I asked anxiously. His Adam's apple bobbed when he swallowed.

"Nothing like what they did to you. They beat me a lot, to keep me weak. And they kept me on bread and water," Dad sighed again. He wasn't telling me everything.

"What else?"

"I shifted. I finally shifted." He stood and began to pace. He really should have stayed sitting considering he had a broken leg, but I couldn't blame him for needing to walk off all the negative energy that was looming over him like a thundercloud.

"What does that mean?" They had told me that his wolf gene was different than mine, but his had been triggered the same way. More easily, even.

"It means that everything we thought we knew is wrong." He ran his hand through his hair again. "We always thought a first generation Dormant couldn't be triggered. Obviously, we were wrong. The Elders will have a field day with that one."

I sat in shock. Dad had changed, but he was strangely the same too. He was angrier, sadder, and somehow more loving.

"I hated hearing your screams. But what was worse than that was when they stopped. I didn't know what to think." Dad shook his head. "Kale?" He paused. I knew where this was going. "What did they do to you?" he asked again.

I didn't want to tell him. I was no longer ashamed of what had been done to me, of the marks on my skin. I just couldn't stand the thought of causing him pain. He would blame himself, just like everyone else.

"Can you help me?" I struggled to sit up and he stopped pacing.

When my dad reached me, he did his best to help me get situated. When I was as comfortable as I could be, I immediately began pulling the comforter down my legs. I knew if I waited, I would change my mind. Dad gasped as soon as the first inch of skin was revealed.

"No," he whispered, shaking his head.

A groan escaped me. It really hurt to move. When I couldn't reach forward any further, Dad took the comforter from my hands and finished pulling it down. I was wearing one of Ryder's shirts and a pair of sleep shorts. Dad could see almost every single mark covering my legs.

The first one had been the deepest of all the cuts on my legs and had needed stitches. There was still a bandage covering that one and the ones surrounding it.

Lillian had taken all of the other bandages off my legs the day before. The wounds on my arms were all deeper and quite a few of them had needed stitches so Lillian left them covered.

"There's more, isn't there?" Dad whispered. I knew it hurt him seeing me like this, maybe even more than it hurt Ryder.

I nodded, bowing my head. I couldn't look at his face while he stared at my shame. I realized that I *was* ashamed. I had been weak.

"Where?"

"My arms and torso." I gestured to my upper boy with my head.

I was whispering, too. I wanted the marks to go away. Lillian had said most of the ones on my legs and torso wouldn't scar, but the ones on my arms and the stab wounds in my shoulders were another story all together. Samuel had been precise in how deep his cuts were. While cutting me up, he said that Brendan had a weakness for a woman's legs as well as her chest and he couldn't risk marking me permanently in either of those places, but my arms were fair game. A canvas he could truly paint.

"I'm so sorry, Kaylee," Dad choked on a sob.

Seeing him cry for his deceased family was one thing, but seeing him cry for me was more than I could handle. I may have been weak under torture, but I could be strong for my father.

"Don't apologize, Dad. None of this was your fault. Ryder said Samuel should have been dead, *everyone thought* he was dead. There's nothing you could have done." I reached forward and pulled my father in for a hug, ignoring the pain as best I could.

No matter what he thought, he would always be my hero.

Epilogue

It had been two months since the kidnapping and four since the move. I had mostly finished healing a quick three days after my talk with Dad. The wounds in my shoulders took another week or so after that.

Lillian eventually came to the conclusion that my five-day coma was most likely the result of my body being forced to shift and adjust to new attributes. Which is also why it took my body so long to heal. My triggered wolf gene did end up helping with the healing process by keeping the scars to a minimum.

After scarring, the gouges in my shoulders looked almost like bullet holes. I called the puckered scar on my calf my tiger stripe. These were my war wounds, and I wore them proudly. I finally felt strong.

My entire body had healed to practically as good as new.

The exact details of how they had found us were described to me in bits and pieces. Ryder knew where the house was located and they essentially stormed the place with tranquilizers and handguns after knocking out the guards.

Lisa apologized profusely when she saw me for the first time—which was the day after I learned about my deceased family. Ryder had been trying to keep my life as stress free as he could. The only people he had let see me while I was in my drugged stupor were our moms.

Despite Ryder's good intentions, I gave him an earful for trying to control who visited me. Lisa felt guilty for not going to Ryder first, and I told her to shut up because she had nothing to be sorry for.

The pack had also caught Elizabeth Berri and thrown her, along with Brendan Asher and his goons—the men who had beaten Dad and Carter—into our prison. Which I found out was essentially a more humane dungeon. Samuel was finally and *actually* dead, like Ryder and Lucas had always thought he was.

It had taken me quite a while to get the courage to tell Ryder than Samuel killed his father. He had been heart broken when I told him, but he hadn't been surprised.

Broddy and Lisa had decided to move to the other pack. Now that Brendan was no longer Alpha, that left the position for Broddy, seeing as he was the only blood relative left.

The packs were only a few miles apart, so I didn't need to worry about never seeing them. I also didn't have to worry about how their lives would be there. The majority of the Coldmoon pack had welcomed them with open arms, as well as the end to Brendan and Samuel's tyranny. There were a few members who rejected the idea of Broddy being their Alpha, but that was to be expected as it is with all leadership changes. Lisa and Broddy were excited to get their relationship well and truly underway without the U.S., Canada border in the way.

Mom and Dad were happier than ever. They were reunited and completely in love. Dad was adjusting to being able to shift, much like I was. Apparently, he had been in wolf form when Broddy had found him in that house.

Dad and I spent much time after healing learning about being wolves. The adjustment was easier for Dad, as he had been around wolves his entire life and mostly knew what to expect. But Ryder was good support for me and helped me whenever I needed it. Whether we were in human or wolf form, he was there for me. He even came with me when Dad took me to the house he had grown up in. Dad and I had both cried.

Lucas found his mate in Broddy's little sister, Maya. But she was only fourteen, and he was sixteen, so they had a couple years to wait before they could actually date. However, they were becoming close friends fast. I was happy for him. After growing up the way he had, with no father and a mother who was depressed for years, he needed someone to talk to.

Lillian had decided to throw another party, now that everyone was safe. It was sort of a goodbye party for Broddy and Lisa, as well as a birthday party for Blake and me. Broddy and Lisa were officially moving in a couple days and Blake and I both had birthdays right around the corner. Blake was turning twenty-one and I was about to turn eighteen.

Blake had crawled back into his shell after he helped with the rescue, and the night of the party I had decided I had had enough. I went in search of him and found him in the big training room in the basement.

"Blake!" I shouted, getting his attention. He noticeably flinched at the sound of my voice, halting mid-swing at the punching bag in front of him.

"Kaylee." He nodded politely before punching the bag again.

"Really, Blake? You wanna give me a cold shoulder? You've been doing it to Ryder too. Why?" I tried to keep my voice as soft as possible, but I was kind of frustrated that he hadn't come to talk to any of us about this.

Something was obviously bothering him. I thought we had grown close over the weeks I had spent bedridden from one thing or another.

Blake sent me a scathing look, as if to say *really?*

"Talk to me, Blake." I was practically begging. I knew it had been two months, but I missed him. I missed my friend. And Ryder did, too. "What's wrong?"

Blake sighed and began picking at the athletic tape he had wrapped around his hands. "I killed my father, Kaylee."

He leaned his forehead against the bag and closed his eyes. His shoulders were tense and his spine was rigid.

"You did what you had to do. Any of us would have done exactly the same thing if it were us. You have to know that." I took a step closer.

Blake's family was gone. The only people he had were his cousins and aunt. And me.

"I do. But it still doesn't change the fact that it was me who pulled the trigger." Blake pushed himself away from the bag. "I know he wasn't a good man, but he was still my father and I stopped his heart. He abandoned me and Mom. He killed and killed. But he was still my dad."

There was a pang in my heart at the resignation in his voice.

"He told me he killed your mom," I said softly.

"He killed her and my mate. Just like he killed everyone else." Blake sighed again and I knew he was melting.

Samuel had gloated about his ongoing role in the deaths of our family members, but he hadn't mentioned his son's mate.

"I'm so sorry. I know that will never be enough, but I am. How old were you?" I took another step toward him.

"When he murdered my mom? Eleven. He killed her in the middle of the night. I didn't know she was dead until I woke up," Blake spoke with such monotony, I knew he was trying to hide his emotions. He blamed himself, just like everyone else. "I found her along with a note that said 'you can't trust women. Love, Dad.'"

"How do you know he killed your mate too?"

"I had the fever when a girl named Julianna Smith was born. She died the same night as my mom, and then her family moved away."

"It's not your fault, you know. Your mom's death, or you mate's, or your father's. Samuel killed your mom and Julianna when you were just a child. And there was no way he was getting out of that house alive, you just happened to the be the one to pull the trigger." I rested my hand on his shoulder in what I hoped was a comforting gesture. I wasn't sure what his boundaries were.

A series of emotions played over the Beta's face until finally peace won.

"Thank you, Kaylee." Blake smiled at me. It was a sort of sad smile, but it was still a smile. "You're good for him, you know? And this pack."

His words made me blush a slight shade of pink, but they also made me feel very proud of myself. I smiled back at him and gave him a quick hug. I made sure he was going to the party and retreated back to Ryder's—our—room.

Which is where he found me later.

The party was in full swing when Ryder finally managed to drag me from our bedroom. Everyone was there. My family, the Perrys—including Carson—Lillian, of course, and Blake. Lucas and Maya had gone as a friendly item. Broddy was there with his and Maya's parents, Shelby, and Michael Hendricks, who were amazing people. Even Carter was there. He had decided that, after everything that had happened and after everything he had seen, there was no way he could return to his life as it was, and had applied to a nearby college for the winter. Lillian had even invited Julie—the caterer. I'm sure it was a sign of forgiveness on Lillian's part. And a sign that there were no hard feelings.

Ryder pulled me straight onto the dance floor, teasing me about not knowing how to have fun at my own party. I stuck my tongue out at him and he laughed. It was such a nice sound. It rumbled rich and deep in his belly and made me tingle all over. Planting a big, silly kiss on my mouth, he tickled my sides and this time—finally—it didn't hurt. I laughed in return and he brought his lips to my ear.

"I love you," he whispered, his mouth brushing the shell of my ear.

"And I love you."

That day, surrounded by the people we love, I realized that I truly was his Soul. And he was mine.

www.ingramcontent.com/pod-product-compliance
Lightning Source LLC
Chambersburg PA
CBHW051513170626
46811CB00002B/793